About the Author

Jack Collett was educated by the state in Wiltshire, Bath and Oxford. He has spent twenty-five years teaching in the West Country. Jack lives in rural Wiltshire and has two daughters. Written mostly in periods of COVID-19 lockdown, this is his first novel.

To receive the latest news about Jack's writing, visit www.troubador.co.uk/bookshop

For Florence, Lila and our via occulta
and
for my grandmother, Lucy Mary, who taught me to read
my first word: quiet

Prologue

Oxford - December, 2019

In Alfred Street, gathered around a fireside table in a pub, a group of undergraduates supped their pints. Michaelmas Term was over, and half the city would soon go home for Christmas. By a window, a very old man sat alone with his whisky and a dry, rasping cough. He wore black gloves and a pork pie hat.

'He spent the rest of his life fighting for women's rights,' concluded Angus, his foppish fringe falling over his forehead.

'How good of him,' retorted Dotty. 'So as soon as he discovered she wouldn't receive a penny of her dad's money, he was out of there. Great guy.'

'It makes for a fine story, though,' added Ollie, his ruddy, chubby cheeks bursting with a smile. His eyes darted across the table to catch Dotty's reaction.

'It's your turn, Dotty,' said Angus.

'I don't really know any ghost stories,' she said. 'But I'll have another drink.' Ollie keenly jumped to his feet.

'Same again?' he said.

'Only if we get to hear a story,' teased Angus in a boorish tone learned at a minor public school. He pulled a paper across his tongue and rolled a cigarette tightly between his forefingers and thumbs.

'I could tell you a story from Cornwall. I suppose it harbours ghosts.' Ollie returned with drinks carefully cradled in his forearms. 'Thank you,' Dotty said and smiled at Ollie for a second or two more than she had intended.

'Just going for a fag.' Angus took his phone with him. 'I've only got fourteen per cent.'

'You'll miss ye old tale from the West Country,' called Ollie. The man by the window was coughing furiously. Every now and then he would turn to the students' conversation, perhaps listening, maybe not.

'His Insta story's obviously more important,' Dotty said waspishly.

'Tinder more like,' replied Ollie, and he quickly realised his mistake. 'Sorry, I didn't mean to suggest…'

'It doesn't matter. I know what he's like. A total player.'

'I don't know what you see in him. I mean, he's a mate and all that, but…' For the second time, Ollie's well-meant words were interrupted.

'Okay. I'm back. Let's hear that story. Wales, wasn't it?' Angus took a gulp of his beer almost before he'd finished speaking.

'Cornwall,' corrected Ollie. Dotty leaned forwards and sat upright. Her blue eyes came alive, poised and sparkling. She began her story.

One

North Cornwall - Summer, 1940

A thick, dense haag had cloaked the coast for three days. Nobody could remember anything like it before. The fishermen and the farmers stayed at home, doing odd jobs in their sheds and on their boats, biding time before the weather set them free. The children played in the lanes, in the fields and on the cliff tops. What there was of schooling was finished for a while. The women and their men bickered, if the war hadn't taken them away. The land was silent but for the sound of the ocean. A mile or so out in the water, the sea lapped against the dark hull of a submarine.

'How much longer, Schult?' the captain demanded in a roaring whisper. There followed a series of metallic clanks and thuds, dull and distant in the depths of the big, iron fish. Then, all was silent but for the sea.

'It's no good, Kapleu. I need a valve, wire and oil. We have none of these,' replied the chief engineer, hollering from the black space below. The captain did not answer; he turned to another man.

'When will this fog lift, Weddigen?' the captain asked calmly.

'Soon, is my guess, Kapleu,' replied the navigator. 'The sea fog on this coast can come and go in minutes.'

The conversation paused. Somewhere near, a herring gull cried. Visibility was no more than a few metres.

'The weather will change soon,' spoke the captain in a half-question, half-statement, not addressing anyone in particular. He lit a cigarette and inhaled deeply. 'I looked upon the rotting sea, and my eyes drew away.' The captain's words drifted into the weather and he climbed down the ladder of the conning tower and into the guts of the submarine. The two mariners looked at each other, not puzzled by the captain's behaviour – they were used to his eccentricity – but with a knowing and urgent feeling that time was burning like a cheap match.

*

High above the bay on granite cliffs, two children were sitting and staring into the fog.

'I like the gorse flowers in April. They smell like coconut then. I like the colour too. Yellow like…like moonshine,' said the boy.

'Moonshine? What's moonshine?' replied the girl. 'You don't even know what moonshine is. And anyway, gorse smells like gorse not coconuts. That's like saying that figs in summer smell like blackcurrants. They don't. They smell like figs.'

'I love it when there's a fog,' continued the boy dreamily, undisturbed by the girl's disagreement. 'It's like the rest of the world can't find us and we are safe, protected – you know, like hibernating creatures.'

'Moonshine,' laughed the girl. 'Anyway, there's something more interesting hibernating out there in the bay – I can feel it.'

'Something out there?' The boy had woken from his dream and seemed anxious.

'Not like a sea monster if that's what you're imagining. No. There's a boat out there. I can feel it and I can smell it. I can sense these things – just like my grandfather; he has handed down that skill to me. It could be a navy boat on a secret mission or a collision. That's what I think. Two Cardiff tramps have collided in the fog. Imagine that. All that coal falling to the seabed. Come on – let's row out a bit and see what's there.'

'You're mad,' said the boy. 'I'm not going out in this. You're crazy.'

'Oh, come on, Eddie, please.' She yearned and pleaded like an infant.

The two exchanged disagreement for a couple of minutes before the boy's gentle nature surrendered. The children clambered down the cliff path to a small cove. On the foreshore was a small wooden dinghy.

'Now you really are mad, Rosie,' Eddie protested half-heartedly.

The children heaved the boat into the water. It was eerily calm – perhaps as flat a surf as they had ever seen. The tide would soon turn in, but for now the current was with them and the children edged out into the bay. They knew not to go far. The North Atlantic waters here were as treacherous as anywhere in the world.

*

Kapitänleutnant Kramer sat in his tiny cabin scribbling pencilled notes into a small, cloth-bound book. On a narrow shelf above his desk was a framed photograph of a pretty, half-smiling girl with thick, dark hair. But at least his space was his own. The rest of his men were cramped together in stinking bunks: snoring, brave oafs – usually laughing, occasionally quiet and one or two even on the brink of tears. Kramer was beginning to warm to his men but was distant, if not aloof, from them at the same time. For their part, the crew of U3276 were unsure of their new commander – he seemed competent, yet eccentric, but was not battle-tested and therefore a novice. Some still held their private doubts.

Kramer sighed, rose and made his way to the control room. The air was an unpleasant mix of diesel, men and damp. He climbed the conning tower to the open air to hold conference with his officers.

'Well, gentlemen, what are we to do? Lange – what is the engine report?' Lange was a tall, thin subaltern; he was twenty-two years old, but his eyes were old and red.

'We do not have the materials to fix the engines, Herr

Kapitänleutnant. I regret to inform you that we can do no more.'

The officers' talk proceeded to discuss all combinations of technical possibility, but the conclusion remained the same: the submarine was stranded no more than a mile from shore in the lee of a chain of rocks. While the fog and its tamed sea held, they were safe. As soon as it lifted, the submarine would be clearly seen from the headland.

'I looked upon the rotting deck and there the dead men lay.' Kramer spoke wistfully. His thoughts were in Hamburg, before the war. 'Gentlemen, we have only two options I can see. The first is we scuttle the boat and surrender. The second is we go ashore, and we find what we need to fix her.'

Lange and the other officers, Mertens and Forstner, looked at each other with bafflement and incredulity. Mertens, a shaggy-bearded, oval-faced veteran of thirty-five, chewed on his bottom lip. They waited for the captain to explain further, but the captain stared once more into the grey gloom seemingly lost in dreams. Mertens lit a cigarette. Forstner was beginning to look impatient and he exhaled some of Mertens' smoke deeply through his nose. A sweep of seconds passed and overhead a gull squawked mockingly. Finally, Kramer spoke.

'We go ashore and get what we need.' Said with such conviction and clarity, for a moment at least, no one in the tower had any doubt this couldn't be done.

'What was that?' Forstner alerted in an anxious tone barely above a whisper.

'I didn't hear anything,' said Mertens, exhaling from

the flimsy French cigarette he pinched between forefinger and thumb.

'I thought I heard a scream in the water.' Forstner moved to the guard rail of the tower, listening again for a sound. But all he heard was the laughter of a turning tide.

*

'You don't know what you're doing, Rosie,' shouted Eddie. 'This isn't like paddling around in the cove. You need to turn around.' Rosie too was losing her nerve. Eddie was right. The water was becoming unpredictable, even though they were so close to shore. With tiring bodies and trembling strokes, Rosie tried to keep their bow straight to the oncoming waves.

'Come on, Rosie! We need to go back,' Eddie pleaded. The water was calm, but the currents were strong. Eddie was highly agitated now and his anxiety was fast turning to panic. As Rosie heaved to turn the boat for shore, Eddie shifted his seat. He stood briefly on one leg, but it was enough to rock his balance beyond control. He slipped, and as his body slammed against the gunwale, he crashed backwards into the water. Rosie instinctively dropped her oars and leaned to the side of the boat. The dinghy was unstable now. Eddie was spluttering in the water, afloat though drifting and soon to vanish in the murk. The children were screaming for each other, but they were losing their battle with the sea.

*

'Kapleu, I can hear something out there. It sounds like voices – listen.' Forstner was leaning far over the rail straining his ear to hear the mysterious sound from the water. Kramer listened and then he heard it too. So did Lange, but he looked less interested and sheepish. Mertens seemed oblivious; he coughed uncontrollably into his tobacco smoke.

'Be quiet, Mertens,' instructed Kramer. The men listened intently and then above the rhythm of the lapping water and the distant wash of the breaking shore, cries could be heard. Indistinctly at first, but then as their ear trained to the sound, the men could hear the unmistakable, high pitch of children's screams. Mertens was the first to react. Without needing instruction, he slid out of the tower, along the deck and lifted a hatch in its casing. Within no time, Mertens was paddling towards the cries in the fog. Kramer gave orders for two more dinghies to join Mertens' search.

'This is madness,' complained Lange. 'We are at risk of exposing ourselves.' Forstner, who had remained on deck, smiled mischievously and shared a conspiratorial glance with his captain.

'What else would you have me do, Lange?' Kramer asked his subordinate. Lange shuffled uneasily and did not pursue his doubts. Kramer thought of his young fiancee in Hamburg, the Neustadt park they walked in on Sunday afternoons, and of the baby she was carrying. For a few seconds his mind drifted, but he regained his composure and stared into the crying fog.

Mertens too was a family man. Besides submarines, his wife, his six children and their tumbledown house near Bremerhaven were all he lived for. Mertens was not a National Socialist, he was a sailor. He loved the sea, but he loved his family more. It was an instinct of undiluted paternity that drove Mertens to the noises in the water. Furiously, he paddled towards them, their call clearer with every stroke of the oar. Two crewmen, Witte and Emmerman, were almost alongside Mertens when Witte cried, 'There!' A few metres away was a very small wooden boat. It seemed to be empty. The screams that had brought the sailors here had stopped and all was silent. The dinghies approached the boat slowly. Emmerman and Witte hooked their oars to its rowlocks. It was empty.

'Nothing,' shouted Emmerman to Mertens and to a third dinghy launched from the submarine. With some difficulty, Mertens steered his craft around the stern of the dinghy. He held its gunwale for a few seconds to catch his breath. I'm too old for this, he thought. As he looked up, Mertens saw two bobbing heads, arms and hands clinging to the rudder. Shivering, scared faces of two children. Mertens was overcome with compassion and an urge to do all he could to get these poor souls out of the ocean. Even in midsummer, the water temperature barely got above sixty degrees. Mertens started to talk to the children softly. He tried to joke with them and then realised they would not understand a word.

Rosie and Eddie shivered uncontrollably. They were unblinking in terror as five men in military uniforms peered over at them, talking in a language they did not understand. The children were too cold to talk and too numb to resist the help from the men. Mertens directed his comrades. The German sailors gently lifted Rosie and Eddie from the water and eased them both into the dinghies.

'Get them on board, get them warm and give them something hot to drink – soup, give them soup. Quickly!' Mertens barked his instructions just in time; his voice cracked and tears filled his wide face. He had not felt so happy and so sad for a long time.

Kramer's eyes were still fixed on the water as the gloomy shapes of the returning dinghies emerged from the grey. Soon Witte was calling to the deck requesting assistance. To his astonishment, Kramer saw two children being lifted onto the deck. The crew quickly wrapped them in blankets and brought them to the tower.

'Herr Kapitänleutnant, Leutnant Mertens has told us to keep the children warm and give them soup,' said Witte.

'Then do as Leutnant Mertens has told you, Witte,' replied Kramer matter-of-factly. The children, silent and pale, were taken below deck. As yet, nobody had attempted or thought to talk to them in English.

Mertens had returned to the submarine with the children's dinghy in tow. By now, he was exhausted and in need of coffee and a cigarette. A sallow-faced young rating handed Mertens a mug of coffee and offered a match to his cigarette. Mertens nodded his thanks to the teenager who promptly vanished.

'Quite a haul, Mertens,' offered Kramer with a wry twist to his tone.

'You would have done the same, skipper,' replied a relaxing Mertens. 'You could have stopped me. But I think you were thinking the same things as me – what if those were our children out there?' Kramer did not reply and turned to face the sea. Mertens continued, 'So what do we do now?' A louder, larger wave had exploded into the cliff face some thousand or so metres to the east.

'We take them home,' replied Kramer. 'We take them home.'

The tide turned and started to spill its spume over the sand.

*

Mrs Trewithen was sitting in a damp ditch. Her hands were stained a deep red. Surrounding her was a minor catastrophe.

'Murder. Bloody murder,' Mrs Trewithen muttered to herself. The old lady cursed and sighed and tried to uplift herself from her flattened backside. 'Dorothy! Dorothy! Where are you? Come here!' Dorothy Trewithen could clearly hear the voice but could not see its owner. 'Dorothy!' yelled the grandmother in an urgent, maddening wail. When Dorothy found her, she burst into laughter. Gladys Trewithen had managed to forward roll into the shallow stream beneath a bank full of bramble and thorn, her enormous bottom turned skyward like a picnic rug spread over a knoll. Dorothy untangled her grandmother from the impossible position and stood above her with hands on her corduroy hips.

'Blackberrying already, Granny?' Dorothy enquired teasingly.

'No – baking a bloody sponge cake. What does it look like I'm doing, girl?' retorted Granny Trewithen. But her sarcasm and ill-humour didn't last long. They never did with Dorothy. Because Dorothy was her daughter now. And she loved her more with every greying day, after each and every graze. She had raised her, fed her, clothed her and held her close all those nights when Dorothy cried for her parents. And Dorothy held her too, but it was only when Dorothy fell asleep that she let her own tears fall and run in streams into the night.

'Look! I have lost hundreds of them. Thousands of them. Look!' Mrs Trewithen's face and hands were red and purple, bruised by the early fruit. But at least half a dozen of them had made temporary residence in her tightly curled hair.

'Come on, Granny, we can save some of these.' They collected what they could, carefully placing a few dozen berries in a basket, and climbed on to the path.

'Do you still want to go to Porthrowan? Maybe we should go back to Penrose, Granny.'

'Of course we're still going – that fiend Bob Chapman owes me five bob. He never pays up. He's a sore loser is Bob Chapman.' Mrs Trewithen had regained her fieriness, if not all her composure.

'I think you like it that way, Granny. I mean, at least this way you get to see more of Bob Chapman,' offered Dorothy with more than a hint of mischief.

'Crumbles,' replied the grandmother. It was an unusual expression and one with no particular history or association with anyone apart from Granny Trewithen.

The footpath followed the stream for another half-mile before it rose a little way, passed the old mill and arrived at a small cluster of cottages that formed the hamlet of Porthrowan, living quietly above a bay of the same name. The fog was not as thick here, but it was difficult to see beyond the wooden five-bar gate at Quarry's Turn, a mere twenty yards away.

'Right, Bob Chapman, let's be having that money of mine.' Mrs Trewithen rapped on the weather-eaten cottage door. When no reply came, Gladys peered through the low, small window into the blackness, her hand saluting to shield any glare. She could make out the dark outlines of Bob Chapman's armchair and a bureau which was probably overflowing with clutter, and which, given half a chance, Gladys would happily set alight.

'He's in there alright, sneaky little frog,' growled Gladys. 'I would like to put a hornet in his long johns.' Dorothy was keen to reply but thought better of it. At that moment, a voice greeted the two women.

'Good morning, Mrs T,' greeted a warm voice from the murk. 'How are we, young Dot?'

'Very well, thank you, Mr Chapman,' smiled Dorothy.

'Someone doesn't look like they're full of the joys of summer,' the villager winked at Dorothy.

'Five bob, Bob Chapman, if you please,' demanded Mrs Trewithen with a vague gesture of restraint. Bob Chapman looked at Gladys with blue eyes the colour of an April ocean. His voice was as rich as treacle, his skin chestnuts in autumn.

'Now, Mrs T, do you remember 1921?' said Bob Chapman in a storyteller's hush.

'1921?' Gladys Trewithen tried hard to resist the memory, but her resolve was melting like frost in the morning sun.

'The long, hot summer of 1921. When it didn't rain. The wells dried up and the earth was cracked like biscuit,' reminisced Bob. 'The sky was as blue as a blackbird egg.' Bob caught Dorothy's glance and the two smiled with their eyes. Gladys teetered on the edge of loveliness, then checked.

'You still owe me five bob. Pay me tomorrow,' instructed Mrs Trewithen.

'Shall do, my dear, shall do,' and Bob Chapman began to sing an old song, 'and when my love comes a-calling, comes a-calling at my door, the clouds they part, the rain will stop, and the sun will shine forever more.' Dorothy thought she heard her grandmother pick up the tune, humming through her closed lips. Above, briefly, the light brightened as if the weather were about to lift, but whatever it was disappeared, and the fog lay still again.

'I think we should go home now, Granny,' said Dorothy plainly.

'So do I,' replied Mrs Trewithen. As they turned towards the footpath back to Penrose, a woman's voice called out.

'Glad. Is that you? Glad!' A breathless woman appeared. She was dressed simply in a grubby cotton dress, wore a pair of tatty gum boots and, as she spoke, revealed only a few remaining brown teeth. 'Glad, you'll never guess what's happened.'

'What, Vera, what is it?' Mrs Trewithen asked in a way that suggested that this pattern of exchange had happened many times before. Vera Craddock, who for decades had smoked a clay pipe full of tobacco she grew herself, regained what was left of her lung capacity.

'The Merriman children are missing,' Vera revealed. Vera was pleased she was first to tell Gladys Trewithen this news.

'Missing? What do you mean missing?' Gladys asked with an undeniable mixture of some concern but more excitement.

'Gone. They've vanished. Old man Merriman was expecting them back at the farm for their dinner – before one o'clock. They're not back and it must be nearly four. Four hours! And the boat's missing from the cove. You know what young Rosie's like – anything for adventure. Could be lost in the fog – that's what Stump thinks. Mrs Merriman is beside herself apparently. They're out on the cliffs now looking for them.' Mrs Trewithen and her granddaughter exchanged worried looks. Everyone knew everyone and everything about everyone in Porthrowan. People were tough and uncomplicated here. Guided by the chapel but ruled by weather and the sea, the routine of life here was unshifting like the seasons. Porthrowan's children were often wild, untamed and free, but like their parents, they obeyed the instructions and the rules laid down before them. Rosie and Eddie Merriman would have come home by now.

'I will help look for them,' said Dorothy. 'Where should I start?'

'Most of them are about the cove, Dot. You could start there,' replied Vera.

'I will stay here and look around the houses with Vera. And, Dot – be careful, it's rum weather.' Gladys Trewithen's eyes were unblinking and black. She squeezed her granddaughter's hand and let her go.

*

The path at the southern side of Porthrowan Bay ran close to the cliff edge. With such poor visibility, Dorothy's progress was slow. The path was dry and she knew it well, but there is only so far anyone can walk blind. Her canvas shoes slipped on the uneven ground and her breathing became heavy. The roar of the ocean was everywhere, a power and a magic that never went away. The tide was beginning to slide into the bay now. Beneath her, she knew the waves would quickly fill the pools and caves. She thought about poor Rosie and Eddie. Maybe they were just lost in the fields, disorientated by the fog. The path steepened a little and fell southwards. Dorothy knew she was leaving the bay. A little further along the path, she reached the top of the cove. The path to the sand was no more than a breach in the cliff face, made hazardous by a thin stream making its way to the ocean. Dorothy could hear familiar voices. Edging her way along the face of the rock, she jumped onto the sand and made her way towards them.

'There's no sign of them at Pentire,' said one of the Merriman labourers.

'Nor at High Cove,' somebody else added.

'What about Trescore?' the children's father asked.

'The boat's gone, Tom,' an older man said grimly.

The young labourer noticed Dorothy's arrival. 'Afternoon, Dot. No joy, I'm afraid.'

'Is there any news from the village, Dot?' Mr Merriman was struggling to keep his usual calm composure. Terror was beginning to fill his unblinking eyes.

'No, Mr Merriman. Nothing when I left,' Dorothy replied. The talk muted and the villagers looked about them and out to sea, helplessly.

'They only have a few hours of daylight left, poor souls.' Terse, laconic and Cornish to his core, Stump was barely five feet tall, about sixty years old with thick, grey hair like metal. His eyes were deep and dark. Anybody else making this comment would have risked being thrown into the surf, but Stump was part of the sea like salt and part of the earth like worms. When he spoke, his words were new spells. And Stump was right. They didn't have long to find the children.

*

'What is that noise?' demanded Leutnant Lange as he climbed through the partition into the cramped officers' quarters. 'Be quiet, all of you!' His long, wiry frame was unsuited to service in a submarine.

'Choco-latte, choco-choco,' sang an officer dressed quite differently to his fellow submariners. The officer had Mediterranean and rugged good looks. He stopped his merry tune and turned to the German subaltern. 'May I remind you, Leutnant Lange, that I am your superior officer and I will tell you when to be quiet.' Kramer appeared.

'Capitano di Fregata Cossato – I did not know you had such a beautiful singing voice,' complimented Kramer with good-natured and heavy sarcasm. Kramer looked at Cossato's audience. Some colour had returned to Rosie and Eddie's faces, but the children were tired and, most of all, frightened.

'Have you had enough to eat and drink, children?' Kramer said gently in English.

'Yes, thank you,' replied Eddie.

'You don't have to say thank you, Eddie. These people are monsters. Sea monsters.' Rosie spoke with defiance that masked her terror.

'Sea monsters?' Cossato queried. He and Kramer then laughed heartily.

'Lange,' Kramer turned to his junior officer, 'coffee, I think.' Lange beat an unwelcome retreat to the galley.

'Children, my name is Kapitänleutnant Hans Kramer. I am the commander of this submarine. A German submarine. This is Capitano Luigi Fecia di Fregata Cossato of the Regia Marina, the Italian Royal Navy. Capitano Cossato is also a guest on my submarine.'

Cossato laughed again and with a grand sweeping gesture of his hand said, 'Please call me Signior Cossato.' Kramer smiled.

'I don't know why you are trying to be nice to us. Singing stupid baby songs and feeding us soup.' Rosie had enjoyed the soup. 'What are you going to do now? Torture us? Kill us? Take us back to Germany as prisoners?' Kramer and Cossato were both surprised at the girl's vigour.

'No,' Kramer said clearly. 'We are going to take you home.'

'Home? When?' said Eddie eagerly. His soft, round face was regaining some colour.

'Now,' replied Kramer and turned to go back to the control room in the middle of the submarine. Mertens had appeared and allowed Kramer to pass. He held mugs of coffee in his hand.

'How old are you?' Mertens asked Rosie and Eddie in heavily accented English.

'Twelve,' answered Rosie, reluctantly.

'Twelve,' repeated Mertens fondly. 'My daughter is twelve also.' He paused as he thought about Marta, his eldest child. 'Would you like some chocolate?' Mertens held out a block wrapped in dark blue paper. The children didn't answer but reached out gratefully for the offering. Rosie nearly smiled. Cossato looked to Mertens. Inside, both men were weeping.

*

It was now late afternoon. The fog was thicker and showed no sign of lifting. Merriman was busily organising the search party. A shopkeeper, Reddie Bland, had brought his ancient Ford van to the edge of the bay in case an emergency journey was needed. How he navigated his way there nobody was quite sure. The outlines of the cliff shapes were uncertain and indefinite, if visible at all. Dorothy looked out to the water. She thought she saw a moving shape but decided it was shadow on the water. Instinctively, she looked again. This time there was no mistaking movement. Here was a boat rowing in on the tide.

'Look,' called Dorothy, 'there they are!' The group of villagers, now about half a dozen in number, ran to the water's edge. Three men galloped into the water, the surf quickly slowing their progress. It was clear then that there was not one boat but four – the dinghy that belonged to the cove, Caerwen, and three small rubber inflatables. The men who ran into the waves stopped, puzzled. The craft came closer. Men were jumping out of them, heaving their boats onto the sand. The Cornishmen backed away, less in fear, more in disbelief. The men from the sea were armed. Merriman's face was white with fear. From two of the inflatables blanketed bundles were lifted and carried to the sand. Merriman sank to his knees. Kramer approached him.

'Mr Merriman, I presume?' Merriman looked at Kramer in utter disbelief. 'Your children are safe.' Two crewmen from the submarine brought the farmer his twins as if they were new born. Kramer pinched the peak of his white cap by way of informal salute. Merriman noticed a scar above his right eyebrow.

'They're bloody Jerries. It's the invasion,' bawled a farm hand called Mallett. 'Come on, we need to tell St Mawgan.' The labourer was about to turn and run towards the cliff path when Kramer interrupted.

'Wait,' he said with calm authority. Two German crewmen had aimed their rifles at the fleeing man. 'We will not need those, men.' Kramer looked at the assembled party. 'My name is Kapitänleutnant Hans Kramer. I am the commander of a German submarine which is in the bay behind me. Our engines are broken and we must repair them. This is not an invasion. It is not an attack. Today, some of my men rescued your children from the water after they had got into difficulty with their boat. We do not wish to harm any of you here. However, we must repair our submarine quickly and leave before the weather changes.'

Kramer had said all he wanted to for the time being. He drew a cigarette from an American carton in his breast pocket. Cupping his hand around a match, he lit it, turned and walked to the water's edge. The tide was gathering quickly along the bay. The German mariners formed a horseshoe either side of Kramer, guns lowered. The villagers gathered. Merriman held his children close to him, their eyes closed with tiredness.

'We should make a run for it. It would take a lucky shot in this fog to kill a man,' Mallett whispered loudly. He was hostile and afraid.

'And risk getting killed? For what? They're not going anywhere if their engines have failed,' added Merriman's cousin, Dinky Young.

'The children need to get home. They have seen enough today,' said Merriman quietly.

'They have been well cared for,' Dorothy added. A few looked at Dorothy as if she had said something traitorous. Nobody had noticed that Stump had slipped away and was talking to Kramer.

'How did you find them?' asked Stump.

'One of my officers heard screams in the water about a hundred metres from our boat.'

'They must have rowed out a fair way.'

'Yes, but then the currents here are very dangerous. You do not need me to tell you that.'

'Indeed they are.' There was silence between the men and the thin edge of the tide licked their boots. 'Thank you for saving them.'

'I am sure you would have done the same.' Kramer flicked his cigarette end into the ocean.

'So, Captain, what is it exactly that you need?'

Stump trudged back to the waiting group. It was still light but darkening slowly. Gulls were crying above the cliffs, playing at this time of day. The fog held – impenetrable and awful and still.

'What did he say?' Mallett still seemed eager for some kind of combat.

'He wants forty-eight hours,' Stump informed them.

'And if we say no?' asked Dinky Young.

'I don't think he is considering that option,' said Stump. 'He said that if they have not fixed their boat in forty-eight hours, he and his crew will come ashore and surrender – to us.'

'Why should we help a bunch of murdering krauts?' Mallett was not the only one to share this view. There seemed to be no consensus of opinion.

'Because they saved the lives of our children,' said Dorothy, and she turned to look Mallett in the eyes.

'And if we do help them? Isn't that some sort of

treasonable offence?' said Baker, a young artist billeting with the Merrimans, who would not receive his draft papers for another year. There was a lull as each woman and man gathered their thoughts until Stump spoke once more.

'This is Cornwall, not London, lad. It's a different country here.' Stump turned to the group. 'I say we give them what they ask for. We say nothing of this beyond ourselves. And, Merriman – keep the children at the farm until Tuesday afternoon. We will say the children rowed out too far and got home late.' Nobody protested. Stump walked back to Kramer. They talked briefly. After that, Kramer and his men waded into the water with their boats. One of them quickly turned as if forgetting something and ran to the villagers. It was Mertens. He knelt beside the children and Merriman. Warmly, he placed his hand on Rosie's shoulder. She was barely awake. 'For you,' he said, and he tucked the bar of chocolate inside her blanket.

'Thank you,' whispered Rosie in a sleepy breath. She fell asleep. In minutes, the bay was deserted.

Two

London - Summer, 1985

It was a dry and sunny early July. The plane trees in St John's Wood were tiring and the air was heavy with diesel fumes as the clock approached noon. Black cabs and buses busied the streets, braking and accelerating in rhythms at traffic lights across the city, but otherwise north London was dozing. Frank Fox slipped out of the grandstand and made his way quietly to the North Gate. Behind him, he could hear the thin applause of a sparse crowd as Australia moved another run closer to beating England. He passed the mower sheds and the practice nets and nodded to a West Indian steward who was leaning against a turnstile. He crossed the main thoroughfare into Wellington Place. Frank didn't want to see the end – it would be over in a few minutes just before the scheduled lunch interval. There was often little drama to a match that finished on a Tuesday morning. Cricket was not a game Frank had known as a boy, but he had grown to love its stories, characters and endless mathematical puzzles. Others too were hurrying away from the grand old ground. Pale blue shirts, bacon-and-egg ties; it was a male parade.

He wandered leisurely around the block towards St John's Wood tube station. Frank was an old man now – not in body, he was lissom and lithe, but his mind was weary. More and more, his thoughts drifted into the past. The present was not a pleasant place to be. Passing a newsstand, Frank bought a paper. He sat down on a bench just inside a small park. The headlines were international. The Soviet Union had appointed an obscure diplomat as their president. Famine was ravaging East Africa. And an Irish pop singer was staging a global music concert to provide Ethiopia with relief aid. France was completing a nuclear test somewhere deep in the Pacific region amidst growing criticism and environmental protest. Frank stared into the empty green space and thought about time he had spent in Polynesia – good times, mostly. He threw the paper in the litter bin. As he did so, he noticed something unusual, disconcerting, at the opposite side of the park. Frank moved quickly, keeping to the circumferential path. Frank could see a struggle between an adult and a girl. But it was not a parent admonishing their child. The adult was male, dressed in an ugly tracksuit and baseball cap – he may have been in his twenties or thirties; the girl was probably eight or nine years old, dressed in a blue school uniform summer dress. The man was covering the girl's mouth with his palm. He was forcing the girl against a tree that was screened by dense shrubs.

Frank quickened his pace. He looked for a way to get behind the tree without being seen by the assailant. Finding an opening in a dark yew hedge, he stumbled through. Sweat was bubbling in his pores. Emerging from the back of the yew, he made for what must have been the perimeter wall of the park. Creeping along it, he quickly found the man and the struggling child. Frank did not hesitate. He stepped towards the attacker and crashed a mighty punch to the base of his skull where it met the neck. The man fell forwards, letting go of the girl, who froze and clutched the tree. He then turned, snarling like a dog, and lunged at Frank with all the clumsiness of a deadbeat street yob. Frank had lost none of his skill or reflexes. As the arm rose to meet Frank's face, he dipped to the left and deflected it with his right forearm, and in one motion rolled it clockwise before slamming his left hand down vertically on his opponent's elbow joint. The bone cracked like a nut. The man fell, screaming in pain, his head colliding with a gravestone. Blood poured from his mouth. He lay still, groaning in agony and shock.

Frank was struggling for breath. He stared at the man briefly and for a second pitied him – vile, pockmarked skin; dirty, baggy clothes; thin red hair underneath a cheap cap. The girl was terrified. Her breathing was tight. She was too scared to cry.

'Come on,' said Frank, 'we must get you home.' The girl did not want to leave the safety of the tree, but Frank insisted, and with reluctance the girl complied. The two walked to the park gates. They passed an elderly woman walking a dog. A couple were laying a picnic blanket across the grass by a war memorial – they were laughing and joking, enjoying a lunch break perhaps. Nobody looked up or noticed Frank and the little girl. Frank took the girl to the newsstand.

'Do you have a phone, please?' Frank asked the girl in the kiosk.

'No, sorry, love,' replied the girl. She sensed something was wrong. 'But there's a phone box on Wellington Road near the tube station.'

Two police cars arrived and pulled in sharply to the kerbside. A female officer coaxed the little girl to sit in the back seat with her. Frank got into the other. The cars swam into the London traffic, tin boxes glinting in summer sun. The little girl's eyes were swollen with fear as they peeped above the door frame. Oblivious, the city scurried on. Within minutes, the police were taking statements in Paddington Green station. Pasty, overweight officers recording elliptical fragments of the event. Stale cigarette smoke, sweat and unanswered telephones. It was grim work in a bleak building with little air and few windows. Even on a fine summer's day, its rooms were ablaze with strip lighting.

The girl's ordeal, here at least, was nearly over. Her mother arrived just before half past three. The same female police officer walked them out of the building to a waiting car. They left together and did not return.

'Is she okay? Alright? The little girl?' asked Frank. He was sitting in a scruffy interview room in a corridor behind the reception of the station. Opposite him, a faded anti-crime poster hung by a corner above a bulky police sergeant. The officer was methodical and kind with his questions, his face pink like sweating pork luncheon meat.

'Physically,' said the sergeant, 'besides a slight bruising mark to the face, she seems okay. It seems like he didn't get a chance to do anything else.' Frank breathed angrily through his teeth. 'But tell me,' the sergeant continued, 'you are seventy-two years old – is that correct?' Frank nodded. 'And you overcame the assailant with one blow, you say?' Frank sensed the sergeant was puzzled rather than suspicious.

'Yes. Like I said, I hit the man on the neck with my right hand, then when he tried to attack me, I forced him to the ground. He fell and cracked his head – his mouth maybe.'

'I don't disbelieve you,' said the policeman, 'but you say the man was in his twenties? Six feet tall? It just seems – different.' It was an unusual word to use, but the sergeant had seen a gamut of human strangeness in decades of Metropolitan service. Frank knew very well why he had chosen to describe Frank's actions as different.

'Is there anything else you can remember?'

'I think he had an accent. Scottish or Irish perhaps.'

'You have a slight accent yourself, Mr Fox, if you don't mind my saying so.'

'Can I go now?' Frank asked.

'Yes. I don't see why not. But we will be in touch, Mr Fox.'

'In touch?'

'Yes, I'm afraid so. No doubt that scumbag will roll up at a casualty department when the pain gets too much – unless he can find a private quack, but I doubt very much he will have the contacts, or the cash for that matter. Give it forty-eight hours and he will be in a cell somewhere in the city. Here probably.'

'So why will you need to speak to me?'

'There are two sides to every story, Mr Fox.' He looked coolly into Frank's grey eyes. 'But I'm sure you are aware of that.' The police sergeant left the room. A limping tea lady appeared and, without looking up, collected the empty mugs from the table, and left the room to continue the journey down the corridor with her trolley. Frank rose from his seat. His body was stiff, shaky and aching. He made his way out of the building and into the bright heat of a London afternoon. The city was revving its engines for rush hour. Two men dressed in dark city suits were standing, deep in conversation at the foot of the steps of the police station. They glanced at Frank as he walked past.

'The Secretary of State?' Unusually the man wore a hat on a summer's day.

'Yes, Popplewell,' replied the other. Frank shuffled away, just another Londoner making his way home.

*

In West Hampstead, Charlotte Groves was sitting on the sofa with her mother, Anna. Charlotte was explaining how she was waiting by the school gates as she had been told to do by her mother and by her teacher, Miss Grafton.

She didn't know if she was early or her mother was late, but a tall man with a cap had told her that she could not wait where she was but must move to the park where her mother would collect her. Charlotte had thought this was not right, but the man had been very clear and stern; he told Charlotte he worked for the school and showed her a card with his name and the name of the school printed on it. Charlotte had remembered that her mother and father had always said how important it was to see a stranger's identification.

'Mummy, have I done something wrong?' asked Charlotte in a voice as honest as snow.

'No, my love. No, you haven't done anything wrong.' There would be many more questions that Anna couldn't answer, and there would be anger and rage over which Charlotte would have little control. The little girl closed her eyes and snuggled into the fur of her cat, Jasper. Anna held her daughter tightly. Tears were forming, warm and large in her ducts like blood. She felt deserted and helpless, but most of all she wanted to put a knife through the heart of the animal that attacked her daughter.

*

It was nearly seven o'clock when Frank opened the door to his flat in Goldhurst Terrace. He had tried to make something of the small patch of garden in front of the tenement – he had planted asters, some potted geraniums, even a few strawberry plants, but he was fighting a losing battle against his fellow residents: a nocturnal French fitness fanatic, an Egyptian rug dealer, who was forever moving large rolls in and out of the hallway, and an ancient Jewish widow who emptied her teeming ashtrays into what remained of a thin mahonia struggling beneath the ground floor window. Everything seemed destined to die in these lonely red brick blocks. He moved along the ground floor corridor, which was cool at least, but dark. The hallway light needed a bulb and Frank collided with the handlebars of a bicycle that hadn't moved for at least two years. He put his key in the lock and entered.

The flat was small with narrow rooms and tall ceilings. There wasn't much natural light, only that which filtered through the limp netted curtains. The front of the apartment faced roughly east. Afternoons were darker here. Frank took a small tumbler from a kitchen cupboard, and from a cabinet in his sitting room, a bottle of Dutch apple liqueur. He switched on the cream Bush radio with its red circular tuner full of frequencies and station names. The BBC headlines rumbled like a slow freight train, the sober tones of a well-spoken newsreader turning like an engine. England had lost the Test Match by four wickets and the weather would be mostly hot and dry tomorrow. Frank turned off the radio. He was restless. He switched on the television. None of the four channels seemed to offer anything of interest, especially one with its chat show full of attention-stealing celebrities and obsequious host. Particularly irritating was a young comedian in oversized glasses, feigning both a cockney accent and dissent towards Margaret Thatcher's government. No doubt he will be promoting his latest work and accounting his appearance fee later, thought Frank, accurately. Within minutes, with television laughing and clapping in front of him, Frank was asleep in his chair.

The slow, shrill ring of the telephone in the hallway woke Frank from a dream of the sea. He ignored it, but the caller was persistent. Reluctantly, Frank moved slowly to the receiver.

'Hello.'

'Mr Fox?' The voice was male, light and reedy.

'Yes?' replied Frank, disorientated.

'We know it was you who attacked the little girl today.'

'What?' howled Frank in bewilderment.

'Quiet, Mr Fox. We will call again tomorrow morning at ten o'clock. Until then, let us hope the police do not find out.' The line went dead as the caller hung up.

Frank's shock almost overcame him. He staggered back to his chair gasping for breath. His body shuddered with cold, clammy fear. He reached for another shot of spirit. Dazed by tiredness and confusion, Frank's thoughts leapt about his consciousness. He felt sickness and repulsion. Frank downed his drink, then went to the kitchen and retched in the sink. He splashed water on his face and through the fringe of his thin, receding hair. Looking to the small kitchen window, the light had almost gone; it must have been nearly ten o'clock. Frank sat at the kitchen table, his palm supporting his forehead. He would call Paddington Green immediately. He rose to do so, but then something made him stop. First, he needed to go through the events of the day. Had someone been watching what happened in the park that afternoon? Whoever it was, how did they know his name and get his number? How many people were there in London with the name of Fox? Frank was suddenly startled by a series of low thumps and thuds. The Frenchman upstairs had started his workout.

*

In Mayfair, Sir Charles Gifford, Patrick Fitzmaurice and Nicholas Ogilvy-Veal were meeting for drinks in one of London's oldest gentlemen's clubs. They were joined shortly afterwards by a tall, younger man, James Ward-Lock, and a guest not yet introduced. The men greeted each other in the drawing room.

'Hello, Charles.'

'Hello, James. How are you?' The two shook hands firmly.

'Charles, may I introduce Armand Rouvier from the French Embassy.'

'Enchanté, Monsieur Armand.' Sir Charles extended a large, steady hand.

'Pleased to meet you, Sir Charles,' reciprocated the diplomat.

'Come, we must have something to drink.'

But for a dozing club member slumped near a window seat, the men were alone and sat in brown leather chairs in the corner of the room. Whisky and water were brought to them by a silent young waiter. The old boy at the window coughed, chewed on air and went back to sleep like a deaf basset hound. Fitzmaurice tapped an untipped cigarette on the arm of his chair and lit it from a book of matches on the table in front of them. Rouvier's eyes cast a 180-degree arc around the wooden panelling of the room before settling on the tumbler cupped in his hands.

'Thank you for coming, Monsieur Rouvier. You may know there has been a slight issue this afternoon,' said Ogilvy with a degree of understatement, habitual to the British upper class.

'A slight issue?' replied Rouvier, accentuating the adjective.

'What Nicholas is trying to say,' interjected Fitzmaurice, 'is the matter is being dealt with. In fact, we expect it to be resolved tomorrow.' Rouvier placed his glass on the table. He hadn't taken a sip.

'Gentlemen, you must all realise the importance of our undertaking. There can be no disruption. And I am sure you all quite understand how much we value your involvement. I think we have made that clear, don't you think?'

'Of course, of course,' Sir Charles agreed in cheerful defence. Fitzmaurice spat out the last of his cigarette smoke, extinguished the stub in a heavy glass ashtray and picked a shred of tobacco from his tongue.

'Then may I remind you, gentlemen, that our government's testing resumes in the autumn. You will agree then that this matter must...' Rouvier paused and carefully selected his vocabulary; his command of the English language was both brilliant and exact, 'must conclude.'

'Dénouement,' concurred Sir Charles. He raised his glass half-heartedly and quickly thought better of it.

'Good. Then I shall leave you all to enjoy this beautiful weather. How the weather so often improves in an English summer evening.' Rouvier, accompanied by a now rather awkward Ward-Lock, walked briskly out of the club. Fitzmaurice spoke to those remaining at the table.

'Where is O'Brien?'

'Safe enough,' replied Sir Charles. 'In considerable pain, but he will live, for now anyway.'

'Lucky then that the old fool didn't call for help at the scene, don't you think? Quite extraordinary that a man of his age could do that,' commented Ogilvy.

'Yes, more than extraordinary, I think. Something about it. I don't know.' Sir Charles's words faded as he thought about the events of the day.

'And the girl?' Fitzmaurice was keen to fill the gaps in his narrative.

'Unharmed,' said Sir Charles. 'The old man and the police seem to think it was some kind of sex attack or child molester.'

'Good,' said Fitzmaurice, with some relief. Sir Charles sat forward in his chair.

'Then I suggest we get an early night, gentlemen. I'm sure there will be a little bit of work to do tomorrow.' The three men drank what was left of their whisky. They left in silence. Outside in the streets of St James's, the evening sky was the darkest of blue. Somewhere in the direction of Westminster, church bells rang midnight.

*

In a small, comfortable maisonette in West Hampstead, Alex Groves could not sleep. He had returned home from work after a frantic, desperate call from his wife. Alex worked as a freelance lawyer and adviser to environmental charity organisations. The job was just about the lowest paid he could get in his line of business, but he believed fervently in his work. Alex could sense the world was catching up with his way of thinking. He had travelled and had seen the wounds the human race was inflicting on the planet and the ugly scars left on its skin. Far from the safety and luxury of western life, Alex had breathed in the squalor of India's slums, Africa's famine and the war-torn, arid landscapes of the Middle East. He was on a mission to change things for the world Charlotte would inherit.

But tonight, Alex cared less about global problems. His only daughter – a child he and his wife thought they may never have – could have been lost: killed, raped, he didn't know. But for the intervention of an unknown, old man. Anna was asleep in their bed, almost silent, her breathing faint and slow. He looked out of the bedroom window onto suburban north London. He glanced at the glowing red digits of the clock radio on his bedside cabinet. It was 3.15 am. Satisfied that Charlotte was sleeping, he made himself coffee from powdered granules in the kitchen, sat at the table and pulled a set of documents from his case on the floor. He checked the contents: itinerary, flights and tickets to New Zealand; a list of names and contact numbers; thick files and reports, some stamped 'Top Secret' and sets of data – figures, charts, graphs. Alex tidied the paperwork, placed it tidily back in the case, sighed and rested his face on his forearms across the table. He was due to fly to Auckland on Thursday.

*

In a side street of Piccadilly, Sir Charles Gifford buzzed the intercom of a windowless, metal door in the side of a brick-faced, featureless building. This wasn't a thoroughfare, more the backside of a showpiece street full of well-to-do shops, department stores and offices. It was dark and there was no street lighting here. Sir Charles gave his name, the door opened, and he edged gingerly over the ledge into a dimly lit stairwell. Climbing concrete stairs, he appeared at a small landing. More stairs double-backed behind him, but Sir Charles tapped on a door set back in a small recess. The door opened, its keeper not revealed. Sir Charles stepped inside to a smudge of bare bulb light.

'Good evening, Manning,' said Sir Charles affably.

'I think it may even be good morning, sir,' joked the gatekeeper. Manning was tall, in his late fifties, with an overgrown military haircut and an accent born beneath the Bow bells. 'He's through there, sir.'

'Thank you.' Sir Charles made his way down a short passage and into a large room with a low ceiling. It looked like it might once have been an office or a shop floor of some kind. Lying on a tatty makeshift bed, surrounded by water bottles and takeaway cartons, was a bandaged man of about thirty with reddish hair and a poor complexion. His arm was in a sling. It was Charlotte Groves' attacker, one Neil O'Brien, ex-Irish Guards and Special Air Service.

'You missed the cricket then, O'Brien?' said Sir Charles with sarcastic jest. 'I thought you would have enjoyed seeing the Aussies whip us Poms?'

'Hilarious, Gifford, really,' was O'Brien's surly reply. He moved slightly to get comfortable and winced sharply as a bolt of pain shot through his body.

'Well, you were busy doing other things, weren't you? Had your eye on the ball elsewhere, or rather off it.' Gifford's usual avuncular tone had changed to something at least partly sinister. O'Brien was visibly losing his nerve; he looked anxious and ill. 'You see, you rather let the side down, O'Brien.' Sir Charles was warming to his extended sporting metaphor.

'I was jumped, Gifford. Whoever that guy was, he wasn't some do-gooding pensioner who just happened to be passing by,' said O'Brien disarmingly.

'You see, the thing is, O'Brien, most of the Met is looking for you. They're looking for a pervert with ginger hair, bad skin, a broken arm and a Belfast accent. Not too many fitting that description, even in London.'

'Yeah – well, I need to lay low for a bit. Get out of town for a while.'

'Good idea, good idea.' Sir Charles walked behind O'Brien who could not see him now. Manning looked uneasy as Sir Charles slipped his gloved hand inside his summer overcoat. 'But would you lay low, O'Brien? Could we trust you to do that? We gave you another chance, remember – after the debacle in Antwerp. We all very nearly paid the price for your careless talk.' Before O'Brien had time to reply, Sir Charles drew a small handgun with silencer and shot O'Brien through the temple at point blank range. It was a surprisingly clean kill. Manning, a tough ex-paratrooper turned East End hard-man, was beginning to sweat, his skin the shade of birch bark.

'Tidy it all up, Manning, please. Over and time, wouldn't you say?' Sir Charles was gone. Manning stared at the carnage and wondered if he had just witnessed murder or an assassination.

*

The telephone rang just after eight o'clock. It was the police, a Chief Inspector Richards – polite, courteous, but formally requesting Frank attend Paddington Green again at four o'clock that day. Frank declined the offer of a car to pick him up; he would make his own way there. He reset the receiver and sat on a kitchen chair. He didn't move until his decision was made. He took his wallet, keys, coat and stick. There was a lot on his mind and much to do. The ten o'clock caller would just have to wait. He closed the front door quietly and slipped into the leafy terraces of Swiss Cottage. Above him the morning sky was blackbird egg blue and despite the city's carbon breath, a clear day was forming. Frank dug deep in his pockets, tore a peppermint from its wrapper, gobbled it like a pill and moved on down the street. A rustle in a garden startled him. A young hedgehog snorted and scuttled under a gate. Frank admired the tenacity and solitariness of the little beast, so visible in daylight but seemingly unconcerned. A wisp of wind licked the side of the street, the English seasons always undecided. Frank shivered slightly, exhaled sweetened air, his silhouette fading into the haze.

*

In a quiet mews house in Belgravia, Sir Charles scoured the morning papers. He chewed on toast and slurped a cup of tea. The telephone rang.

'Yes?' he answered.

'Your car will be there at half past nine, sir,' informed the caller.

'Very good – thank you,' said Sir Charles and he put the phone down. He adjusted his reading glasses, licked the tip of his index finger and turned a couple of pages in a small address book. Lifting the Bakelite handset, he turned the dial seven times for a local number, each time the dial rotating clockwise then back again with a fast-ticking sound.

'The Secretary of State, please. It's Sir Charles Gifford.' A red admiral butterfly briefly fluttered at the window and then flew with the gentle breeze. 'Jon, it's Charles. I'm afraid we've had to kick up a bit of dust this end. Can't have Paris getting cold feet now. There will be some unforeseen expenses – ten should cover it for now.' There followed some anxious words at the other end of the line. Sir Charles once more ignited his charm and guile. 'I will call you later, Jon.' There was a knock at the foot of the stairs. Outside a car engine was running. The driver looked into his rear-view mirror. 'Swiss Cottage,' said Sir Charles. The Rover pulled out of the mews and headed north.

*

St Barnabas Church of England School was not an inconsiderable distance from West Hampstead, but when Anna and Alex Groves had moved homes a year ago, they didn't want Charlotte to move schools. She had made friends and she enjoyed her education. The school was quite old-fashioned in its ethos. Conservative and traditional appealed to Charlotte's liberal parents, as it did to so many middle-class professionals in the suburbs. The school crest was distinctive: a green cross set on a white shield surrounded by green olive leaves. Frank had recognised it when he saw the girl's uniform. He was now at the school gates. It was busy. It occurred to Frank that he hadn't been in a school for over fifty years. Children were running and shouting and playing. Parents were talking in huddles. A teacher with arms folded was greeting children. Frank felt conspicuous that he hadn't a child with him, but nobody took any notice of him. He was probably just a slightly confused grandparent called on at the last moment to do a school drop-off.

Hurrying out of the reception office was a face Frank recognised from Paddington Green police station. Dressed simply in jeans, T-shirt and trainers was the girl's mother. Her brown hair blew about her face as she hurried to exit the site. It was now or never. Frank backtracked slightly and cut across the playground bumping awkwardly into two mothers as he did so. Apologising profusely, he gathered his pace and was almost running as he caught her. 'Excuse me. Excuse me.'

She turned and looked at Frank, who was catching his breath. She looked tired and nervous.

'Good morning, can I help you?' she asked.

'You are Charlotte's mother?' That much about her he did know. She looked horrified and turned to the school, as if to call for help.

'Yes.' The reply was hesitant and full of fear.

'I am the man who found your daughter yesterday, in the park.' The woman's expression changed instantly. Fear melted and was replaced by some kind of relief, some kind of joy. 'I saw you at Paddington Green yesterday when you collected Charlotte. I recognised her school uniform. Is she... is Charlotte okay?' Frank felt like the whole school must be watching him. But nobody was. A bell sounded, and within a few moments the children had vanished and the site was quiet.

'She is sleeping at home.'

'I am sorry but I must talk to you. Something has happened and I fear I may be in some danger. Is there somewhere we can talk?' Anna looked uncomfortable.

'Okay. You know Panzer's? There is a small café nearby with a red and white awning. I will meet you there.' She smiled faintly, distantly, then walked out of the gates, turned to the left and was gone. The morning cloud cover was quickly burning up. A blackbird stood beneath a shrub. It had caught a caterpillar in a tree next to a line of large waste containers belonging to the school. Frank watched it hop away. A crisp packet drifted across the ground. Frank lifted it with his stick and put it in one of the open bins. As he left for the rendezvous with Anna Groves, Frank felt divorced from the very nature of things.

*

The traffic was getting heavier on the east side of Hyde Park. Rather than do battle with the chaos of the Edgware Road, Sir Charles's driver darted through a maze of squares and side streets. In seemingly no time, the Rover was under the Westway, continuing north to NW6.

'We should be early,' chuckled Sir Charles, 'just in time for coffee.' And he laughed some more.

'No more than ten minutes now, sir,' updated the driver, his voice deep like Tilbury silt. Sir Charles closed his eyes. He still loved the thrill of the chase. Ever since his Chindit days, it was his ill-found destiny – a mixed and confused desire for misplaced patriotism and pursuit of natural selection. The air in the car was stale. Outside it was sickly sweet with fuel fumes. But his mind was in the teak forests of Burma. The driver had expertly avoided Marylebone. Sir Charles checked his watch and the contents of the case beside him in the empty passenger seat. Covert operation. Deep penetration behind enemy lines. Special forces. Aged men were forever like their boyhood selves, mostly. The sun caught the windscreen, and for a second, a blinding flash of light struck the car.

*

The Mountain Lodge was a peculiar name for a café in St John's Wood. But then London was full of random names seemingly unrelated to their place in the city. Frank arrived first, chose a table in the cool, quieter space away from the window and pavement. A beautiful, tall waitress, no more than twenty years of age, smiled politely, ready with a notepad. Frank ordered coffee and lemon cake. He wasn't hungry, but he needed sugar. He watched the waitress walk back to the counter and noticed her glossy, brown hair tied into a ponytail with a silver band and two Biro pens. How the young could wear anything and look divine. On the walls were a series of black and white photographs – cyclists, skiers, mountaineers. Recognising a couple of figures – a Belgian pedalling somewhere high in the Pyrenees, an Austrian careering down an Alpine slope – Frank's mind once more fell into the past: this time to the summer of 1939, or was it '38? He couldn't pin the memories down today. At that moment, the café door opened to the signal of a cheery bell.

Frank raised his hand slightly, but he needn't have bothered. Anna had seen him first. She sat down at the table. The café was empty except for two elderly women who had just taken a window seat. The waitress finished noting down their order and before taking Anna's. 'Just a coffee, please,' said Anna and she did her best to smile. Frank wasted no time in starting the conversation.

'I am sorry to have alarmed you,' said Frank, but Anna interrupted him.

'Was she hurt? What happened? I need to know. The police told me very little.' Frank paused and sat a little lower in his seat before replying.

'No. Not really. I saw almost the whole incident.' Frank chose his words sparingly and carefully. 'He covered your daughter's face with his hand and was dragging her in to some bushes.' Anna's eyes were wide with horror. 'But he didn't touch her.' Frank felt awkward. 'I mean, he didn't harm her in any way.' Anna knew what Frank meant. She was crying, but she looked relieved.

'Thank you,' she said. 'Thank you. For what you did.' The waitress brought their orders and Frank nodded thanks to her. Anna took a paper napkin from a diner-style dispenser and blew her nose. 'I'm sorry,' she said, 'but I just had to know.'

'Of course,' said Frank comfortingly. He picked up a fork and cut into the cake. There were a few moments of silence curtailed by the loud, aggressive growl of a passing motorcycle.

'You said you were in danger?' Anna looked into Frank's eyes.

'Yes. Possibly. Something very strange happened last night.' Frank explained the phone call to Anna.

'Why haven't you called the police?' Anna asked. It was a reasonable question.

'They want to see me today at four o'clock. I was planning to tell them then. But,' and Frank lowered his voice as if somebody might be listening, 'if they – whoever called – know my telephone number, who's to say they don't know my address?'

'Somebody saw you in the park – or at the newspaper kiosk maybe?'

'Maybe,' said Frank, 'but unlikely.'

'Somebody saw you, followed you to the police station. A prankster with a sick sense of humour?'

'I don't think so. Only the police knew it was me at the crime scene. The police and the attacker – that's all.'

'You think it was Charlotte's attacker who called you?'

'Again – I think it unlikely, but who else could it be?' Frank spoke earnestly. 'Anna, please listen to me. I will tell the police everything about the phone call this afternoon, but please believe me – I had nothing to do with the attack on your daughter.'

'I believe you, Frank. Charlotte has not wavered from her story.'

'There is something more, something bigger to this, Anna.' They sat silently, sipping their coffee. Anna left a pound note on the table. She scribbled on a napkin and passed it to Frank. Hitching her bag strap to her shoulder, she left. Frank pushed the uneaten lemon cake to one side. The young waitress returned.

'Was everything okay for you?' she said, looking at Frank's plate.

'Very good. Very good – thank you,' replied Frank absently. He unfixed his gaze and tilted his head to the girl, smiled thinly and got up to leave. The small bell rang as the door closed behind him. The puzzled waitress cleared the table.

*

The pale blue Rover carrying Sir Charles Gifford turned into Goldhurst Terrace shortly before ten o'clock. It pulled into a kerb-side space in front of a builder's skip. A young labourer threw some old floorboards into it.

'I won't be long. Wait here.' Sir Charles looked up and down the street and walked into the garden of Frank's apartment block. He took a passkey from his inside pocket and turned it with gloved hand. Avoiding the bicycle in the corridor, Sir Charles knocked at Frank's door. He knocked again, only slightly harder. There was no reply. Sir Charles took a piece of metal shaped like a file and inserted it into the door frame. With another skeleton key he applied pressure to the door. A metallic click confirmed he had successfully unlocked it, and he put his housebreaking implements back in his pockets and pushed the door ajar. The flat was silent. On the table was a half-empty cup. Sir Charles took off a glove and dipped his pink finger into the coffee. It wasn't yet cold. He snarled an expletive, careful not to raise his voice. He looked at the small chimney piece above the electric fire. There were some framed photographs – all of them taken many years ago. One stood out. It was a group of young men in military uniforms, standing relaxed as if on leave or celebrating. Sir Charles was angry as he left Goldhurst Terrace, angry he had failed to hunt down his quarry, but somehow relieved to be leaving a place that felt haunted by a melancholy he couldn't explain.

*

A few envelopes tumbled through the letterbox. The outline of the postman evaporated in the frosted glass.

Charlotte sat at the kitchen table colouring in a jungle scene with bright felt tip pens. Thoroughly absorbed in her activity, her father watched over her protectively. The sky was clear and blue, disturbed only by a few wisps of stratus cloud and expended vapour trails. London's comfortable northern suburbs were quiet this Wednesday morning. Alex picked up the mail. There was little of interest other than a white envelope addressed to him in a scrawling, handwritten slant. Inside was a neatly folded sheet of writing paper. There was no watermark, nor address – simply a typed note. Alex's heart was racing and his mouth was dry.

'Daddy, can I have a drink, please?' Charlotte did not look up from her drawing book.

'Sorry, darling, what did you say?'

'Can I have a drink, please, Daddy?' she repeated.

'Yes, of course, my love.' The front door lock turned. Anna had returned. Alex quickly stuffed the letter into his pocket.

'Hello, you.' Anna wrapped her arms around Charlotte and squeezed her.

'Careful, Mummy. Look at the tiger's ear now.' They both giggled.

'Sorry, Charlotte.' Anna turned to her husband. 'How has she been?'

'Fine. Fine. Quiet. She asked why she didn't have to go to school today.'

'What did you tell her?'

'Just that she would be very tired today after having to talk to the policewoman and she should stay at home to rest.' There was uncomfortable quiet between them. 'You were a long time – at the school.'

'Mr Barnes was seeing another parent, so I had to wait. And then it took a while to explain everything.'

'What did he say?'

'He was anxious, obviously. They're going to send a letter to all the parents today. And the police are going to talk to the children about stranger danger.'

'And presumably the children will wait inside the school from now on?' said Alex angrily, his face reddening beneath his newly cropped greying hair. There was more awkward silence.

'You're not still going on Thursday, are you? Surely not.'

'I don't know, Anna. We've been working on this for over two years. It's not like somebody else can just step in – who would have that kind of knowledge? I don't know. Maybe it can be delayed.' Charlotte was singing a song by a Norwegian pop group.

'Maybe?' Anna's fury was rising. 'Look at your child, Alex! Do you really think that flying to the other side of the world is the right thing to do? After all of this?' She looked at him for a few seconds and then went to have a shower. Alex peeped over his daughter's shoulder.

'That's beautiful, Charlotte,' he said. But for all the guilt that he was beginning to feel, his mind was on another side of the planet.

*

Emerging from Camden Town tube station, Frank's eyes narrowed in the bright light of late morning. He hurried along the Holloway Road and turned right into a narrow, ugly street and stopped at an Italian café. He tapped the brass knocker of a black door. It was opened by a diminutive older man dressed in loose-fitting jeans and an old office shirt unbuttoned to the waist. The man peered above his glasses and met Frank with a beaming smile.

'Frankie,' said the man, almost singing, 'Frankie, Frankie, Frankie. Come in, my boy,' the man continued with warmth and a little ceremony.

'Thank you, Carlo.' The little man shut the big door.

'So, you are in trouble, Frankie, yes? That is why you call me?'

'Possibly, Carlo.'

'Then we will talk.' Frank and Carlo's history was rich, colourful and long. Both were immigrants either during or just after the Second World War. London's blitzed landscape was then a magnet for displaced Europeans whose own lives, families, homes and cities were equally ruined, if not worse. In those first few months after the armistice, Europe crawled like a disturbed ant nest. Carlo had been an Italian prisoner-of-war. On some forgotten date in 1941, he had been sent to collect water from a well near an arid crossroads at the edge of the Libyan desert. His truck was caught by a strafing British aircraft and he was left stranded over five miles from his unit. Luckily for Carlo, he was able to surrender to a British patrol before thirst and snakes got him. Carlo was a lucky man. His battalion was all but wiped out a few days later. Surviving a torpedo attack on the sailing to England, Carlo had spent the rest of the war in the fields of Essex and Kent digging for victory. Like many of his countrymen, he wisely bided his time and before too long found himself back on the winning side. Here he had learned the native language, but perhaps more importantly, the values of the common Englishman. If he hadn't known already, Carlo quickly realised that ordinary men the world over, whether they are from Calabria or Colchester, are very similar.

After a tiring explanation, Frank settled back in a chair and sipped his espresso coffee.

'You must stay here. At least for a little while. And you must go to the police today. If you do not, it will look suspicious. I will arrange a taxi for you. Rico can drive you and bring you here afterwards. Everything will be okay. We have lived through much worse, my friend.' Carlo touched his friend on the shoulder and went to make a phone call. Frank felt suddenly overwhelmed by fatigue. Maybe it was the strong Italian coffee, he thought briefly, but who was he kidding? It had been a frantic twenty-four hours and there was still a long, long way to go.

*

Outside the Richmond Arms in Chelsea, on a stepladder, the landlord was tending his hanging baskets that were full of geraniums. Water dripped on to the pavement to be quickly burned up by the midday sun. Inside the pub, Sir Charles was sipping a pint of Fuller's ale.

'I adore the smell of a pub at lunchtime, Jon. The hoppy staleness of it all.' Dust particles hung like stars in the shafts of light that pierced the opaque, decorated glass. Jonathan Popplewell lit a tipped cigarette with a gold lighter. He sat cross-legged with a decided look of impatience on his brow.

'I would prefer it if we weren't here at all, Charles. I must say, this whole thing is a bit embarrassing. Frankly, it's a cock-up.'

'These things happen when you play for high stakes, Jon. The gambler in you must see that.'

'Yes, but we are running out of time,' the Secretary of State whispered urgently. The red vessels in the whites of his eyes were numerous.

'Then we raise the stakes,' added Sir Charles. It was a gambling metaphor this time that added to his drama. He fanned away the minister's tobacco smoke.

'You are going to have to stop talking in riddles, Charles. Speak plainly, for God's sake.'

'Then let me be clear. O'Brien is dealt with – the police won't find a body somewhere along the Thames. The old man has been warned off. My contact at the Met tells me he is due for interview at four. We have, shall we say, found a witness who will testify that the hero of the story is in fact the villain.'

'I don't understand. It seems convoluted.'

'We don't know what was said between them. There can be no loose ends, Jon, no scraps of paper blowing in the wind. The police only have the girl's statement and the old man's. Who's to say he didn't persuade her to change the story?' Sir Charles was still struggling to convince Popplewell, who looked queasily uneasy. 'Jon, we needed the girl to get to Groves. Groves is due to fly to New Zealand on Friday and there he will meet with his bearded, hippy friends. They will cause anarchy down there. They won't stop until the whole programme is halted. That cannot be allowed to happen.'

'No, it can't,' said Popplewell soberly. 'Under no circumstances.'

'I think a subpoena will be just the ticket. I am sure any decent father would want to be there for every step of the trial.' It was clear from his fat, smug smile that Sir Charles was pleased with this latest perceived stroke of brilliance. As he shifted the beer jar from left to right, his fingers were sticky like morning slugs.

'Trial? So, you are framing an innocent man?'

'Only tell a big lie, Jon – little ones don't work. It should be second nature in your line of work. Anyway, consider the great work you are doing for Queen and country – not to mention a few hundred thousand in preference shares. You are helping to protect the civilised world. Millions of people. What is that compared to the life of one busybody old man?' And he left Jonathan Popplewell to his frayed nerves and his chain-smoking.

Three

North Cornwall - Summer, 1940

St Eval Church stands in a remote spot a mile or so from the coast. In mist and fog, there can be few places on Earth that match it for eeriness and ghostly atmosphere. At six o'clock a few hardy parishioners gathered for evensong. The service was mercifully short. The Reverend Dunning was as keen as any to get to the 'Lord's Prayer' and go home. As the last of the prayer books were collected from the pews, only Stump was left.

'A short service, Vicar, thankfully,' said Stump not even attempting to hide irony.

'Well, I thought it best, given the weather,' Dunning replied diplomatically.

'If you say so.'

'Well, don't you think so, Mr Trelawny?' The vicar was

stung by Stump's sarcasm, if that's what it was. Stump was the verger at St Eval. He had returned to the Anglican faith out of loyalty to his ancestors after a brief affair with non-conformism in the parish.

'I do,' said Stump idly. 'But given folk had come out all this way this evening, perhaps you could have given them a little bit more?'

'Look, Ezra, I did my best in the circumstances. There is a war on.'

'Indeed there is,' said Stump with a twinkle in his granite-grey eyes.

'And we... I am very grateful for everything you do – especially the churchyard. But why do you keep coming here if you disagree with the ways we do things?' It was a question that neither of them could answer.

'A word of reassurance, Vicar,' said Stump.

'I beg your pardon?' replied the vicar indignantly.

'A service to reassure the parish. Everyone knows invasion could happen any day now.'

'But not here, surely? The Germans can't land here. It's impossible.'

'It doesn't really matter where, but any coastal community will feel vulnerable at present. If you were to give a special service, to unite the parish, to bring us all together in the house of God,' Stump could see he was appealing to Dunning's ego, 'it could be the making of you, Vicar.' The clergyman looked to the pulpit and then back at Stump.

'But when? Next Sunday perhaps?'

'No, sooner would be much better.'

'Sooner?'

'Yes.' Stump paused. 'Tomorrow.'

'Tomorrow?' gasped Dunning.

'Strike while the iron's hot.'

'But how would we let people know?'

'Leave that to me. Six o'clock tomorrow, then?' As Reverend Dunning scurried home with a headful of ideas for tomorrow's sermon, Stump got on his bicycle and slowly disappeared into the fog.

*

'You say they got lost in the fog? Well, I never,' said Gladys Trewithen. 'That Merriman girl will get into real trouble one of these days. Just like her mother, she is.'

'They are safe, Granny. That's all that matters, surely,' said Dorothy.

'I dare say,' and she carried on shuffling the washing-up. 'And you'll never guess what.'

'What?'

'Bob Chapman paid up that five bob.'

'Really?' replied Dorothy with genuine surprise.

'And there's something else. Look at this.' Gladys pushed an envelope across the table to where Dorothy was sitting. Dorothy looked on hesitantly. 'Go on, open it.' Inside was a greetings card. On the outside was a country scene – a hedgerow, a dog rose and bindweed. Inside was some handwritten verse. Dorothy read aloud: "'My love she sings at dawn with the lark, her song as sweet as the dew, and when day is done and so sets the sun, I want to be there with you." Blimey, Granny. It's not even Valentine's Day.' But Granny Trewithen wasn't paying attention – she was somewhere in her mind's morning dew.

'Of course, this changes everything.' Granny eventually returned to the conversation she had started. 'He is obviously going to ask me to marry him.' Granny snatched the card and envelope away from Dorothy as if they were jewels.

'Well, I'll be very happy for you both,' congratulated Dorothy with a teasing grin.

'Thank you, my love,' said Gladys. Then her eyes flicked towards Dorothy again. 'I'll kill you,' she barked, and chased her granddaughter around the table armed with Bob Chapman's love song.

*

Light was murky at the cove. Stump Trelawney stood at the edge of high water. Three figures were approaching, two dragging a small inflatable onto the sand.

'Good evening, Mr Trelawney.'

'Captain Kramer.'

'Do you have any news for me?'

'You will have two hours tomorrow evening between six and eight o'clock. Maybe a little more. There is a machinery workshop in the village at Quarry's Turn.' Stump had prepared a crude map. 'It belongs to a man called Rowe. He won't be there. Rowe fixes engines, farm implements, anything at all. His shed is a treasure cove of spare parts and all sorts of rubbish. He might have something. If you find what you need, take it. That is the best I can do.' Kramer took the map and shook Stump firmly by the hand.

'You have done more than enough, but can I ask one question? Why are you helping a German submarine crew?' Stump looked towards the sea and sighed heavily.

'In the last war, Captain, there was slaughter beyond all imagining. I was in France. My company – from a Cornish regiment – were attacking the enemy line. Most of my pals were killed in the first wave. Somehow, I almost got to their wire when a bullet ripped through my thigh. I lay there all night in a shell hole full of mud. When the pain got too much, I let out a cry and I must have passed out. When I came to, a German orderly was hovering above me. I thought he was going to kill me, but he was dressing my wound. He just said "go" and I crawled back to our trench. Our commanding officer was disgusted – told me I should have killed the Jerry. He was a right royal one, that major. But I have never forgotten that kindness, Captain Kramer. I owe my life to that German, whoever he was.' The sea broke harder and the surf hissed at their feet.

'Few of us are animals – even us Germans.' The two men laughed and Kramer lit a cigarette. He offered one to Stump who refused. 'Thank you, Mr Trelawney.' Kramer saluted in a traditional fashion. The inflatable slipped into the fog. Stump watched it vanish and then plodded along the dry sand to the dunes. His dreams would be full of demons tonight.

*

In the summer of 1940, the British people were bracing themselves for invasion by the German armed forces, even if very few in high government thought such a threat was credible. But for the new Prime Minister, Winston Churchill, the invasion scare was a useful propaganda tool, keeping his fellow countrymen well and truly on their toes. Throughout the south and east of England mines and sea defences had been laid. The Royal Air Force, and its pilots from all over the world, were scrapping for their lives high above the home counties and across the Channel. Along the north Cornish coastline, things were quieter – just. Airfields had been quickly built and planes were buzzing about across the water in search of the enemy in the air and beneath the waves. But the skies were empty this Monday morning. Nothing was flying in the fog that refused to shift.

'There's a service at St Eval this evening we're all supposed to attend,' said Gladys with a hint of disdain. The rooms in her slate cottage in Penrose were dark despite the fog being a little thinner here.

'On a Monday?' Dorothy replied. She was rolling pastry on the parlour table. 'Seems a bit odd. Who told you?'

'Ruth Mallett. Whole parish is going apparently. Important announcement from the vicar,' said Gladys with a sarcastic grin. Thoughts of yesterday afternoon at the cove flashed across her mind. Had word got out? If it had, there would be no surprise where it escaped from, but Billy Mallett wouldn't cross Stump – not if he wanted to be seen in Porthrowan again. She tried to banish these kinds of thoughts.

'Well, it might be fun, Granny. Especially if Bob Chapman's going to be there.' And she continued to work on the pastry.

'Bob Chapman in church? Pigs might fly.'

'Well, if Ruth Mallett's going...' started Dorothy.

'Ruth Mallett in church? She'd bring the devil for company.'

'She doesn't need to – she's got her husband,' added Dorothy with a little spite and grit.

'Too true. Have you seen him lately? Looks like Ruth has been working him harder than Merriman. He's hardly the rampant bull – more the tired old dog.' And both women dissolved into laughter.

*

On board U3276 the mood was tense. Kramer was planning with his officers.

'Herr Kapitänleutnant, I must protest. Three men is not enough. What happens if we meet resistance?' Lange was in combative mood and keen for action.

'No, Lange. This is a covert operation. No fireworks. The fewer of us the better. I will go with Mertens and the chief. You will stay on the boat. Forstner will take charge in my absence. You will deputise.' Lange revealed a defiant expression. 'That is an order, Lange, not a request.'

'Yes, Kapitänleutnant,' Lange acknowledged.

'We have two hours to get in and get out.' Kramer revealed the map. 'The tide will help us a little. If the fog holds, we should get ashore okay.'

'And defences – are there any?'

'No. The beach isn't mined. There is some wire, but there are two clear gaps. Here and here.' Kramer pointed to them. 'We take this one. Here there is a small bridge. We cross this and enter this field – over a wooden gate. We keep to the edge of the field next to the road. There is a short, steep hill. We climb this. There is an inn on the hill. Beyond the inn is the road to the village. The workshop is the first building on the right as we enter the village. We enter this building by the door at the back. Does everyone understand? Good, then let us prepare. We leave in two hours.'

Kramer retired briefly to his cabin. He closed the curtain which offered a modicum of privacy. He lay on the bed and thought of home. Of Hamburg. Of the canals and the lakes. And the unmistakable smell of the Elbe. He pictured Clara in her parents' apartment in Hamburg. Clara with child. Not his child, but theirs nonetheless. He had known her since kindergarten school. Her parents and his had been friends before both of them were born. Clara and Hans, sister and brother. But when Clara's fiancé had been killed in Poland in the first hours of the war, Hans had vowed to look after her. When he had left Kiel in late July, he promised to marry her when he returned. But the war was casting spells with every passing day. There was talk among the senior officers that Germany's submarines would be moved to France. Kramer breathed deeply through his nose. Everything smelled and tasted of diesel. He took his revolver from the drawer, without any intention of using it at all.

At a few minutes to five o'clock, the small inflatable was quickly taken from its deck compartment. Kramer, Mertens and the chief engineer, Stuckmeier – gaunt, haggard and the oldest man in the crew – took to the boat and paddled toward the shore. Lange was watching carefully from the tower.

'I doubt we will see them again,' he said absently.

'That sounds like defeatist talk,' Forstner joked, but Lange had not understood the humour. 'I don't think that would go down very well in Berlin, do you?' added Forstner drily.

'I didn't mean anything by it, sir,' apologised Lange. Forstner didn't reply and went below deck.

The ocean was loud and playful, but benign by its own standards. Kramer's boat skidded into the sand. The three men efficiently disembarked and towed the dinghy to a small cave at the northern edge of the cove. A towering arch of granite soared above them, its outline partially visible in the mist.

'Like a cathedral,' admired Mertens.

'A photo opportunity,' joked Stuckmeier. The men laughed and enjoyed a few peaceful moments before heading out of the cove and along the bay. The tide was far out and the large expanse of firm, wet sand made for easy progress. Kramer was the first to notice.

'I think this fog is beginning to lift,' he said quietly, 'don't you think, Mertens?'

'I think you're right, Kapitänleutnant. The air temperature is changing.' They moved swiftly along the southern side of the bay having crossed it diagonally. It wasn't long before they reached the small road bridge that Stump had described to Kramer the previous evening. The shallow stream beneath poured underneath the arch as the three men crouched beside it.

'Opposite is the gate. On my count we go.' Kramer counted to three. Just as they were about to cross the road, a young couple trotted over the bridge, giggling as they went. The young woman had seen Mertens.

'Who's that?' she called. Mertens froze, daring not to breathe.

'There's nobody there, Lizzie,' her boyfriend replied. 'Come on or we will be even more late than we already are. That will give your father something else to say.' The lovers hurried on their way not stopping any longer to look for phantoms in the fog.

'Come on,' urged Mertens. Kramer and Stuckmeier followed, and they each climbed over the gate. Following the hedgeline up to the pub took no more than five minutes. The plan was running to schedule. In a short time, they would be searching Rowe's junkyard emporium for the pieces they needed to fix the submarine's six-cylinder engines. Pale smudges of orange light marked the windows of the tavern. It wasn't far now as they picked up the track to Porthrowan hamlet. There in the early evening grey was what must surely have been the workshop. Kramer checked the map. They were at Quarry's Turn.

'This is it,' confirmed Kramer.

*

The Reverend Dunning stood proud and upright in the pulpit of St Eval. Never had he seen the church so full. The congregation stood to sing the first hymn, 'Nearer My God to Thee' – an inspired choice thought Dunning: sombre and brave. Prayers and readings followed, including Stump's chosen passage from Luke's gospel about helping a neighbour. The organ cranked up for the next hymn, an obscure and interminable song from the mid-nineteenth century. Very few, if any, knew the melody. When the sermon commenced, the church was silent. Dunning had chosen to construct an elaborate metaphor around the theme of bees. Without directly referring to invasion, he compared the hive to the community, working and protecting its queen, fighting off weather and wasps, as if in a war. Punctuated by meticulously chosen references from the New Testament, Dunning was convinced he had pulled off a master stroke of oratory. When he had finished some forty-five minutes later, he was surprised to see so many bewildered expressions in front of him.

The baffled villagers filed out of the narthex. Dunning wished them well, blessing all with God's love.

'What on earth was that all about?' muttered Gladys.

'I'm not altogether sure, Granny,' giggled her granddaughter.

'Very good, Vicar. Very good indeed. My congratulations to you,' said Stump, shaking Dunning's hand firmly.

'Really? Do you think so?'

'Of course – just the right length as well,' Stump added as he wheeled his bicycle along the church path. The reverend scratched his balding pate. Yes. Pretty good, he thought. A bit of tweaking perhaps needed for next time. He went back inside the church. It was nearly eight o'clock.

*

Silently, the three submariners approached the corrugated iron door at the back of the shed. Kramer tried the handle and, to his good fortune, found it unlocked. Opening the door emitted a loud scraping noise. Mertens cursed. The disturbance seemed not to have caused alarm. Once inside, all was still and spookily quiet.

'Mertens, by the door. Stuckmeier, all yours.' The chief engineer – or simply The Chief as he was affectionately known – was in his element. His life was diesel engines and electric motors, ballast tanks and torpedo tubes. Like a mouse sniffing for food, Stuckmeier searched quickly, his thin torch flicking between shelves, in and out of drawers, in jars and boxes. Mechanics the world over, it seemed, shared their own inscrutable codes of chaos. Stuckmeier handed Kramer the end of a very fine piece of wire, the width of cotton thread.

'Hold the end.' Stuckmeier expertly unwound a length of wire, made a neat cut. He repeated the process twice more and put the coils safely in his coat. Kramer watched him, fascinated. The torch beam moved its way through the near darkness like a searchlight. Stuckmeier then grinned madly. He held up what looked like a very ordinary lump of metal, as if he had found a precious stone. The hunt continued.

'I need a container,' whispered Stuckmeier, holding a can of oil. 'I don't need very much.'

'Can't you just take it?' said Kramer.

'That wouldn't be right,' answered Stuckmeier mysteriously. He extracted some of the oil and decanted it into a jar, screwing the lid tightly.

'Ready?'

'Ready,' confirmed Stuckmeier. Mertens suddenly spoke.

'Quiet! Shush!' Behind the workshop door was a rustling noise. Moments later the scraping of the door was followed by a shaft of daylight entering the building. The three sailors crouched, their eyes waiting for movement. Standing in the doorway, silhouetted by the fading daylight, was Rowe. His ponderous, chubby frame stepped into the workshop. Rowe's torch beam slowly edged the floor. It didn't meet Mertens. Stuckmeier was kneeling behind the carcass of an old Austin. The flashlight failed to find him too. As it swung around and traversed the far wall, it caught something in its beam. It was Kramer.

'Who's that?' yelled Rowe. They needed no instruction. Mertens powered past Rowe and sent him spinning off balance, the mechanic's palm clutching the edge of his lathe as he regained control of his bulky frame. Stuckmeier followed, his wiry frame well trained in clambering around cramped, darkened spaces full of metal. But Kramer was boxed in as he tried to follow them. Rowe was now standing upright. Kramer could not be sure whether he could see him.

'Let's be having you then, thief,' growled Rowe. 'Not at church, then? Thought you'd help yourself to my valuables, did you?' Kramer realised his identity was protected, for now at least. He had to think quickly before Rowe raised any more alarm. He moved alongside the old car. Rowe's torch beam was less patient now and so was Rowe. The big mechanic moved into his workshop, but it was an unwise decision. He approached Kramer, still unseen and lurking by the now open passenger door.

'Oh, I see,' said Rowe extending his hand carrying the torch into the vehicle. Kramer timed his move perfectly. He slammed the door against Rowe's protruding forearm. The door closed on it with a vile cracking sound. Rowe let out a high-pitched yell of pain as his radial bone fractured. Kramer scurried out of the workshop. In the lane he thought he heard voices nearby. The light was poor and he was momentarily disorientated. At Quarry's Turn, he hurdled what he thought was the field gate that would take him to the hill and to the bay. Instead, after careering down a slope, he reached a path next to a small stream. Presumably the path to his right would lead to the sea? He would take that risk. As he did so, he could make out a female voice faintly singing. The song was getting closer. Kramer turned, but slipped as he did so, landing painfully on his side. As he sat up, a woman's face looked down on him. It was the girl he had seen yesterday at the beach. Her beauty overwhelmed him, and he was lost for words.

'Shouldn't you be fixing your submarine, Captain?' the girl said with cool calm.

'It seems I am lost,' replied Kramer, and he laughed wryly. Dorothy looked at the fallen sailor with curiosity and interest. His eyes were kind, and she could see he meant her no harm. The moment was interrupted by the approaching clamour of busy conversation. The parishioners were heading home. Instinctively, Dorothy made a decision.

'You had better come with me,' she told Kramer. Kramer had only seconds to agree before the game was up. He got to his feet, badly bruised perhaps, but not injured greatly, and followed Dorothy along the ever-darkening path to Penrose.

The blue twilight was falling on the small village which nestled in farmland and the remains of an old quarry, about a mile from the sea. There was little here to interest the outside world and rarely did the outside world disturb its peace. A small village store and a postbox were the only concessions and connection to a more modern way of life. Otherwise, the squat, slate cottages sat in the land as they had done for generations.

Dorothy led Kramer along the path. The trees and hedgerows now loomed high above them both, meeting at intervals, creating a tunnel-like effect. Kramer considered this woman's courage, or was it recklessness? Here she was leading a German officer out of danger, betraying her own countrymen even, shielding an enemy soldier. But she wasn't the only one. There were plenty in his own country who would gladly get rid of Hitler and his cronies if they weren't so terrified of the regime. There were those too in England who would happily strike a deal with the Führer. One of them used to be King. No, thought Kramer, there are no sides in war – just those who organise and profit from it, and those it happens to.

They stopped at a gap in the hedge. Enclosed in a mass of honeysuckle and ivy was a scruffy wooden picket gate. Without motion or sound, Dorothy led Kramer to her grandmother's cottage. It was obscured from the path by fog, but Kramer could make out a garden abundant with vegetables and fruit. In a nostalgic way, it reminded him of the garden villages on the outskirts of Hamburg. How he longed for home and its simple comfort. Dorothy opened the door to the cottage. She lit lamps and candles in an assured routine that suggested it was a house without electricity supply.

'Who else is here?' said Kramer with a hint of nerves about his voice.

'No one,' Dorothy replied.

'No one?' Kramer was relieved, but unsure.

'I live here alone with my grandmother. She won't be home tonight. She is staying with her…' Dorothy hesitated and almost laughed, 'with her friend.' Kramer knew what she meant and did not say anything. There was a not uncomfortable silence. Dorothy fetched two glasses and a corked bottle, pouring out blue-purple liquid.

'Blackberry wine,' she said. 'Last year's.' The alcohol was strong and warm and medicinal.

'Thank you,' said Kramer. He took another sip of wine. 'What is your name?'

'Dorothy, but most people call me Dot. Yours?'

'Hans. It was my uncle's name. He was killed in the last war.'

'So was my father,' said Dorothy quietly. A beat of sadness struck her face.

'I'm sorry,' said Kramer. Dorothy seemed keen to tell her story to the stranger.

'He died in the last week of the war. I never knew him, and he never met me. My mother was heartbroken and couldn't live without him. She threw herself off Trevose Head when I was a toddler. They say her body was washed up on Booby's Bay and that she looked still and at peace. But I don't believe that. I think my grandmother told me that to make me feel better. Have you seen the cliffs at Trevose? The waves there? Nobody could survive that in one piece.' Kramer again said nothing.

'Where is she now – your mother?' For a moment, Dorothy didn't know what he meant, then understood.

'She's buried at St Eval. My father in Belgium. That's the irony – they're not together even now.' She poured herself another drink and refilled Kramer's glass. 'And you, Captain, what is your story?' Kramer told her about Clara and his life in Hamburg. How he had been lured to the sea by tales of adventure told to him by his father's friends who had served in the German Imperial Navy.

'It's funny,' he said, 'many of those tales were about Cornwall. How the U-boats would wait in the Channel for English ships on their way to Bristol and Cardiff. Many ships were lost here. But our submarines do not come close to the coast anymore – there are too many aeroplanes hunting us.'

'And you thought you would follow in the footsteps of your fathers?' Kramer didn't understand the humour.

'We made several errors. We should have turned back and gone home when the engines started to fail. But I was eager to prove myself to the men. This is my first command.'

'Several errors?' Dorothy asked.

'I, my officers and the navigator mistook Trevose for Lundy Island. By the time we approached the Quies, it was too late.'

'What will you do if you can't fix the boat?'

'We will surrender,' said Kramer gloomily, 'as the entire German armed forces will do one day.'

'Really? You think you are losing the war?' said Dorothy with surprise.

'We were losing from the day we started,' continued Kramer. 'Do you know how many U-boats are on patrol in the Atlantic at the moment? How many submarines we have out there hunting your ships?'

'No. I have no idea.'

'Eight, maybe nine. Like looking for needles in haystacks.' Kramer gave a wry laugh. 'So, you see, we are not the invincible foe you might think we are.' The room was still and then Kramer looked up. 'How long do you think the fog will last?'

'Not long,' said Dorothy. 'We haven't had one like this in my lifetime.' She continued, 'It will be gone in a day or two.' A clock above the fireplace chimed the half-hour.

'I must get back to the boat,' said Kramer.

'It would be madness to attempt that in darkness. Wait until first light, then go. There is a small wooden skiff in the cove, to the left of the path that runs down from the cliffs. It belongs to the village – anybody can use it.'

'Thank you,' Kramer said, but he realised the word wasn't strong enough. Dorothy poured some more wine.

'Why did you save the children?'

'They are children. Who wouldn't have done the same thing?' Kramer shrugged his shoulders.

'But you must have known that it would be risky – that you would come out of hiding?'

'There is a risk to any rescue. We didn't expect to find a welcoming party on the shore.' They laughed at the absurdity and coincidence of the situation.

'Is it dangerous at sea?'

'Sometimes. Mostly it is tedious. Waiting. Watching. Endless empty seas. The weather can be frightening.'

'But you are under the water?'

'Not as much as you would think. We can only submerge for so long. We even attack on the surface.'

'And have you sunk ships?' Dorothy asked the question without hint of judgement.

'Not on this patrol, but yes, when on my previous boat.' He paused and his eyes darkened as he stared into the fire. 'We sank a small steamer in the Atlantic – a few hundred miles west of Ireland. It was small enough that we didn't need to use a torpedo. We used gunfire. The crew clambered into a lifeboat, but they got into trouble as the boat settled and all were lost. All except one man.'

'What happened to him?' Kramer continued, oblivious almost to her question.

'He stood on a piece of wooden decking that had come loose from the bow. It made a good raft. He must have been an engineer or a stoker or something because he was dressed only in trousers and a vest. He was tall, strong, not young. Maybe a father.'

'And you rescued him?'

'He waved to us as we approached. The steamer had sunk. There was lots of floating wreckage. My captain asked the man the name of his boat. Chalfield, I remember him saying. The survivor motioned to us as if asking to come aboard. One of our men climbed onto the hull. I remember vividly because he slipped on the casing and water was washing over it in the swell. He threw the man a canvas bag containing some brandy, food and a compass.'

'And you left him?' Dorothy was disbelieving.

'A few of us protested to the captain. An argument broke out in the tower. I and another junior officer were nearly put on charges for insubordination. The commander was a loyal Nazi.' Kramer wore a haunted look, vulnerable, guilty. 'I will never forget that man's face as we left. Desperate. Alone on that cold ocean swell.' Dorothy pokered the embers in the grate.

'Would you like to wash and clean up a bit? You could probably do with it,' Dorothy joked quite deliberately. Without waiting for an answer, she prepared hot water, soap, even a razor, adding lavender oil to Kramer's bath. In a small bathroom that doubled as a laundry, Kramer lay back in the enamel tub. He thought about Dorothy – her dark, sad eyes, her slim hips and the long brown hair. There was something about her that made him feel deeply, to reflect, to forget. He dried himself down and, dressed only in the towel she'd given him, walked into the sitting room. There was no sign of Dorothy, nor his clothes. He called out, but there was no reply. His pulse began to quicken. A trap maybe? A steep, narrow staircase led Kramer upstairs. There were two doors; one was open.

He walked into the bedroom. Half covered in crisp white sheets lay Dorothy, naked and still. She had pulled the bedsheet around her just enough to cover her breasts. Her long legs were sculpted in the cotton.

'It will soon be sunrise,' she said, looking at Kramer without blinking. Outside, the fog was lifting.

*

Aboard U3276, lookouts stood in its bandstand-like tower searching the sea with binoculars. Lange, particularly, was anxious and fidgeting.

'They should have returned by now. I don't like this,' he said, 'I have a bad feeling about it.'

'Do be quiet, Lange,' retorted Forstner, paying him no more attention.

'I can see them, port-side bow,' called one of the lookouts. Mertens and Stuckmeier pulled alongside while the crew roped them in and helped them get aboard.

'Where is the captain?' enquired Forstner of Mertens.

'I don't know. One of the villagers surprised us.'

'Do you have what you need, Chief?'

'Yes, I think so,' replied Stuckmeier.

'Then, get those diesels fixed and let's get out of here,' Forstner advised.

'With or without the Kapitänleutnant,' added Lange. Forstner stared hard at Lange, but he didn't disagree. While two lookouts remained above deck, the rest of the men slid into the belly of the boat. For the engineers, it was going to be the longest night of their lives.

*

First light was just after five o'clock, the blue twilight of dawn clearer now as the mists were beginning to lift. Dorothy had made tea with mint from the garden. Kramer was once again dressed for combat. Dorothy placed the tea, some bread and jam in front of him. He wasn't hungry but ate nonetheless. A stillness, quiet, sad and mournful, floated in the room like dust. Outside, a wood pigeon called from a walnut tree. Kramer looked at Dorothy, dressed in a tatty dressing gown, hair tied loosely at the back. She was beautiful and brave. Her honest passion had disarmed him completely. Young and lonely and thrown into a cauldron of war that neither of them understood, nor wanted – in circumstances like these, there is no right or wrong, no map, no compass guide that leads to the exit signs. Kramer thought of Clara and felt a pang of guilt. But he didn't love her, and Clara knew that too. For all her physical frailty, her mind was made of iron. Perhaps he should surrender? His men wouldn't know what happened to him. It was a fleeting fancy. He was a man of duty, and this wasn't going to change now – he owed that to Dorothy at least. It seemed like she was listening to his thoughts.

'You must go,' she said. 'You know the way – you're sure?' There was only slight tremulousness in her voice.

'Yes,' he replied, reassuring her. 'Thank you, Dorothy.' He couldn't look at her for too long. His eyes began to warm and moisten, tears that could become a tide.

'Go – and remember, follow the path all the way to the bay. Don't go through the village.' These were her final instructions. He wanted to stay, wanted to tell her that the war would not last. That his people, in Hamburg, in Bremen, in Kiel, hated the Nazis. That Germany would not win the war. But instead, he grabbed both of her hands and pulled her towards him one last time.

'Take this.' She placed a metal charm in his palm.

'What is it?'

'A piskey. For good luck,' she said. And then Kramer was gone. Dorothy closed the door to the cottage. She ran upstairs and fell on the bed. The sheets still had the scent of lavender oil and her lover. For the first time in her life, she understood how her mother must have felt. More than that, it was her mother she yearned for now.

Kramer saw no one as he ran light-footed to the cove. He found the wooden dinghy easily enough, upturned in a shallow cave. It was heavier than he had imagined, and he wondered how on earth two children could have manoeuvred it so easily. The oars had seen better days but were serviceable. Tide was almost at high water. He had to get away. Easing the small craft into the water, he climbed into the rocking boat and pulled against the surf. The lapping, splashing water was cold, but awakened his senses. He spat some salty water from his mouth and briefly looked to the shore. He was now about a hundred metres from the sand – if he could see this, the fog was clearing. He hastened his stroke and heaved with all his strength. Sunlight was now piercing patches of fog. Kramer was tiring. He stopped and turned to look out to sea. He could just make out the looming, black shapes of the Quies and the white surf breaking at their base. The lighthouse at

Trevose was still hidden by the weather, but it wouldn't be for long. As the sun burnt through, the British resumed their hunting. After an hour and at the point of collapse, Kramer was nearing the hulk of the submarine.

Mertens was on deck – loyal, terrier-like Mertens. He could barely contain his joy when he saw his captain. Others quickly scurried across the deck casing and hauled Kramer aboard. There was no time for storytelling – for this, Kramer was grateful. Consumed by urgent tasks, the crew were making final preparations to leave.

'What is the mechanical report, Forstner?' enquired Kramer.

'The chief is ready to start engines, Kapitänleutnant.'

'Then what are we waiting for?' Kramer said with winking irony. Forstner communicated to the engine room through the intercom, giving the order to start engines. With a slow, screeching moan, the pistons of the two big diesels started to come to life, billowing clouds of black smoke from the exhaust system as they did so. The noise was deafening. But somehow, Stuckmeier had worked his magic.

'We must get out into open water fast,' said Kramer. 'We must charge the electric motors before the weather changes completely. The British will be flying as soon as they can.' Stuckmeier wanted more time to test his engines, but Kramer was impatient. He stayed in the tower with Forstner. The spirits of the men were lifting with the fog. Somewhere below decks in the officers' quarters, Capitano Cossato was lying on his bunk singing a Tuscan folk song.

'A weary time! A weary time! How glazed each weary eye – when looking westward, I beheld something in the sky.' Forstner glanced at Kramer but didn't say anything of his captain's lyrical expression. The U-boat edged out of the shelter of its hiding place and slipped away into open sea. By noon, the haag would have burned up and gone, but by then, U3276 would be somewhere in the North Atlantic.

Four

London - Summer, 1985

Rico arrived promptly just before three-thirty in a big square saloon. He was red-faced in the afternoon heat despite his Parmanese heritage. In his late-thirties, prematurely receding and full of wide smiles, he was every inch his uncle's favourite nephew.

'Rico, my son, please make sure my friend Mr Fox is punctual,' said Carlo flamboyantly. He could have been auditioning for the part of a minor villain in a James Bond movie.

'It would be my pleasure, uncle,' Rico replied, maintaining the drama.

'Just tell them the truth, my friend.' Carlo was shaking his friend's hand.

'But in the wrong hands, truth is worse than lies,'

said Frank darkly. Carlo did not reply. He shrugged his shoulders and closed the front door to his house.

They exchanged only a few words during the ride to Paddington Green. Frank sat in the front of the car, gazing at London's vast Victorian skyline along the Marylebone Road. Arriving at the police station, Rico explained to Frank that he would wait in a neighbouring street. The desk sergeant greeted Frank with a perfunctory nod, then stepped into the back office to talk with a colleague. Frank did not have to wait long. Chief Inspector Richards was a physically unimpressive human being. Smartly dressed in over-ironed uniform, his manner was not unfriendly, or initially intimidating. Frank thought him abjectly dull – the sort of career policeman whose life ambition was to be Assistant Chief Constable one day.

'Mr Fox, thank you for coming today. I would just like to go over a few things with you,' Richards began in an estuarine twang. Frank recited the previous day's events with clarity, but he sensed the chief inspector wanted more.

'You say this man was in his twenties or thirties? Can you be exact, Mr Fox?'

'It is difficult for me to be precise, Chief Inspector. I am seventy-two years old. Everyone younger than fifty looks the same to me.'

'This isn't a joking matter, Mr Fox.' Frank wasn't trying to be funny.

'And you say the man didn't look like a typical criminal? That is rather an odd statement to make, don't you think?'

'What I mean is, he looked like...' But Frank was stuck

for words. He wanted to say he looked like a professional, but what on earth did that mean? Frank couldn't explain it. The chief inspector was poised to attack again, but Frank anticipated this. 'He looked like a military man.'

'A military man?'

'Yes – the way he carried himself, the way he moved. Have you ever served in the armed forces, Chief Inspector?' The chief inspector shook his head and bit the end of his pen. 'Then it is difficult to explain.'

'And you are a military man, Mr Fox?'

'I was. In the war.' And Frank's memory bank played like a camera roll.

'Mr Fox, I have to inform you that some evidence has emerged. My team are working through this as we speak. I must ask you formally not to leave your house this evening and not to leave London. We will see you again tomorrow at ten o'clock. This time a car will collect you.'

'New evidence? I don't understand. Am I under arrest?'

'No, Mr Fox, you are not under arrest. You are helping us with our inquiries.' Shocked, but somehow not altogether surprised, Frank got up to leave.

'Chief Inspector?' Richards looked up. 'Please may I use a telephone?'

'There is a payphone in the reception area,' said Richards curtly. Frank fumbled for change. He pulled out the scrap of paper Anna had given him and called the number. He pressed the coin into the slot as her voice answered the call.

'Anna? It's Frank. I need to see you.' Anna spoke a few words. 'About an hour.' He put the phone back in its cradle and walked briskly to where Rico was dozing. He got in and awoke the taxi driver.

'Everything go okay, Mr Fox?' Rico yawned massively.

'I need to go to Swiss Cottage briefly, please. Then West Hampstead.'

'Bit of shopping, eh?'

'Something like that,' said Frank, tired of explanations. Rico whistled and pulled onto the main thoroughfare. So did the car that was about to follow them.

*

A brooding, bitter tension was eating up Alex and Anna Groves. Charlotte was quietly playing in her room, seemingly undisturbed by the toxic silence in the kitchen.

'Are you going to tell me what's wrong, or are you going to just shut me out as normal?' Anna was a mixture of anger and hurt. 'Well?' Alex knew he owed her some kind of explanation.

'I received a note – in the post,' he said. His voice was shaky, brittle even.

'What sort of note?'

'I don't know – a warning, I suppose. It doesn't say who it's from – just a typed message.' He took out the badly folded piece of paper from his pocket and handed it to Anna. She read it. It contained one typed line: 'Do not go to New Zealand if you want what is best for your family.' She handed him back the note.

'You don't seem very surprised?' Alex said.

'It could be from anyone. There are enough people

who know who you are and what you do – corrupt businessmen, politicians, who knows? It's not as if you haven't encountered threats before. Remember Portsall Rocks?'

'Yes, but don't you think this is a bit more…' and as he searched for the right word he glared at Anna, 'sinister?'

'Given everything that's happened to Charlotte, I think it's sinister you are even considering going to Auckland.'

'Then you agree with this?' Alex held the note in front of her. They didn't speak for several seconds. And then Alex caught a glimpse of an expression, a wild glint in Anna's eye.

'You know something about this, don't you?'

'Don't be ridiculous.' Her long, thin fingers pushed a chopping board across the kitchen worktop.

'Don't lie to me, Anna.' The veins in his forehead were bulging. He was insistent in his statement. Anna knew he would not let this go. More seconds passed. They could both hear Charlotte moving upstairs as she went to the bathroom.

'Okay, so what if I did write it? What difference would it make? What will it take for you to realise that your family comes first? Not the planet. Not the protest. Not your bloody ego. Us. Us is what matters.' Alex had given up listening after her admission. Consumed by blind fury, the breach in trust was too great for reason to act. He walked past her and upstairs. She could hear drawers opening and closing, and then her husband talking softly to their daughter. He returned to the kitchen a few minutes later with a suitcase and a rucksack. Picking up the box of paperwork, he took out the contents and transferred them to the case.

'What are you doing?' Anna asked him incredulously. 'Where are you going?' Alex didn't turn around or say goodbye.

'New Zealand.' And he left his family, the door wide open. Anna stood at the doorway.

'I didn't write it anyway,' she shouted, but Alex had moved quickly and was gone. A neighbour's curtains twitched. Anna went back inside.

*

At Goldhurst Terrace, Frank was careful not to arouse the attention of his neighbours, not that he had spoken to any of them for months. The silver saloon that had been following slowed a little then glided away, its powerful engine purring. In less than ten minutes he had collected changes of clothes, a few personal items and a packet of bank notes from a wall safe hidden in a cupboard, savings that, until now, he didn't think he would ever need. But he had a strong feeling that somebody had been in the flat. A photograph in a slightly different position. A chair askew. He inspected the front door. No apparent sign of a forced entry, but a blister to the paint work and a tiny chip of wood dislodged. Even in these twilight years, Frank's eyesight had never failed, not even when he needed to read. He trusted his senses and was pleased to get back inside the cab.

The drive to West Hampstead was quick and easy as London rolled north into the suburbs, greener and steeper as the land climbed away from the Thames. Rico knew these streets like the back of his hand. Wardour Court was a modern block of flats not far from the Finchley Road. Frank asked a puzzled Rico to wait. He had little trouble finding the first floor maisonette. Anna quickly answered and let him in. Frank instinctively felt her upset, an atmosphere damp with tears. Indescribably, she was pleased to see him and felt a little less anxious now he was here.

'He's left. My husband – he has gone to New Zealand. I don't know what to do.' Her usual resilience and fortitude had fallen apart. Charlotte appeared in the hallway. She smiled at Frank, and Frank smiled back.

'Hello again,' he said gently, and in that brief exchange, Anna had no further reason to doubt the truth in the old man's story.

'Would you like to see my drawing?' Charlotte asked.

'I would very much like to see it.' In the midst of their panic and fear, Frank calmly listened to Charlotte's elaborate narrative.

'Very good. Thank you for sharing this with me,' he said.

'I'm going to draw you one now.' Charlotte scampered upstairs to her pens.

'She is coping well, it would seem.'

'I think so, but I am worried about her.'

'Of course.'

'Why did you want to see me?' They were still standing between the hall and the kitchen.

'The police say they have new evidence. They say I am

only helping with their inquiries, but there was something in their tone, the way they implied things. It is hard to explain.'

'You don't have to, Mr Fox. I don't believe this was a random attack on my daughter. I think it is connected to my husband's work.'

'What does he do?' Anna told Frank a little of Alex's environmental quests and his radical political status. He listened. When she had finished, Anna felt as if he had understood.

'From what you say, Anna, it seems we are both in some kind of game that is bigger than either of us.'

'What are you going to do?'

'I am going to get out of London.'

'But you say the police want to see you? In just over twelve hours?'

'If I stay, I could face who knows what – a trial? Prison? Despite what your daughter says. If the outcome is decided, I am a doomed man.'

'Where will you go?'

'I don't know,' said Frank and his words faded. Anna's bottom lip was tucked behind her upper front teeth as she bit a little nervously.

'I do.'

'I'm sorry?'

'You will come with us.'

'With you? What do you mean?'

'Wait. Give me fifteen minutes.' As Frank sat at the kitchen table, Anna rushed around the apartment. An excited Charlotte was soon busily helping her mother.

They were both soon standing in the hallway with two cases. Charlotte was clutching a floppy kangaroo soft toy.

'This is Brucey,' she said.

'Did you say you had a car outside?'

'Yes,' replied Frank hesitantly.

'Then it can take us.' Anna grabbed her keys. Frank carried her case. The three of them walked to the car. A bemused Rico opened the rear doors for his new passengers and put their cases in the boot.

'Right. Camden Town at last, then,' Rico said with mock cheeriness.

'Sorry, Rico. There is a change of plan.'

'I should have guessed. Where to now, Mr Fox? The Dartford Tunnel?'

'No. Cornwall.' Anna and Frank spoke the words together. It was as if one knew what the other was thinking.

*

Later that evening, Sir Charles was dining in a restaurant near Sloane Square with Jonathan Popplewell. It was another balmy English evening. As Sir Charles salivated over his lamb cutlets and minted peas, Popplewell nursed white wine in a long-stemmed glass.

'These really are very good. Are you sure you won't have something, Jon?'

'No thank you, Charles. I am really not that hungry.'

'Suit yourself, old boy.' Sir Charles ploughed on, the juices of the meat spilling over his lips and chin. An adventurous pea bounced off the plate and away in the direction of the nearest table. 'I think we've covered all bases, Jon,' he continued, eating, talking, hiccupping and burping at the same time in a whole spasm of digestion. 'Fitzmaurice followed our man back from Paddington Green this afternoon. He's back in his hutch for the evening. Just have to make sure Richards isn't too involved.'

'Richards?'

'Chief inspector down there. Good sort but plays with too straight a bat for my liking. We need somebody a bit more Botham than Boycott, if you know what I mean.'

'I think so.' Popplewell took a cigarette from a white and purple packet on the table.

'You go ahead. Doesn't bother me.' Popplewell lit his cigarette, inhaled deeply and blew a funnel of blue smoke from the side of his mouth. He sat back, cross-legged in his chair, seemingly a little more relaxed.

'I'll get on to it first thing and speak to my contact.'

'How is Rouvier?'

'Ward-Lock hasn't been in touch, so I assume all is well.'

'And Groves? What do we know of him?'

'Nicholas arranged for his apartment to be watched from dusk till dawn. Latest report suggests he hasn't left home for days.'

'And if he does?'

'I doubt very much he will. Nicholas had the ingenious idea of sending a little note. Just to wake him up a bit and suggest he stays put.' Popplewell seemed to infer what Sir Charles meant.

'Groves won't get to the Pacific, then? Without him, they shouldn't be able to proceed.'

'No leader down there from what we can make out. I have my doubts whether Groves would have pulled it off anyway, but best to be on the safe side.'

'And this untidy little plan to kidnap the child and use her for ransom can be forgotten about. But I still don't understand why you have to go after the old man?'

'Like I said, there must be closure – no trail, no wake. Even the tiniest scrap of information could be traced back to us. We just don't know if anything was said between O'Brien and the old man. The tiniest scrap – it would ruin you, Jon, if any of it were to get out.' Sir Charles closed his dinner plate and wiped the fat from his mouth with his napkin. Popplewell looked at him with barely concealed disdain.

'The whole thing is really quite despicable.'

'Yes, we are, Jon, we most certainly are.' Sir Charles beckoned an attentive waiter and ordered more wine.

*

The sun was setting over the Wiltshire plains like ripening plum skins. Rico had settled to his task having spoken to his reassuring uncle from a payphone in a service station at Fleet. It was past eight o'clock and the roads were quiet. Charlotte had fallen asleep silently as children do.

'I've never been to Cornwall,' said Rico breaking a peaceful silence in the car.

'I used to live there,' said Anna.

'Really? What brought you to the Smoke?' Rico was keen to converse with his attractive, slightly older female passenger.

'I was brought up there.' She was keen to close the conversation down and doze with her daughter, but gave up a little more of her story. 'At school, I was very good at Geography for some reason and I won a scholarship to study in London. That's where I met my husband. I have stayed ever since.'

'Do you like it? Do you miss Cornwall?' Rico's questions were well-natured and genuine. Anna did not mind answering them for the time being.

'We've been to Cornwall once with Charlotte – just to show her what it's like. I go there on my own sometimes – maybe a couple of times a year. Do I miss it? I don't know. It seems like another lifetime ago. It sounds silly, but I haven't had time to think about it.'

'Not at all,' agreed Rico. 'Life tends to get in the way.' Rico then set off on a long monologue about his own family – his wife and their four children, his brothers, their life in Tufnell Park. Anna and Frank exchanged a smile, and every now and then Frank would ask Rico a question, sending him down another biographical diversion. Anna was content to listen and gaze out into the endless fields of barley and wheat. They passed Stonehenge which stood out in the half-light like bad teeth. In less than an hour, night had fallen around them as the car cut a lone shape through the trees of the Blackdown Hills. Shortly before one o'clock in the morning, the taxi pulled up next to a wooden gate. Anna was easing Charlotte awake. Frank thanked Rico profusely and insisted he accept a bundle of bank notes, which he did awkwardly, but gratefully.

'Please tell your uncle I will be in touch, Rico. He is a good man.' The taillights of Rico's car evaporated in the thin black mist. Frank felt strangely awake and alert. The air smelled familiar almost. Distantly, an owl was calling. They stood in the lane as Anna fumbled for some keys.

'Where are we?' asked Frank.

'It's a tiny village called Penrose,' she said. They carried their cases to the cottage. Frank's breathing tightened; he felt dizzy. Stars were clear in the still sky. It was very late. Frank was dreaming that he had been here before. Many years ago.

*

In the early hours of Thursday morning, Alex Groves arrived at Heathrow Airport's Terminal 3, dropped off by a friend he had stayed with since leaving Wardour Court.

'Thanks, mate, I appreciate it,' he said as the friend hauled the suitcase over the lip of the hatchback boot.

'Sure you're doing the right thing, Al?' offered the scruffy-looking friend with kindness.

'All this will be here when I get back.'

'But will she?'

'It's a risk I have to take. I'll see you.' Alex didn't need any further attempts to dissuade him from the course he'd decided upon. He had been waiting his whole life to make a difference and now was his chance. The friend climbed back into the small Japanese car and drove away.

The Air New Zealand flight would board in an hour. The departure hall was quiet. He felt youthful excitement again – the energy and nervousness that so often accompanies solo travel. How he loved his daughter and would miss her, but his purpose was defined. He sat down. The seats around him were peppered with businessmen, a family or two, and what looked like a sports team of some sort, all in matching tracksuits. The random variousness of global travel was both exciting and futile. Alex sipped some more of his watery, tasteless coffee. How this terminal could do with refurbishment, he thought idly, looking about the tired building. None of it mattered, though. Just over an hour later, the Boeing carrying Alex Groves was taxiing across asphalt.

*

'What do you mean he's not there?' bellowed Sir Charles to a shaken caller. 'Where the hell is he, then?' Evidently, Nicholas Ogilvy-Weal's covert operation had fallen apart somewhat. 'And the girl and her mother – don't tell me they have gone as well?' More disagreement followed, punctuated by plosive expletives and a barrage of anger. Sir Charles slammed the receiver down and wiped the sweat that wetted his forehead. He made another frantic telephone call. This time his manner was restrained, if not obsequious. At a quarter past two in the morning, a black cab pulled up outside his mews house. Sir Charles stepped into it. The taxi pulled away and drove to Swiss Cottage, but there was nobody home at Goldhurst Terrace, as he had feared.

Conspiracies formed in his mind. Somebody must have warned them? It was all too much of a weird coincidence. Back at Sydney Mews, Sir Charles poured a large Cognac, then called Fitzmaurice, Ogilvy-Veal and Ward-Lock. By four o'clock, all three were sitting in the club in St James's.

The drawing room was quiet. The three younger men had the look of guilty schoolboys, Ogilvy-Veal especially. Unusually, Sir Charles was nursing a cup of coffee.

'I went to Mr Fox's – that is his name, I believe – flat about two hours ago. He wasn't there. Odd coincidence, don't you think? Patrick, what do you know?' Any of the characteristic avuncular charm had disappeared. The quick-tempered Fitzmaurice retorted in robust manner.

'I followed him back from Paddington Green in the afternoon. He went into the flat. There is no question mark over that.'

'And you checked in at regular intervals?' Fitzmaurice said nothing. 'No, I thought not.'

'Maybe he was scared off, caught scent of something,' said Ogilvy-Veal, trying to be helpful.

'Scent of your cologne,' said Fitzmaurice, looking pointedly at Sir Charles and correctly guessing that he had been to Frank's apartment beforehand. 'And anyway, where is Groves, more to the point? Surely we should be more worried about him.'

'With any luck, he will have taken his family somewhere quiet. Nicholas's letter may have done the trick there.'

'And Fox?' said Fitzmaurice, lighting his customary cigarette. Smoke curled above their table and drifted away into the big square Georgian room.

'You don't think,' said Ward-Lock ruminatively, 'that they're all together? In a sort of... bubble.'

'A bubble?' laughed Fitzmaurice.

'I don't follow,' Ogilvy-Veal added.

'Well, it seems odd they have all vanished at once, that's all. Maybe they had some kind of tip-off or something?' Inadvertently, Ward-Lock had scattered some seeds of suspicion across the table. Whatever his private doubts, Sir Charles was keen to rein in their imaginations and anchor the situation before it got out of hand.

'Impossible,' he said, with as much conviction as he could muster. 'How on earth could that happen? They don't know each other from Adam. Their only contact could have been at Paddington Green, and they were all kept apart. Gentlemen, I am going to call time on our discussion for now. We are all very tired. It has been a long night. I suggest we reconvene when we have had some rest. And by then, I fancy, our quarries will reappear.' The hunting party shuffled away, each unconvinced by Sir Charles's rallying call, and each now a little suspicious of the other.

*

It was a clear, bright morning, early in North Cornwall, with just a hint of autumn gathering on the berries and hedgerows, gossamer webs catching the light. Frank was already dressed and walking in the garden of Trescore Cottage. Anna joined him. She was wearing pyjama bottoms and a huge baggy jumper.

'It's beautiful, isn't it?'

'Yes. It is,' said Frank. A wood pigeon called from an ash tree in the green valley beyond. 'Who looks after it?' he asked.

'Eric Chapman,' she replied. 'He's the local odd-job man.'

'He does a good job. I have tried to keep a small garden at my flat in London, but it is a fruitless task. There is no light. The soil is poor. And the neighbours like to fertilise the geraniums with cigarette ash.' Anna laughed. 'How is Charlotte?'

'She is fine. She will probably sleep late.'

'She has been through a great deal. How old is she?'

'Nearly nine.' An unspoken moment of trust between them had grown. 'Are you hungry?'

'Probably,' said Frank. They laughed and Anna turned towards the house.

'Anna.'

'Yes?'

'Nothing.' She looked at him with half a smile and went into the kitchen to prepare breakfast. Frank pinched his bottom lip with his thumb and forefinger. His mind was scrambled with a collage of images and sensations. He could smell the sea. After breakfast, he would go for a walk and make sure his mind was not playing games with his heart.

*

The car that had been sent to collect Frank returned empty to Paddington Green just before eleven.

'We'll need everything you can find on Fox, if there is anything at all,' said Richards to an enthusiastic young officer, fresh-faced enough to still be at school.

'Yes, sir.'

Richards called another colleague on the internal phone line. 'Send a car to 14 Wardour Court, please, Keegan. Better make sure Mrs Groves and her family are okay. Just a courtesy call, I think. And Keegan, better ask if they have seen anything of Fox. Unlikely of course, but just a routine question.' Richards was flummoxed. He was dubious about the new evidence that implicated Frank Fox. A lone bystander had come forward out of nowhere to report they had seen an old man attacking a young girl, dragging her into undergrowth in St John's Wood Church Gardens. When pressed, the timings didn't quite match. There were discrepancies. Richards was keen to get this witness in, but so far had been unsuccessful. All of it didn't feel right. The chief inspector sat up in his chair, unsettled and unsure of what to do next. There was a tap at his office door.

'Yes?' called Richards.

'Tea, sir?' offered Mrs MacDonald, the station housekeeper, or PG as she was affectionately known.

'Yes, thank you,' Richards said. A nice cup of tea, he thought. As if that ever solved anything. The phone rang. It was the chief superintendent. He wanted to see Richards immediately.

'Thank you for coming so promptly, Richards,' said the chief superintendent. 'Please do sit down.'

'Thank you, sir.'

'I will keep this brief, as I know you are very busy downstairs. What can you tell me about this incident in the park at St John's Wood on Tuesday?' Richards explained the past couple of days' events. He did so with precision and clarity. The chief superintendent warmed to his efficiency.

'And what of the family?'

'We have sent a car to the flat this morning. They are due to call in any time.'

'Well, let's find out, shall we?' Within a phone call, it was revealed that the Groves family were not at home. 'Leave this with me now, Richards. That's all. And thank you.'

'I'm sorry, sir?' Richards replied, stung a little by the ambiguity of the instruction.

'No need for you to pursue this one. Refer it to me.'

'Yes, sir.' Richards left, stuck somewhere between frustration and a feeling that his hunch and doubt about this case had been right all along. Meanwhile, the chief superintendent was making another call.

'Good morning, sir. Yes – I have got the details. Yes, sir – he is very reliable. No, I have told him to refer it to me. I will, sir, at what time, please? I will see you then, sir.' Later that morning, the chief superintendent arrived at Scotland Yard for a meeting that lasted no more than fifteen minutes. He tucked his cap under his arm as he got back inside the car. Paddington Green had been taken off the case.

*

Below London's square mile, not far from Pudding Lane, a group of men was gathering in the tunnels of a disused tube station. There were dozens of these places, abandoned in the warrens of the capital's subterranean transport network. But very few could obtain access to such exclusive, dank meeting spaces. Three distinct groups assembled, each sheltering in the shadows of a platform recess or what was once an exit point. To add to the macabre drama, some were wearing hats or glasses, masking identities.

'We are running out of options and what's more, gentlemen, we are running out of time. There have been a series of alarming coincidences. Almost unbelievably so, some might say. I have just received information confirming that AG is on board a flight due to land in Auckland at around midnight. Our plans to keep him here have failed, leaving a lot of mess to tidy up. This has been an expensive operation and there have been multiple failures. Of course, these debts will have to be called in.' The voice was calm, chilling and final. 'We can only hope that the Polynesian testing goes ahead without a hitch. Otherwise, it is my opinion that the deal will be off. Are there any questions?' A cough reverberated around the tunnel.

A male voice with a south-east English accent spoke.

'Do we have a contingency plan?'

'We have a clean-up plan, if that's what you mean? Gifford will disperse his squad.'

'And the St John's Wood incident?'

'Closed pending whereabouts of Fox et al.'

'Do we know the identity of Fox?'

'No, but the evidence suggests he is working for an agency linked to Groves. Seventy-year-old pensioners just don't fall from the trees and roll over a marine highly skilled in hand-to-hand combat. Further questions?' The silence suggested not. 'In that case, gentlemen, that is all. Gifford will stay behind.' Sir Charles had been dreading this summons. He was damp under the collar, pins and needles in his wrists.

'Well, Gifford, you understand the seriousness of this?' It was a rhetorical question. 'It goes to the very top, you understand.'

'Yes, I do understand,' he replied gravely.

'But it can't go to the very top. You understand that as well, don't you?' The intimations spoke more clearly than any explication. 'If Paris cancels its orders with us, we will hold you at least partly responsible. And you will appreciate the clarity, I'm sure.' Before Sir Charles could offer any meagre resistance, leather soles tapped away into the darkness. He stood alone in the silence, somewhere beneath the roaring streets of the Embankment. A tremor of fear was soon supplanted by acid-like thoughts of revenge. He would hunt down the old man, Fox. If this ship was to sink, it would go down with all hands.

*

Emerging from the underworld in mid-afternoon, Sir Charles adjusted his eyes to the sunlight. He made a quick call from a telephone box, hailed a black cab and, despite heavy traffic, was in West Hampstead in an hour. It was easy to get into Wardour Court – cheap locks in cheap buildings. There was clearly no one there. On the kitchen table was a note: 'If you have changed your mind, we are in Penrose.' Presumably written by the wife to her husband. But Penrose – where was that? Wales, Lake District? Sir Charles looked around the flat. In a small sitting room adjoining the kitchen, he found plenty of family photographs. There were many books lining the shelves – novels and travel journals mainly. And a road atlas. He checked the index. Penrice, Penrioch, Penrith... Penrose. 'Gotcha,' he said triumphantly. A quick calculation estimated a six-hour journey by car. He scanned the map again and put it back on the shelf. Sir Charles was closing the front door of the maisonette when a neighbour peered over her doorstep.

'I'm Uncle Peter,' Sir Charles bellowed, somewhat unconvincingly. The bent old lady stared at him pointedly. 'You don't know where they've gone? Only I was dropping off a present.'

'Left yesterday,' the old woman said.

'All of them?'

'Just the mother and the girl.'

'Not Alex?' added Sir Charles, feigning an air of familiarity.

'No. They're always arguing,' said the woman in a thick North London twang, pleased of the company and the chance to share her gossip. 'He left the day before.'

'So just the two of them, then?'

'No. There was another man. Didn't see his face, though. Probably a bit older, I would say.'

'What did he look like?'

'Like I said, I didn't see his face.' The woman was becoming a little suspicious and called for her cat. A fat tabby trotted in around her ankles. She looked at Sir Charles again and closed her door. With the engine and meter running, Sir Charles took the taxi back to his Belgravia home. There he telephoned to book a room, under a false name and address, in a large Victorian hotel just south of Penrose. He packed a bag and from a locked cabinet took out a British service revolver, wrapped in soft cloth. Outside the mews cottage, he unlocked the garage doors. The twenty-year-old, powder blue Mercedes started with the first turn of the key. If only the British could make cars like this, he thought to himself. Sir Charles was soon speeding through south-west London, keen to avoid the rush hour, and keener still to make last orders at the Blue Bay Hotel bar.

*

The breakfast had been wonderful. Poached eggs on fresh, crusty, toasted bread. How difficult it was in the modern age to find decent bread. Frank finished his coffee.

'If you don't mind, Anna, I would like to go for a walk,' he said.

'Of course. Turn left out of the gate and follow the path all the way to the sea,' she replied brightly. There was an ease to her company that seemed so natural. 'There won't be too many people around. The school holidays don't start until next week.' In the cottage garden, wood pigeons were calling. Frank picked a sprig of mint and twisted the leaves between his fingers and popped some in his mouth.

The walk to Porthrowan took less than an hour at a gentle pace. The summer green shades were darkening, snoozing their way to autumn. Blackberry flowers were pink in the hedgerows. In an odd way, summer was a dying time. Frank followed the path beneath the village which stood above the sloping field to his right. To his left was a whispering silver stream. He paused and breathed quickly through his nose, trying to prevent a tear from falling, but it was no use. The emotions were too raw and the current too strong. The wind picked up a little from the sea. He walked on and the path descended into a large square car park lined with a row of about a dozen houses. At the entrance to the car park was a road junction shaded by trees. A van sped past. Frank crossed the road, past a small beach shop, and followed a path that quickly became sand, then dunes, then the sea. Before him was Porthrowan Bay, long and narrow. The tide was out, breaking about quarter of a mile distant. Frank had stood here in the summer of 1940, but this was the first time he had seen its stark beauty.

He strode out to the foreshore, across rippled wet sand. A couple of walkers tossed a ball to their dog. Nearing the grey surf, the smells and sounds of the sea refreshed him. The tide was out far enough to get to the cove. Funny how the past surges in a torrent when it breaks through the dam that has been holding it back. The great granite arch towered above him – just like the cathedral Mertens and Stuckmeier had joked about. He reached the spot where they had brought those children ashore, where he had stolen the little wooden dinghy to row back to the boat, on that morning when he had left her, the scent of lavender oil still lingering on his skin. Looking out to sea, the four black shapes of the Quies loomed like giant shark fins, and the white lighthouse at Trevose Head stood strong like a sentinel. He sank to his knees. Hiding most of his life, here was another great escape, only there was nowhere left to run. Hans Kramer felt like he was kneeling at the edge of the Earth.

Five

North Cornwall - Spring, 1941

'Looks like Dot, I'd say,' said Vera Craddock, breathing heavy tobacco smoke over the baby. 'Got her cheekbones. Not her hair colour, though. Father blond, is he?'

'He is,' confirmed Gladys.

'When we going to meet him, then?'

'Meet who?'

'The father, the fiancé.'

'The husband, you mean. When he's next on leave.'

'When will that be, then?' Vera was annoying, and persistently so. It was clear she was not altogether convinced by what Gladys was telling her.

'Any day soon, Dot says,' Mrs Trewithen replied without taking her eyes off the little face in the pram.

'I will be pleased to meet him,' continued Vera through

pursed lips and squinted eyes as she relit her pipe. 'I like a man in uniform.'

'Don't we know it,' teased Gladys. Vera glared at her old friend.

'Some of us weren't lucky enough to keep ours.' It was rare for Vera to be ambiguous. Gladys kindly squeezed her wizened friend's arm, and they exchanged knowing, sad smiles.

Emily had been born early in March. Dorothy had confided in her grandmother. She alone understood. And so Gladys had devised a plan to spare her granddaughter and great-grandchild the embarrassment of having a child out of wedlock. Dorothy had quickly joined the Women's Auxiliary Air Force. She had been posted to a base in Kent just as the Germans had started their Blitz on British cities. The training, the uniform, the people – all had opened her eyes to a bigger, wider world. Most of all she had relished the sense of purpose and direction. In the autumn she had met a pilot, now grounded due to injury and fatigue. One night, following a dance in the local village, she had told him her story. She had expected him to balk, to run, to quit, but he had not. He bore no prejudice, or judgement. War causes crazy circumstances. Later that month, he vowed to stand by her and the child, raise it as his own. They were married in London before winter.

'Granny, Granny,' called Dorothy, rushing through the gate. 'He'll be here this evening. George will be here this evening.' She had returned from the village having used a telephone belonging to an elderly doctor.

'That's wonderful news,' replied Gladys. 'Well, I'd better get the house ready. So, Vera, if you'll excuse me.' She hauled the heavy pram towards Trescore Cottage, smiling smugly at her friend as she did so.

'Hello, Vera,' said Dorothy.

'Dot,' she acknowledged. The exchange was polite, but no more than that. Dorothy caught up with her grandmother who was struggling with the pram along a narrow stretch of path.

'This is like trying to push a tank, Dot. Would be a lot easier just to carry her, you know,' complained Gladys.

'But not as comfortable for Emily,' she replied. 'And George wants the best for her.'

'He sounds too good to be true, your George.'

'I can't wait for you to meet him.' Gladys was noticing changes in her voice – new phrases, rising inflexions, a diluting of her Cornish vowels. She was cross with her and proud at the same time. Dorothy was pleased to be back in Penrose, even if it was only for a few days. She would go back to London with George; he only had seventy-two hours of leave. Bob Chapman was working in the garden when they reached home.

'Supper's in the porch,' he said with a little mischief. Hanging by the door were four rabbits tied together around their necks with string.

'You can skin them,' instructed Gladys.

'As long as you cook them, my love.' Bob's weathered face smiled at Dorothy.

'You sound like an old married couple, Granny,' Dorothy joked.

'Old indeed, but not married,' Granny replied. 'He doesn't think it's worth it. Says we'd look ridiculous at our age. Suppose we would really,' she added wistfully.

'There's still time, Granny.'

'I suppose you're right.' Dorothy was sitting on a kitchen chair.

'She will need feeding soon,' said Dorothy. 'I might go upstairs.'

'Feed her here.'

'I would rather not.' Dorothy was reticent and coy. There was an unusual distance between them. Dorothy took Emily to her bedroom.

'I will make this stew, then,' called her grandmother, and she wiped away an onion tear from her cheekbone. At that moment, Bob stood in the doorway.

'Doesn't she look well?' he said. Gladys glared at him.

'Take off those filthy boots,' she hissed. Bob Chapman hurried back to sewing vegetable seeds.

*

Flight Lieutenant George Drake's journey was nearing its end after eight hours. The small locomotive was pulling only a couple of half-empty carriages alongside the Camel Estuary. It terminated at Padstow's small station. George alighted from the third-class car, put his suitcase on the platform and lit a cigarette. The last of the spring twilight had faded to black and there were stars above the water. At the station exit, he was greeted by Reddie Bland, ever helpful in his reliable old Ford van. It was a short trip of a few miles to Porthrowan, winding along the coast road, through the straggling village of St Merryn.

'How is the war going in London, Flight Lieutenant?' said Reddie Bland. George smiled. Reddie was only half joking. The threat of invasion may have passed, but there was still conflict in this part of Cornwall – lone raiding bombers peppered the airfields. Sea planes and fighters scrambled in and out of St Mawgan and St Eval. Military vehicles buzzed about the lanes, but it was a quieter world than much of Europe under occupation from a monstrous regime.

'London has been hit hard,' George said.

'As bad as the papers suggest?'

'Worse,' continued George. 'Not just London. Bristol, Cardiff, Sheffield, Liverpool – all the cities really.'

'We don't get it so bad here, but it happens. Twenty-one killed up at St Eval in January. Last October, Padstow was bombed too. Three people – three generations from one family – were killed in New Street. Dozens of buildings were hit.'

'They get everywhere.'

'Mind you, we give as good as we get. One of our boys put one of their Heinkels in the sea at Stepper Point a few weeks ago. We picked them up out of the drink as well. What about that for service?' George laughed. 'Are you a flier?'

'Was,' answered George. 'Shot down over Sussex last year. Broke my collar bone when I baled out.'

'But otherwise okay?'

'Burns to my back. And...' George misted over, 'and, well, let's just say it was a bad day.' Reddie had pressed enough and knew better than to push further. His curiosity was satiated. The old van bounced along the road and was nearing the village.

'Thank you, Mr Bland,' said George. 'Can I give you something for your trouble?' George reached inside his pocket for his wallet. Reddie cut in quickly and patted his passenger on the shoulder.

'No, no, Lieutenant. It is I who should be thanking you – for everything you fellows have sacrificed.' The van pulled away. Wisps of mist hung in the lane. George shivered a little and an owl hooted in the trees. The cottage looked inviting, windows glowing orange. The blackout didn't extend this far. George knocked on the door. When Dorothy answered, she threw her arms around him, pulling him into the cottage.

Bob took George's case. Gladys was bringing food to the table. George's mouth watered as a pot of rabbit stew arrived, served with vegetables and bread.

'Simple food, I'm afraid,' apologised Gladys.

'It is simply delicious, Mrs Trewithen, it really is.' And he was not fibbing. The repetitive air force diet was miserable. The latest experiment had involved whale meat steaks, after which there had nearly been a mutiny in the mess hall. Bob poured some more wine.

'Dandelion,' he said anticipating George's curiosity. After the rabbit, Gladys served mulberries in syrup with thick cream.

'That is the best meal I have had in years. Thank you.' Dorothy smiled, proud of her husband and her grandmother. Dorothy went upstairs to settle Emily who had started crying. Gladys cleared the table, refusing all offers of help from George. Bob put a beech log on the fire, poking the flames into life.

'Dot says you were shot down – lucky to be alive, she said.'

'She's right. I am lucky.' There was a comfortable pause in the conversation. 'Do you mind if I smoke?'

'Not at all,' called Gladys from the kitchen. George shook the match to extinguish the flame and threw it on the fire.

'It was July last year. I had just scored my first kill. It was a Dornier – a slow bomber. I watched it smoke and fall away. One of the crew got out, but his chute didn't open. At the time it felt good, and I was running on adrenaline. I should have pulled away, but I waited too long. A 109 appeared from cloud and I couldn't shake it off. It took out my fuel tanks and the engine started to burn. I flipped the Spitfire and dropped out. My chute opened and I drifted to the ground. I saw my Spit break up, pieces falling on a village. I landed badly – wrecked my collarbone and I'd also been burnt on my back.'

'Quite a story,' Bob said admiringly.

'It didn't end there. I later found out that my plane crashed into a house and killed an elderly couple who were having an afternoon nap. Can you believe that? I spent two months in hospital. But I lost my nerve. Couldn't sleep. I wasn't in a good way.'

'You had been through a lot.'

'Yes, but I couldn't reconcile what I had done. And I felt so much guilt. You know what stayed with me?'

'What?' said Bob in a soft tone.

'The image of the German airman whose chute didn't open. I imagined his fear and terror. Some poor lad, my age, plunging to his death.'

'You were doing your job, son. It was him or you.'

'I know, but somehow that didn't help. Then I met Dot and things began to change.' The fired burned evenly.

'She has that effect on people – a bit like her grandmother,' said Bob, lightening the mood a little. George sensed he was perhaps saying too much too soon. He changed the subject.

'I'm sorry you both couldn't come to the wedding. It's difficult to plan anything in wartime. We just wanted to do the right thing.'

'You've done more than that, my love,' said Gladys coming back into the sitting room. 'She's a very lucky girl.'

'I'm the lucky one,' said George humbly. He stared into the dancing flames, his eyes moistening.

'Well, it's late and I am tired,' said Gladys. 'I will see you in the morning, George. Goodnight.'

'Goodnight, Mrs Trewithen.' Bob followed her to bed. Presently, Dorothy appeared.

'She's sleeping.'

'Sorry – think I might have blabbed on a bit. Must have been that wine.'

'Not at all. It's brave of you to talk about it.' Dorothy sat with her back between his legs. He stroked her neck and she kissed his hand. The fire started to burn lower. They were both asleep within minutes.

*

Strange rumours had surrounded the village in the late summer of the previous year. They had become so wild, few believed there was anything to them. Unsurprisingly, Billy Mallett had attracted the first of the unwanted attention. He had been drinking heavily one night at the end of the harvest season, holding court around the bar of a pub in Trenance. Mallett's loose tongue and fiery temper weren't only stoked by beer, but by news he had received earlier that day that Tom Merriman had terminated his employment at the farm. Mallett retold the story accurately without embellishment, but few thought his tale was anything but alcoholic pantomime. A cursory search of the bay by a detachment of St Mawgan Military Police and an extra roll of barbed wire was about the only consequence of Mallett's story. His drinking worsened during the winter as bitterness and anger ate away at him. Before spring, he was living with a widowed aunt in Bodmin.

The careless talk hadn't stopped with Mallett's leaving the village. The Merriman children, especially the free-spirited Rosie, had shared their stories among friends – how they had been kidnapped by enemy invaders from the sea. A few days after the incident, Mrs Merriman had discovered a chocolate wrapper in Rosie's room, a wrapper with foreign writing. She challenged Rosie, who appealed to her father. The children were sent to their rooms again, while their parents argued ferociously downstairs. A tense silence held the household for a week or more until the family gathered around the kitchen table and all swore an oath of secrecy.

Elsewhere, the village and surrounding farms muttered, but never spoke. Dinky Young volunteered for action and adventure, hoping for posting to distant battlefields and bars of beautiful dancing girls. So far, he had spent week after week shivering under rain and canvas in the depths of Yorkshire. The young artist Lionel Baker was declared medically unfit for service. Tuberculosis would claim him before too long. Another of Merriman's young labourers, Roche, died that summer, gruesomely in a haymaking accident. It was as if a curse had fallen upon them. As winter turned to spring, there were new tales to tell, and the old story withered and began to die away. Those who were left didn't talk about what had happened. Porthrowan closed in on itself as remote rural places do, the lines between fact and fiction vague and redrawn. The laws of the village were largely their own, known only to those who had stayed and lived long enough to learn them.

*

'A fine morning for a walk over the cliffs, don't you think, Dot?' said Gladys. Dot concealed a yawn.

'I am just so tired, Granny,' she replied.

'Then get some air. We can look after Emily here. When's she due a feed?'

'It seems like all she's done all night is feed. She's asleep, thankfully.'

'Morning, George,' said Bob as he refilled his cup from the pot. 'Sleep well?'

'Yes, thank you,' said George rather awkwardly, as if a little embarrassed by his talk from the previous evening. 'In fact, I haven't slept that well for years.'

'Wait until you get some of that sea air, then you'll sleep like a baby,' added Gladys. From upstairs Emily started to grizzle. Dorothy and her grandmother went to her. Unsurprisingly, she was hungry. Without saying a word, Bob put George at ease and the two men enjoyed their food.

'Fresh eggs,' George said.

'They're not rationed in this part of the world,' joked Bob. 'At least, not in this village.'

After breakfast, Dorothy and George walked out onto the cliffs and to the headland just south of Porthrowan. The spring sky was big and wide.

'This is my favourite spot,' she confided. 'You can see for miles. There are occasionally dolphins. And grey seals.' She pointed to a patch of water some 200 feet below them. George had rarely been close to the sea. His boyhood holidays were usually spent in the Peak District with his father who was very keen on rock climbing.

'Are these seas dangerous?' he asked.

'Very,' she said. 'Even in peace time. The weather gets a few every year.'

'Storms?'

'And fog. That's why there's a lighthouse over by Quies,' and she pointed to Trevose Head a couple of miles to the north. A search plane climbed above them, lumbering out to sea.

'Looking for Jerry,' he said. There was a moment of quiet between them.

'They'll have to go a long way. They stay well away from the coast – too dangerous. There are minefields out there as well as planes. Not like the last war. Granny says you could see boats sinking from up here on the cliffs.'

'It seems pretty calm out there today, don't you think?' He hugged her close and they walked on a bit further.

For a few minutes as they approached a tumulus, Dorothy's thoughts tangled in her emotions like brambles. She thought about Hans – out there somewhere beneath the ocean, alive or quite possibly dead. She loved George. He was an honourable man – a good man. But part of her was always looking out to sea, over the breaking surf and to the curving earth beyond. George too was lost in reflections and images. Somewhere over England, thousands of feet above the fields of Sussex, forever replaying those brief seconds in the air. How it is the lost part of ourselves that keep us alive, she thought, and how our fears bind us together like ivy and thorn. The wind picked up a little from the south-west. Rain would close in before too long. The seaplane was merely a speck in the sky now, a black fly without a sound. Dorothy tugged George's sleeve. He looked at her, smiling warmly. They turned for home, hand in hand, as close and distant as they would ever be.

Back at the cottage, Gladys was preparing for an afternoon tea party. She was busily rushing in and out of the house and barking instructions to a patient Bob who was raking soil.

'What are these tables, Bob?' said Dorothy.

'Your grandmother is hosting a tea party this afternoon,' replied Bob, and he raised his eyebrows.

'A tea party? Why?'

'To celebrate young George apparently – the hero of the RAF. And to raise a cup of tea to the married couple.'

'Oh no. He won't want that. We have to stop her.'

'Bit late, I'm afraid. Half the village has been invited and most of them are bringing sandwiches or cake.' George, who had been side-tracked by wonders in the vernal hedgerows, appeared at the gate. Dorothy looked at Bob and closed her eyes in exasperation for a few seconds.

'Good walk, George?' called Bob changing the subject for her.

'Yes, thank you. I didn't realise what a beautiful part of the world this is,' he said.

'A pleasant change from London, I would imagine,' Bob said. George became aware of the activity in the garden. Gladys was now unravelling bunting and Bob had been instructed to find the stepladder.

'Bit of a party, I'm afraid,' apologised Dorothy. 'My grandmother's idea.'

'Right,' said George nervously.

'She just wants to show us off to the family. You don't mind, do you?'

'No. No, I don't think so.' He didn't sound convincing. Gladys interrupted them.

'Dot – go and find where he's got to with that bloody ladder,' she said. And she blushed, having sworn in the presence of her grandson-in-law. They all burst into laughter.

*

Albert Rowe was beating a piece of metal beneath a muted lightbulb. His wife, a small mouse of a woman with shiny eyes, came into the workshop in a shaft of natural light.

'You need to be getting ready, love,' she said.

'I'm not going,' Rowe replied with disinterest and continued with his noisy work. Skilled in this particular and peculiar style of conversation, his wife replied between blows.

'You will. We've been invited.'

'I can't stand that woman, or her granddaughter.'

'Starts at three, so you'll need to be ready soon.'

'Collaborators they are.' He cursed and growled under his breath, but Mrs Rowe had already gone. A farm cat appeared, disturbed in its sleep by the voices. It meowed and brushed itself against Rowe's ankles, hoping to receive a scrap of food. Rowe's temper flared as he struck out with his boot sending the scrawny creature into the darkest recesses of the shed. Rowe put down his tools and trudged miserably to his adjoining cottage, fists clenched as if bent on some kind of revenge.

*

The wind dropped after lunch. It was a bright afternoon, but not warm. At three o'clock, if not before, villagers from Penrose, Porthrowan and a few from St Eval arrived at Trescore Cottage. Most were laden with things to eat and, despite the time of year and the rationing, it was a fine community effort. George was attracting much attention, resplendent in azure, Air Force blue and peaked cap. Dorothy rarely left his side. She wore a simple cotton dress of spring colours. Little Emily, drunk on milk, was snoozing obliviously in her gigantic pram. Reverend Dunning was first to introduce himself, and like so many clergymen, talked exhaustively about himself, having asked a few perfunctory questions of his hosts. Dorothy was relieved when he helped himself to more Victoria sponge and was accosted by a bell ringer wielding a cake knife.

'Just to warn you, this is Vera Craddock – wicked witch of the north and village gossip,' whispered Dorothy.

'She looks quite formidable,' replied George, only half joking. Vera approached confidently; she was on home turf. Dorothy wondered how she would cope in a tube station during a raid.

'Mr and Mrs Drake,' greeted Vera, 'congratulations to you both.'

'Vera, this is my husband, George. George, this is Granny's friend, Vera Craddock.'

'Pleased to meet you, Mrs Craddock,' said George extending a hand. Vera declined the handshake – not out of impoliteness, but more out of unfamiliarity with social convention. Dorothy smiled to herself but covered her expression with her hand.

'We were all sorry to miss your wedding, Mr Drake,' Vera said.

'Well, we wanted to seal things quickly,' he said. George was tiring of this expression.

'I'm sure you did,' Vera cut in ambiguously. Dorothy and George ignored her mischief-making. 'What a beautiful baby Emily is. You must both be very proud,' she continued.

'Yes, we are,' said George, pleased they could agree on something.

'Lovely blonde hair she has too,' said Vera peering into the pram. 'Is that your side of the family, George?'

'Yes, I think perhaps it might be,' said George, taken aback. 'My uncle was very blond.'

'Your uncle? Well, it won't be from Dot's side. They were all very dark, weren't they, Dot?' Dorothy didn't answer. 'Well, I must go and say hello to Mrs Merriman. It's lovely to see you both. Look after each other, won't you.' And off she went, giddily.

'Is she always like that? I didn't care much for her tone,' said George with considerable restraint.

'Don't worry about her. Did you smell her breath? It wasn't just tea in that cup. There's more than a drop of barley wine in there.' Dorothy gave her husband a reassuring clasp of his forearm.

The sound of a fork banging against the side of an enamel mug quietened everybody down. It was Gladys. She wanted to make a speech.

'Thank you, everybody. Thank you for coming today and for all your contributions. Especially Mrs Merriman's sponge.' There was a slight ripple of applause and a few chuckles. Mrs Merriman feigned a curtsy. Gladys continued, 'As you all know, my beautiful granddaughter has tied the knot. We were wondering if we'd ever get rid of her. But she met this very brave airman who has sacrificed so much in defending our country, and together they are starting a new life in London with baby Emily. Although we will miss them very much, I am sure they will visit us as often as they can. So, ladies and gentlemen, please raise your glasses, or tea, and toast the married couple. To George and Dot.' The guests repeated the toast, and this was followed by a heartier round of applause. George looked relieved, his ordeal seemingly nearing an end.

At that moment, a loud male voice called from near the back of the gathering. For an instant, it didn't cause alarm, more surprise. Then, the aggressiveness and anger of its speaker became clear.

'I thought our Dot would be marrying a kraut – not one of our boys.' It was Billy Mallett. There was a collective gasp. Somebody told him to be quiet. Billy was clearly inebriated. His words were slurred and his gait staggering. 'Don't sound so bloody surprised. You lot know what I'm talking about.' It seemed that perhaps some did. Vera Craddock was standing, arms folded, waiting for the next instalment. It wasn't long in coming.

'I know what you're talking about, Billy,' said Albert Rowe. 'All sweetness and light standing there. Not all of us were deceived, you know.' Mallett staggered towards Rowe, parting Reverend Dunning's impromptu sermon to a small group of older ladies from Penrose. Mallett put his arm around Rowe and took a swig from a bottle.

'So what do you say about that, then, Mrs Drake?' Mallett spoke with all the bitterness of a lover scorned. Dorothy was dumbfounded and drew upon all her inner steel not to burst into tears. George was frozen, guns jammed, spinning out of control.

'Well, I tell you what I think of it.' Tom Merriman walked straight towards Mallett, his eyes unblinking and furious. Without uttering another word, he punched Mallett with full force in the mouth, sending a front tooth flying out the side of his mouth. Rowe took a step backwards, his nerve deserting him. Mallett attempted to retaliate, but his coordination was wrecked with alcohol. The farmer sent a second fist into the drunkard's abdomen. Mallett coughed and fell forward and collapsed onto a table. Merriman collected his coat from the back of a chair and walked out of the gate.

For a few moments, there was silence. Rowe was steered home by his wife. Mallett was carried out by two burly labourers. The guests drifted away, unsure how to say goodbye, unbelieving of what had just taken place. Dunning offered some words of comfort to Dorothy and George, but for once, at a time when they needed it most, didn't know what to say. Vera Craddock left last, fixing a cold glare on Dorothy before she did so. The wind began to pick up. Bob started to clear away the debris of the afternoon. Gladys was in the cottage, crying over the kitchen sink.

'I'm sorry, Granny,' Dorothy said. 'I'm so sorry.' She tried to put her hand on her grandmother's shoulder, but Gladys pushed her away and hurried upstairs to her room, slamming the door behind her. Dorothy could hear her sobbing into a pillow above her. George was shaken.

'Perhaps we had better go back to London first thing tomorrow,' he said. Dorothy looked at him, expecting more, wanting more. She could feel her wild, free spirit rising to meet the inadequacy of his words, but somehow reined herself in, containing all that felt right and just.

'Yes, I suppose we should,' she said. Outside in garden, Emily had started to cry.

The evening was spent in bouts of silence and truncated talk. Bob did his best to cheer the mood whenever he could, but a rift had cleaved its way between Dorothy and Gladys. No lines of battle had been drawn, no reasons given, no unpleasant words traded. Something unspoken and bigger than both of them had descended rapidly like sea mist, and neither could find a way out, nor get back to where they were. George spent time with Emily. Gladys had agreed to look after her, at least until the bombing had died down. Secretly, Dorothy was pleased. She wanted to go back to being a WAAF, for life to assume some greater purpose beyond these empty Cornish lanes. And as much as she loved her child, every time she held or fed or so much as looked at Emily, she was thrown into a storm of emotions where she quickly started to drown.

George struggled down the stairs with suitcases, the noise suggesting the walls of the cottage might collapse. He was dressed in uniform, as was Dorothy. Gladys was holding a sleeping Emily, and Bob stood by her side.

'Well, thank you very much, Mrs Trewithen. Most delicious food. And thank you, Bob,' George said with pristine politeness and genuine well-meaning.

'You are more than welcome, my dear boy,' said Bob, shaking him by the hand.

'It was lovely meeting you, George. Look after Dot, won't you,' said Gladys.

'I think she will look after me,' replied George, paying his wife a compliment.

'Look after Emily, won't you,' said Dorothy with a brittle plea in her voice. Bob helped George to Reddie Bland's van that was waiting in the lane. Gladys watched them leave.

'I don't know where that man gets his petrol, I really don't,' she said.

'Granny, I am sorry. I know you are upset with me, and you have every reason to be,' said Dorothy.

'It was a wicked thing that Billy Mallett did. Nobody in the village has any time for him. Except Albert Rowe perhaps.' Gladys was still sidestepping, avoiding her granddaughter's apology.

'But, Granny...' Dorothy was interrupted.

'You have nothing to apologise for, girl. There are some in this village have done far, far worse. Some who would sell their own children if they thought there was enough gold in it for them.'

'Thank you, Granny,' said Dorothy and she hugged her.

'Just you look after yourself and get back here as soon as you can.' Gladys and Bob stood in the lane waving as the van pulled away, Dorothy leaning out of the passenger window and George, rather comically, trying to say goodbye from the back of the van. Gladys held up Emily's arm in a mock wave. Dorothy wiped away a tear. Something had been resolved, but something still felt undone. Perhaps it was the loosening of ties. She undid the window and put her face into the wind. The air was warm and fresh as it blew the hair from her forehead. She felt free and for that, did not feel guilty.

The acrid smell of locomotive steam engulfed the single platform at Padstow. The tough little engine would be pulling a mix of passengers and fish. George and Dorothy stepped into the carriage, which was surprisingly busy. They sat in a compartment with an older couple who were impressed and privileged to be sharing their time with two uniformed young people. The journey was glorious as the train snaked along the south bank of the Camel Estuary before leaving Wadebridge for the wooded valleys and the approach to Bodmin. The train to Plymouth where they would connect to London was late. Dorothy and George sat on a bench. The sky was beginning to cloud and there was threat of rain in the grey above.

'What's wrong, Dot?' It was a stupid question, but she knew he was only trying to be kind.

'I'm just missing Emily, that's all.' He held her hand, not knowing what to say. How one's whole life course can be altered by a single gust of wind, she thought. A lone gull flew high above them.

'Here's our train,' George said.

'So it is,' she said. They alighted.

There were plenty of spare seats. A conductor checked their tickets. Cornwall fell behind them, and in just over an hour they were cutting through the suburbs. Plymouth was scarred with rubble, wrecked buildings and craters.

'I didn't know it was so bad here,' said George who had only seen the city in darkness.

'It's a big port, lot of navy here,' Dorothy informed him. Close to the station, what looked like most of a street had been reduced to ruins. What were offices, shops or houses were now only ghostly, precarious shells.

'If this carries on, there will be nothing left,' said George despondently.

'It won't. They are losing the war.'

'How do you know that, Dot?'

'The Germans are in Greece. Hitler's forgotten about dear old Blighty.'

'It doesn't look like it.' The train slowed as they made their approach to the station.

'He would have invaded by now if he meant to. Anyway, the Germans were losing this war the very moment they started it.'

'I don't follow at all,' said George, baffled by his wife's assertions and confidence.

'Don't listen to me. It's just something someone said to me once, that's all.' She turned and looked out onto the people and the platforms. Inside, she was smiling and somehow felt vindicated.

The eastward journey to London was interminable. The spring showers swept in and rapped the carriages with spiteful swipes of rain. Dorothy slept peacefully and noiselessly. George admired her, watching her in the window reflection, her high cheekbones and fresh skin beautiful in the fading afternoon. As the train pulled into Paddington, London was preparing for another night of torment from Hitler's bombers. Passengers and service personnel were scurrying across platforms to exits. Lighting was minimal and the huge ironwork structures of the platform canopies were macabre staging in a grotesque drama. George and Dorothy took the tube to Maida Vale. Home was a rented, modern apartment in a purpose-built block. They had not been here together for some time having spent so much of the last few weeks at their base in Kent. The rain was lashing their backs as they fell through the lobby door in a fit of giggles.

'I want a bath,' said Dorothy.

'I could do with one too,' George said, taking off his wet coat.

'Then why don't you join me?' she said and beckoned her husband to follow her.

Dorothy was lying in the bath, in a mountain of bubbles, her toes playing with the taps.

'No more scullery washing for me,' she joked. George was nervous in his nakedness. His body was pale and battered by war, his flesh a brutal map of scars. He climbed into the water, clumsily at first. Their skin melted together.

'Lean forward – I'm going to wash your hair,' she said. George complied with her instructions. Her fingers tenderly tousled his scalp. Just as he was relaxing deliciously, she poured a jug of cool water over his head. George's shivering reaction sent Dorothy into a fit of uncontrollable laughter. George splashed her and they started flicking water at each other until he pulled her close and kissed her deeply on the lips. He felt her shoulders loosen and fall a little. He brushed the side of her cheek with the back of his hand, and she pulled it towards her breast. 'Come on,' she said, 'let's go to the bedroom and make love.' On the bed, Dorothy rocked gently above him. She placed her forefinger on his lips as he let out a small gasp. Her hair fell forward over his face, and she smiled lovingly. George lifted her into his arms. They slipped into deep sleep. The city was quiet. There would be no raid on London tonight.

*

Billy Mallett did not arrive in St Austell that evening, or the next. His family made every effort to find him, but nobody was able to help them in their search. The men who had removed him from Trescore Cottage said they last saw Mallett walking towards St Merryn. What little police investigation there was found no lead or clue to his whereabouts. Missing person details were printed in local newspapers and posters pasted throughout the county, but not one scrap of information was received. Somewhere in the woodland, or in some ditch of a fallow field, in a disused quarry or mine shaft, or below the waves sunken with weights, was Billy Mallett's corpse. A blunt instrument, a wayside beating or a clumsy knife wound. Lonely, dark cries late at night, carried out to sea by the wind. Whatever it was, whoever it was, the truth slept in the shadows. Perhaps a body or bones might one day be unearthed by a dog, or a fox, or the farmer's plough. Perhaps. But the village, if it knew anything, said nothing at all. New life blossomed in the trees and the land warmed slowly under the spring sun.

*

'I hope they are alright. There's been heavy raids on London again.' Gladys had been listening to the wireless.

'Probably safer at the airfield, I would imagine,' said Bob trying to reassure her. He put a twisted scrap of hawthorn on the fire.

'She's almost three months old.' Gladys changed the subject.

'Have you received a letter this week?'

'Not yet.'

'You could write to her,' Bob suggested.

'I don't like to bother her.'

'Bother her? She will want to know how Emily is doing, don't you think? Must be hard for her.' He went to the kitchen and left Gladys to her worries. Bob was right of course, Gladys thought. She would write to Dorothy in the morning – she could suggest they meet one day between London and Cornwall. Dorothy could spend some time with Emily. She might even try to persuade Dorothy to move back to Cornwall to be with her daughter. Gladys's mind was scrambled. She felt tired, old and, lately, a little less confident than once she had been.

*

Dorothy's life was changing again. Her aptitude for detail and analysis had been noticed by her commanding officer. From Kent, she had been posted to Buckinghamshire and assigned to a newly established intelligence unit. The work was demanding, but Dorothy found it absorbing and purposeful. She spent her time studying thousands of aerial reconnaissance photographs, examining square inches of film for buildings, structures, weapons or anything unusual. Each blemish, differing shade, line or mark was scrutinised, considered and filed. Her life with George was interrupted, and for this she was grateful. When they did see each other, they were friends and occasionally lovers. George remained in his post, fixed and unmoving, his mind still full of memories that would paralyse him until the day he died.

Dorothy had been proved right. By late summer, the war had changed course as Germany tore through Belorussia and Ukraine. Its bombers still came, but there were fewer of them and the raids lighter. In much of England, the skies were dull and overcast, if quieter.

'George, I have to tell you something. Can we sit down?' Dorothy's voice was unusually apprehensive. They found an empty bench. The park was quiet. 'George, I think we are going to have a baby.'

'That's wonderful news,' he said, eyes glistening. 'Are you sure? I mean, how do you know?'

'Do I really have to explain this to you?'

'No, of course not. Forgive me, I'm being dense,' he offered apologetically. 'When? I mean, how long?' He didn't know how to ask the questions she knew she would have to answer.

'A couple of months. Maybe a little more.'

'So that would make…' George was trying to compute the dates.

'February.'

'February,' he repeated. A huge, wide smile broke across his face, easing his troubled mind. 'What do I need to do?' he asked innocently.

'What do you need to do? Nothing. You need to look after me.' A rain shower threatened to break at any moment.

'Come on,' he said. 'We need to get you home before this rain begins.' They walked arm-in-arm through the gates of the recreation ground. An old man raised his walking stick to them, by way of greeting, and shuffled on through the park. The London skyline looked dirty and bruised against the darkening sky, flecked with barrage balloons and cumulus clouds.

'I wonder if it's a girl or a boy?' George said excitedly.

'Maybe we'll have one of each,' teased Dorothy.

'A brother or sister for Emily.' He said it so naturally and so kindly that Dorothy loved him just that little bit more. When they reached home, the shower had started – warm air ascending higher and higher, until it cooled and fell to earth.

Six

North Cornwall - Summer, 1985

The last of the sun was dipping beneath the sea. Cradling a whisky in his fat, pink fingers, Sir Charles Gifford sat in the elegant, if tired looking, bar of the Blue Bay Hotel. His meal had been adequate without being excellent; his room comfortable, not luxurious. Holidaymakers sat around him. Not the company he would wish for when enjoying a fine Speyside single malt, but they were anonymous and harmless – in fact, just the sort of background music needed for this particular mission. He pondered the situation for a moment and remembered that he was a retired colonel visiting his niece in Truro. He ordered another whisky and pulled a long hair from a large mole on the side of his face. Holidays, reflected Sir Charles, were not for sunbathing, surfing and souvenir shops, but for adventure. Shooting, safari, skiing, sailing and some more shooting – these were pursuits one should enjoy in those rare days of vacation. He held the bent white hair to the light, twirled it in his fingers and released it into the air.

'Another, sir?' The soft timbre of the voice was Cornish and female.

'A small nightcap, why not,' said Sir Charles.

'A double?'

'Well, if you insist,' he said.

'I'll put it on your bill?'

'Indeed. Yeghes da!' Sir Charles tipped the Scotch back.

'Are you staying with us long, sir?' asked the barkeeper courteously, while wiping down a surface and spilt-slop tray.

'Just a day or so.'

'Holiday?'

'No – visiting my niece in Truro,' said Sir Charles, warmed by the whisky and the charade.

'How nice. Which part of Truro?' Sir Charles had to think quickly.

'Near the cathedral. I always forget the name of the house.'

'Easily done.'

'I don't suppose you're familiar with the village of Penrose, by any chance?' Sir Charles said, changing the subject casually.

'I know it,' the barkeeper said.

'Is it far?'

'Not really. Five miles, I would think. Nothing there. Not even a pub as far as I can recall.' She sketched a simple map on the back of a paper napkin.

'Thank you, that's very helpful.'

'Visiting someone?'

'Just wanting to pay my respects and lay a few flowers.'

'On a grave?'

'Yes.'

'You'll have a hard job.'

'Why?'

'There's no church in Penrose.' The barkeeper had no further questions but had made up her mind that this old cove was a bit of a rake. Sir Charles thanked his host, slid off his bar stool and retired to his room.

Once inside, he shook off the colonel's character and the effects of the alcohol with a splash of cold water from the sink in the adjoining bathroom. He opened the window and looked out into the black night. The air was warm and full of the sea. He left the window ajar, lay back on the bed and listened to the ocean. Tomorrow he would go to Penrose. Any village without a church or pub couldn't be more than a hamlet. It shouldn't therefore take too long to find Mr Fox and his entourage, he mused. The mission should be straightforward. Back in London by early evening. Report back to HQ. The boundaries between past and present were blurring again. Imagining London at dusk, he pictured the War Office, sandbags and sentries. Sir Charles's eyes were heavy. They flickered and closed. Past and present were merging. Fantasy and reality had ceased to be separate a long time ago.

*

A police cordon had been set up on the banks of the Thames beneath some disused dockland. The flickering blue of a squad car partially illuminated the scene. Local police were taping off areas and searching nearby with torches. Accompanied by a small group of officers from Scotland Yard, the chief superintendent from Paddington Green arrived. They walked to the water's edge beneath the concrete pier. Lying face up, swollen and in the first stages of decomposition was the body of Neil O'Brien. He was wearing the same clothes as on the day Charlotte Groves was attacked. The chief superintendent peered at the body, a constable shining a flashlight on its face.

'Like the banks of the Styx,' he said. The confused constable nodded unconvincingly. 'I said this is a godawful spot, Constable. Do you know where this river gets its name?'

'No, sir,' he replied.

'From an ancient pre-Celtic word, "tamasa", meaning dark river.' The chief superintendent spoke to another colleague. 'That would match our descriptions, don't you think, Wallace?' The accompanying officer agreed, although it was unclear from his expression whether he really did or really did not. 'I think we need to get him to the chiller.' The chief superintendent turned away from the corpse. 'It's getting a little chilly. Autumn will be here soon.'

Neil O'Brien's body was shipped to the pathologist for a forensic autopsy, which was concluded quickly and without fuss. A self-inflicted gunshot wound to the right-side temple causing death instantly – in other words, suicide. O'Brien would be returned to his native County Armagh where he would be laid to rest by his mother and extended family. He left no wife, children, nor any kind of note. It was assumed by his former colleagues, and explained to Mrs O'Brien, that Neil had developed mental illness and post-traumatic stress disorder following dangerous operations in West Africa. That he was a gun for hire, an alcoholic, unreliable and violent was never mentioned. His coffin was lowered into the Irish earth as fine summer rain swept in from Monaghan and Tyrone. In London, the case involving Charlotte Groves was closing, paperwork stamped and filed away.

*

'You have been gone for hours. We were starting to get worried about you,' Anna said as Frank appeared in the porch at Trescore.

'Sorry, I had to clear my mind,' Frank replied.

'And did you?'

'Some of it.' Frank smiled, easing the tension in the room. Anna prepared the table for supper. Charlotte was keenly joining in, laying cutlery.

'Do you eat spinach pie?' Anna said.

'I don't think I ever have, but it sounds delicious, Anna – thank you.'

'Good,' she replied.

'I don't like spinach pie,' said Charlotte. Her delightful honesty restored warmth to the room. Over food, Charlotte asked Frank questions.

'Frank, your voice is a bit strange,' she said.

'Charlotte, that is a rude thing to say,' admonished her mother.

'No, that's okay, really,' said Frank. 'It is, I suppose.'

'Charlotte means you have a slight accent to your voice.'

'That's true too.'

'Is it Swiss?' asked Anna, sharing her daughter's curiosity.

'German,' said Frank. 'I am German.'

'But you speak impeccable English,' Anna added.

'I have lived here for nearly forty years.' Anna did not ask any more questions. She wondered if Frank had suffered some great trauma in the Second World War, lost family in a concentration camp or had been forced to leave his homeland.

'Would you like some mulberries, Frank?' Charlotte offered a jar to him. Frank spooned some into his dish and poured over a little cream. The dark, syrupy fruit was almost caramelised with a hint of spice.

'What are these? They are delicious,' he said.

'Mulberries,' said Charlotte, purple juice spilling from the side of her mouth. 'Do you like them?'

'Very much,' said Frank. After supper, they played a board game before Charlotte had a bath and went to bed. When Anna returned from reading her a story, Frank had already completed the washing-up.

'Thank you,' she said.

'It is the least I can do.' Anna took a bottle of wine from a cupboard and poured two glasses. The liquid was an imperial purple with a faint hint of blue.

'Blackberry,' she said. 'Cheers.' Frank sipped the wine. He felt a warmth and a glow. The taste was new and ancient at the same time. The bubbles on the surface seemed to wink at him.

'This is a family recipe,' he said with certainty.

'Yes, it is. How did you guess?' Frank replied with a question.

'Is this your house, Anna?' She looked a little unsettled, but not worried.

'Yes. Why do you ask?'

'It belonged to your mother?'

'To my grandmother.' At that moment, Charlotte started to cry.

'Give me a moment, Frank.' Anna rushed upstairs to console her daughter who was having a nightmare. When she returned, Frank was leaning against the porch, the door slightly open. He was staring at the heavy, steady rain. She decided to leave him, standing in the doorway alone. She thought about making a fire and having some more wine, but she was tired and wanted to be alert for Charlotte. She called goodnight to Frank, but he didn't seem to hear her. With a little unease, she went to bed.

*

On the other side of the world, Alex Groves was greeted in the arrivals building by a small group of men and women. They drove quickly out of the airport to a wharf in the city harbours. There, on board an old fishing trawler, Alex rested for a short time before briefing his fellow activists on some final details for a plan to halt French nuclear testing in the Pacific Ocean. Debate and discussion raged into the early hours of the morning. Alex occasionally paused with fatigue, but adrenaline kept him going. Sitting at the side of the meeting were two new faces, quiet and sullen. Alex thought them suspicious but was assured by his friends they were good people – Belgian nationals keen to help stop weapon experiments in the Tuamotu Archipelago. As dawn broke, the boat was finally sleeping. The two new recruits slipped away unnoticed.

*

With the scent of danger, Sir Charles's appetite grew. He breakfasted like a huntsman, washing down his kippers and eggs with half a pint of bitter. The day was glorious, the sea fresh and powerful. Before leaving his room, he made some final checks. The faithful Webley handgun was loaded. The reception area of the hotel was quiet apart from the barkeeper from the previous evening. She had switched roles for the morning shift and was receiving the morning mail from the postman.

'Have a good trip, Colonel,' she called.

'Thank you, miss,' he said, smiling like a toad as he walked to the Mercedes. The six-cylinder engine fired up with a syrupy growl and the car pulled away on the gravel, turning left on the coast road north towards Penrose.

The coast road snaked the huge cliff faces 200 yards to the west and the Atlantic Ocean beyond. Nothing between here and the east coast of America. The Mercedes descended along a snake-like road to Mawgan Porth, with its bucket and spade shops and busy beach. Sir Charles took a back road that skirted an old airfield, a relic of the war. Halfway round the perimeter fences of the old runways, he noticed a church standing alone as if on some Gothic film set. He slowed and read the sign: St Eval. Penrose was no more than five minutes away. A farm tractor chugged past him, a terrier sitting precariously on the wheel arch. It may have only been a mile or two, but Penrose was lost in the folds of farmland. Sir Charles emerged in the middle of what he presumed was the centre of the village, a piece of scruffy ground where three roads converged. There were no more than two or three dozen squat cottages, packed into this tiny place. Sir Charles parked his car and got out. It was silent and there was nobody around. He looked like an outlaw in some gold-rush frontier settlement.

Next to where he'd parked was a post office which could easily have been mistaken for a shed. He tried the door and was surprised to find it opened. Inside it was like stepping into night from day. An old woman with white hair and no more than five feet tall appeared from a room even darker behind the counter.

'Good morning,' she said in a broad Cornish voice.

'Good morning,' said Sir Charles. He looked conspicuously out of place, dressed like the county squire.

'Can I help you?' the woman said patiently. Sir Charles felt he should buy something.

'Some first-class stamps, please,' he said.

'How many would you like?'

'Twenty.'

'Twenty? I see.' The woman tore the stamps from a folder and passed them across the counter. Sir Charles paid for the stamps.

'Thank you,' he said. 'I wonder if you could help me. You see, I am looking for an old pal of mine. Name of Fox. Older gentleman. Don't suppose you have seen him in the village?'

'No, can't say as I have,' the woman replied politely.

'Might be with a younger lady and her child, from London.' The lady looked at Sir Charles doubtfully.

'Who might you be, sir, if you don't mind my asking?'

'My name is Hawkins. Colonel John Hawkins. I used to serve with old Foxy in the army.' Sir Charles softened his tone with a smattering of charm.

'I see. Wait there a moment.' The old lady went into the cave behind her and reappeared with a man who was living in his ninth decade. 'My brother says you should try Trescore Cottage.' She explained how to get to the house. 'Young Anna lives there. She might be who you're looking for.'

'Thank you very much. You have been most kind.' Sir Charles doffed his hat in parting. The old brother and sister stood motionless and wordless, then went back into their hiding place.

Hillbilly country, thought Sir Charles disparagingly, and he walked along the lane in the direction of Trescore

Cottage. Anna and Frank were drinking coffee. Charlotte was playing in the garden.

'I think I will take her to the beach today,' said Anna. 'Come if you would like to.'

'Thank you, but I may visit the church you were telling me about. St Evil?'

'St Eval,' she laughed, correcting him.

'Sorry. Or I might stay here and rest a little, if that's okay with you? Perhaps I could do a little work in the garden? Although I might do more harm than good.'

'I suppose I need to think about what to do next.'

'Have you heard from your husband?'

'No. He will be busy trying to save the world. He may have guessed I am here, anyway.'

'Does he like it here?'

'No,' she said. 'I'm not sure he likes it anywhere. He's never still – always moving to the next thing.' She wanted to change the conversation. 'What will you do, Frank? Will you go back to London soon?'

'Yes, I suppose so. There isn't really any other choice. I may call the police today. No doubt they want to know where I am. The fugitive pensioner.' They laughed and then Charlotte ran into the cottage.

'Mummy, there's a man in the garden.'

'It might be Eric. I will go and see.' Anna returned shortly afterwards, followed by a large man dressed in tweeds.

'Good morning,' he said, his speech a mixture of received pronunciation and gravel. He noticed Charlotte looking a little frightened, staying close to her mother. 'I am looking for Mr Frank Fox.' Sir Charles looked fixedly at his quarry.

'I am Frank Fox.' Frank got up out of his chair. Sir Charles was visibly surprised by Frank's height; he was just over six feet tall. Given what he'd done to Neil O'Brien, he was also wary. He flexed his fingers in readiness of an attack.

'Mr Fox, my name is Colonel John Hawkins. I am a former British Army officer. I believe you knew some of my men. I would like to talk with you, if I may.' Gifford was gambling. Anyone of Frank's age must have served in some capacity during the war.

'I find that very unlikely, Colonel,' Frank replied. 'Impossible even.' He sensed menace in this man's behaviour.

'Perhaps,' anticipated Sir Charles, 'if we could discuss this outside, I think it might be more appropriate.' He glanced at Anna and Charlotte.

'I see, then we shall.' Frank led Sir Charles. Anna and Charlotte slipped out of the back door of the cottage, through a gap in the hedge and along the lane to Penrose village.

The two men sat on a weather-eaten garden bench. The flower borders were a spectacular mix of pinks, reds and oranges.

'Such pretty dahlias,' said Sir Charles as a preface to his gambit. 'Mr Fox, I will make this very clear. I want to know what connection you have with the girl and her mother. Furthermore, I want you to tell me how you overcame the attacker in the park.' Frank had guessed there was some sort of connection to this whole, unbelievable affair.

'I have told the police everything I know,' he said. 'What is your interest in this and what is your connection? You are not a former army officer, I presume.'

'Mr Fox, we both know you are not who you say you are.'

'I don't follow you,' said Frank.

'You were told to stay in London by the police, were you not? Have you missed an interview with them?' It was clear to Frank that this man, whoever he was, knew a lot about him. 'And you will follow me now, Mr Fox.' Sir Charles opened the lining of his jacket to reveal a body holster containing a gun. 'Don't try anything silly, old boy. We wouldn't want to spoil the family holiday, now, would we?'

Frank had no choice. He walked in front while Sir Charles gave him directions.

'We are going for a little drive,' said Sir Charles, 'to say a few prayers for the living and the dead.' They approached the spot where the Mercedes was parked. 'I assume you can drive, Mr Fox.'

'Not for some time, but I assume the principles are still the same.' Sir Charles tossed him the keys. 'Drive carefully, Mr Fox. I will show you the way.' Frank turned the ignition key. He had exerted too much pressure on the accelerator pedal and the car growled in disagreement. 'Easy does it. This is not a toy.' They eased forward, gingerly at first, then with a minor wheel spin, pulled away down the hill into the lane between the trees.

From the east side of the hamlet, Anna and Charlotte had made a call from the telephone box. They were walking back to the cottage when an old villager called to them.

'Good morning, Anna,' he said heartily. The wizened old face belonged to Mr Müller, a Swiss artist who had lived in Penrose for years.

'Good morning, Mr Müller,' she replied, hoping the exchange would be brief.

'I have just seen two gentlemen get into a car and drive away as if they were drunk,' Müller said in precise, heavily accented English. Anna was suddenly interested.

'What did they look like?'

'Well, one was short and fat and looked like an Englishman. The other more distinguished, I would say – a military man, perhaps.'

'Which direction did they go?'

'Why – do you know them?'

'One of them.'

'They went that way,' and Müller pointed in the direction of St Eval.

The church at St Eval was empty and locked. However, it was not difficult for an expert like Sir Charles to break in. They walked through the vestry and sat in a pew a few rows from the pulpit.

'Such a simple thing of beauty, the English church. Do you know merchants from as far away as Bristol helped to rebuild the tower after a storm? You see, the church was a recognisable landmark for sailors.' Sir Charles had memorised some facts from his planning and research.

'I did not know that,' sighed Frank, tiring of Sir Charles's cheerless drama.

'But it was not always such a lonely spot.'

'Yes, I am aware there was once a small hamlet here.'

'You are well-informed, Mr Fox. But the houses were demolished, you see. Compulsory purchases. The government in its wisdom built another airfield here. For our aircraft to carry out anti-submarine patrols against the wolf packs.' The church was dark and cool. Somewhere high in the tower there was a flapping of wings. 'And what did you do in the war, Mr Fox?' Frank considered what he might reveal to this man, if only to buy more time, but he needn't have bothered as Sir Charles contrived to plot a little game. 'Let me guess. Just answer yes or no.' Frank's silence suggested he would play along. 'You were not a British serviceman?'

'No, I wasn't.'

'I could tell by your accent.' Sir Charles was enjoying himself. 'You are Dutch?'

'No.'

'Norwegian?'

'No.'

'But you fought alongside the Allies?'

'No.' Sir Charles's countenance altered, twitching as if a horrible truth were revealing itself.

'You are German?'

'Yes.'

'My God, a bloody Nazi.'

'No, I am not a Nazi and never was. I am from Hamburg. If you know your history, you will know most of us there did not support Hitler. Not that it did us much good when your bombers destroyed the city.'

'You fought for them, damn you.'

'I and millions of my countrymen really had no choice.'

'Everyone has a choice, Fox.'

'Why don't you tell that to all those ghosts in Belsen, Dachau, Treblinka, Auschwitz, Sobibor, or the thousands of children who were burned alive in Hammerbrook and Rothenburgsort?' Sir Charles interrupted.

'Enough, Mr Fox. What is your real name?'

'Hans Kramer.'

'And why did you change your name?'

'I think you can work that out for yourself. What is your name? I don't believe you are who you say you are, Colonel.'

'That is irrelevant.'

'Is it?'

'Tell me your connection to Alex Groves and his family. There must be one. Why would you be here in Cornwall, running from the police if you didn't have something to hide?'

'I have told you who I am. I have no connection – only that I saved the girl from being attacked. I am here because I was scared – afraid for my life, that I would go to prison for a crime I did not commit.'

With his back briefly turned, Sir Charles stood and paced through the aisle between the pews. Frank scanned the church for exit points; he could see none. For a second, he thought he heard a noise at the door to the entrance of the church. Wishful thinking. After some time, Sir Charles spoke more quietly and without so much affectation.

'We are both old men, Kramer. We have little time left on this godforsaken earth. But I intend to leave it with dignity. Like you, I fought in the war. Dunkirk,

North Africa, Burma. Mentioned in dispatches once. But after it finished, things got difficult for people like me. Lefties and communists with their hammers and sickles, scything down our heritage and way of life. They did more damage than you Germans ever did. Great families and their estates reduced to rubble and tears. For what? It has achieved nothing. My country is a wasteland. So you see, dignity is all I have left. You and that terrorist Groves could jeopardise that. I will ask you once more – what is your role in all of this?'

*

Eric Chapman had arrived at Trescore. It was Friday and he was intending to harvest some potatoes, mow the grass and do some gentle watering and maintenance. Anna rushed out of the cottage.

'Eric, I need your help. Do you think Mary would look after Charlotte for a bit?'

'I'm sure she would love to. What's wrong?'

'I will tell you on the way. Can you drive me to St Eval?' Eric downed his tools and they walked quickly to the car. With Charlotte safely in the care of Mary Chapman, Anna shared as little and enough of the story as she dared.

'My uncle always said you had your mother's fire about you, Anna.'

'I need it now, Eric. I have never done anything like this before. I called the farm, but nobody answered.' They drove steadily, passing no other vehicle. Morning tipped into noon, the sun was hot and the day began to doze.

Sinister things happen on still, sunny days, thought Anna. The drive to the church was no more than a quarter of an hour. The dark square tower looked bleak, even on the brightest of afternoons. 'I think you had better contact the police, Eric. I didn't get a good feeling about this man.' Eric agreed, but before he drove away, Anna stopped him and said, 'If I am not here, I will make for The Head.'

The approach to the church was open. It was a fearsome spot, treeless and some may say godless too. Anna walked cautiously, listening all the time for voices or movement. All was quiet. She tried the main entrance door; it was locked. She walked around the church looking for another way in. At the eastern side was a much smaller door to the vestry. It was worth a try. The latch moved upwards – it was open. She stepped inside. Her eyes adjusted to the contrasting darkness of the church. Despite the summer temperatures, it still felt cool and a chill blew about her ankles. Anna crept through a curtain to the anteroom which led to the altar rail. The choir stalls and altar were empty. She walked towards the pews. She saw Frank sitting near the back; he was looking at her, his face iron grey and motionless.

'Frank,' she called. No sooner had she done so, than a voice called from behind her.

'Sit down, Mrs Groves.' Anna glanced behind her to see Sir Charles pointing a gun at her. She gasped visibly.

'It's okay, Anna. Do as he says,' said Frank, reassuring her.

'Very wise words,' added Sir Charles.

Anna sat beside Frank and clasped his hand. Sir Charles kept a distance of a few feet. He lowered his gun briefly.

'I am sorry about this, Mrs Groves.' Sir Charles gestured to the gun. 'But you really have given me no choice. I have been explaining to Mr Fox here, or should I say Herr Kramer, that I need to know how you are both connected.'

'Who is he?' Anna whispered. She was pale and felt sick.

'Somebody who means to harm your family,' Frank replied.

'Be quiet, Kramer. Mrs Groves, your husband is at this moment in New Zealand – is that correct?' Anna nodded. 'My organisation believes he is a terrorist. An enemy of the free world. A threat to national security.'

'Rubbish,' cried Anna.

'Do you know why he is there?'

'He is there trying to protect the world from nuclear disaster.'

'A little dramatic, Mrs Groves. He is there because he and his activist friends are trying to stop the French government conducting important research.'

'Testing bombs,' Anna interrupted.

There was silence for a few seconds as Sir Charles considered what he would say next.

'Mrs Groves, you are making this difficult. May I remind you that France is one of our closest allies. Anybody who seeks to upset the entente is walking on thin ice.'

'So you tried to attack my daughter – what, to threaten us?'

'We were going to borrow her. Not harm her.'

'Kidnap?'

'We needed to ensure that your husband stayed in the country.'

'Well, it didn't work, did it?'

'No, which is where this gentleman comes in. Odd, don't you think, that an old man just happened to be stalking the bushes and then fought off a highly trained operative, young enough to be his grandson?' Anna looked at Frank and was momentarily thrown off balance by the comment. She was shaking now. 'I don't believe in coincidence like that, Mrs Groves.'

'So, what is this? Some kind of weird payback?' said Frank.

'This is what I call justice. A German war veteran who has scrounged a life from his enemies and the collaborating wife of a traitor.' Anna's breathing quickened. Her thoughts were with Charlotte. Her mouth felt dry and she found it difficult to swallow. Frank's steely nerve was holding, just.

'And what are you going to do now. Arrest us?'

'I'm not a policeman, Kramer. You will both come with me. Kramer – you will drive. I will sit in the back with Mrs Groves. Nothing silly – we do want your daughter to be safe, don't we? I suggest we go somewhere very quiet to talk this over. I'm sure Mrs Groves can suggest somewhere.' Sir Charles's words slithered from his mouth.

Guided by Anna, Sir Charles instructed Frank to drive to a remote headland just north of Bedruthan Steps. He parked the car next to a dilapidated shepherd's bothy. They walked along a track which ended at the coast path and to the cliff edge, bordered by soft tussock grass. Sir Charles pointed the way forward to a steep, narrow pathway which dropped into the cove below. The descent was nerve-wracking. Anna was wearing boots with a slight heel – hardly climbing footwear. But it was Sir Charles who struggled the most, his portly frame now unsuited to all but the most moderate of exercise. Eventually, they reached the wet sand of the cove. Anna looked back up to the path where they had been minutes beforehand; it must have been a drop of 200 feet or more. Sir Charles motioned towards a small cave in the cliff face.

Inside the cave, there was barely room to stand. The walls were dripping with sea water. At high tide, it would fill with water.

'Here will do. Sit down, both of you. Back-to-back.' Sir Charles grabbed Anna's ankles. She kicked out. He backed away, drew his gun and undid the safety catch. This time, Anna offered no resistance. Sir Charles bound her ankles and her hands. Then he turned his attention to Frank. As he pulled a piece of thin rope around his wrists, Frank lashed out at Sir Charles, glancing a blow to his cheekbone. Sir Charles recoiled and stumbled, but quickly regained composure. He lifted the revolver and coshed Frank's skull with the barrel. Frank groaned. His head fell to one side, blood running freely from the wound.

'Stupid old fool,' Sir Charles snarled viciously.

'You are an animal,' shouted Anna, her cry drowned partially by a breaking wave outside.

'We are all animals, my dear.'

'What – leave us here to drown? How honourable, how cowardly.'

'You have a choice. Tell me how you and this old man helped your husband.' Sir Charles wiped the sweat from his brow and sat on a ledge of the cave wall.

'There is nothing to tell. Frank saved my daughter from that attack – from your kidnapping. You don't understand anything – you and whoever your organisation is. My husband would have gone to New Zealand whatever the cost.'

'How noble,' puffed Sir Charles sardonically.

'Noble. Honourable. Dignified.' Frank moaned quietly, pain throbbing in his head.

'You don't know the meaning of those words.'

'I think I do. You see, I think I know what you represent, why you are so desperate to stop my husband.'

'Do you?'

'This isn't about Queen and country. This is about money. Most of the filthy tricks in this world are. Alex has told me about the arms dealers, the weapons companies, the middlemen. You are one of them. You don't work for the army or the secret service or whatever it is. You work for yourself.' Sir Charles was taken aback by her courage. Women were alien to him – as alien as ordinary life. Her words spat at him, every syllable true. She glared with abject contempt. For a giddy moment, he felt impotent and spent, but soon regained his energy.

'I have given you a chance, but sadly your arrogance and loyalty to your husband means I have no choice. The tide will be in just before dark. Goodbye, Mrs Groves.'

Sir Charles stood briefly at the small mouth of the cave, scanning the cliff path for walkers. Then he was gone.

'Frank, Frank,' Anna called and pleaded, but for now he was barely conscious. The late afternoon sun was slowly falling into the sea and the surf pulled and hissed on the sand.

*

Near Penrose, Eric Chapman was delayed. Firstly, by a dairy herd crossing the road for milking, then a slow tractor. His wife was doing a puzzle with Charlotte at the table when he walked into the living room. She looked up to see him uncharacteristically worried.

'Everything alright, Eric?' But he was too preoccupied with the task in hand. Eric found the number in the phone book and called Wadebridge police station. The duty officer tried to be understanding, but the story Eric described didn't seem to require urgent attention. Two older men having a conversation and a woman visiting a church – hardly the stuff of television drama. The police officer assured Eric that a car would drop by St Eval later. He put the phone down. 'I'm just nipping out for an hour or two,' he called to his wife. He heard her reply something about working at Trescore, but wasn't listening, then got in his car and drove away.

Pentire Farm lay in the fold of a small valley about a mile or so from Porthrowan. The old farmhouse was built of traditional north Cornish slate and stone. Reached by way of a winding track, the grey buildings looked as tough and damp as the weather often was so near this part of the coast. Eric Chapman pulled up outside the house next to a scruffy Land Rover. A collie barked and quickly recognised Eric's footsteps and figure. 'Hello, Alfie,' he said as he gave the dog a scratch behind the ears. A farmer's wife came to the door, dressed in jeans and a checked shirt.

'Hello, Eric,' she said. 'Ed's not in, I'm afraid. He's up on top field somewhere. He shouldn't be long.' Eric sat in the kitchen while Di Merriman made tea. 'Everything alright, Eric? You look a bit twitchy.' Just as she placed a mug in front of Eric, Ed Merriman walked through the door.

'Ewe stuck on the cliff path,' he said, and then noticed his guest. 'Hello, Eric. Not at Trescore today?' Eric's story gushed from his lips in a torrent.

'You say Anna told you to call the police?' Eric nodded. 'I think we'd better go and take a look. If the police work at their usual speed, they might be there by midnight.' The two men took the Land Rover and drove to St Eval.

*

When he reached the cliff path, Sir Charles was in poor shape. Panting and struggling for breath, he loosened his collar. He looked left and right; there was nobody nearby he could see. In minutes he was sitting in the driver's seat of his car, sweat oozing from every sallow pore. As soon as he felt his heart rate ease and slow, Sir Charles started the engine. It was time to go back to London and disappear into its labyrinths. The radio was tuned to a classical station. Elgar's Nimrod was playing. Under a red sky, he exited to the whisper of hesitant violins.

*

Ed Merriman walked quickly back to the Land Rover. There was nobody inside the church as far as he could tell.

'What do we do now?' asked Eric. 'Where the hell have they gone?'

'Might be back at Penrose. We'll go there but stop at Porthrowan first.' They met the coast road north-west of St Eval. As they pulled onto it, Ed slammed his foot on the brake missing a passing car that was travelling at high speed.

'That's it. That's the car I saw in Penrose this morning,' Eric shouted.

'You sure?'

'How many of those do you see around here?'

'Did you see who was driving?'

'No, but there wasn't anyone else in there as far as I could see.'

'I wonder where he's been?' They looked at each other and then together said, 'The Head.'

*

The tide had turned and was beginning to spill over the rocks in the cove. With stronger waves, the sea began to boil and foam in pools. Frank was conscious, but in some pain. His wound had clotted. Anna and Frank were tightly bound in Sir Charles's murderous knots.

'I'm sorry,' he said. 'This is all my fault. Perhaps if I had just let him kill me, you would not be here. Or if I hadn't come to Cornwall.' Frank's voice was fragile and hoarse.

'No, Frank. It is me who should apologise to you. You have done nothing wrong – only the right things. You saved my daughter.' She was beyond tears now.

'Anna, there is something I need to tell you.' Frank could see the ocean outside the cave; it wasn't far away now. 'I don't know if you will believe me, but there has been the strangest coincidence. Your cottage – I have been there before.'

'You have been to Trescore?' Maybe the blow to the head had affected his thinking, she thought. 'When?'

'In the war.' Anna shivered and felt her pulse race. 'Go on.'

'I was the captain of a German submarine. Our engines failed and we were stranded here. There was a great fog for many days.' Anna knew all about the great sea haags from stories her great-grandmother had told her. 'We had to come ashore to get things to fix our boat. It is an incredible story. But I met a very brave and beautiful woman who helped me. In fact, she may have saved my life and those of my crew. She lived at Trescore – with her grandmother, I believe.' The sea was spilling into the cave. Outside, gulls climbed and cried above the water. Anna felt pain and soreness in her wrists.

'Is this true, Frank? Please don't lie to me. I don't know what to believe anymore.'

'Yes, it is true.'

'What was her name?' Frank exhaled and felt a surge of pain across his forehead. Light outside the cave was fading fast. The backwash of a probing wave edged closer. Nobody would find them now.

'Dorothy,' he said in the faintest of whispers. Anna swallowed, tears welling up like high water in the cove. The sea was louder as the ocean began to fill the cave. With bodies tied, they held each other's hands and fingers as tightly as they could. Closing their eyes, they didn't let go.

Seven

London - Autumn, 1942

Baby Anna was nearly five months old. She had her mother's beautiful big black eyes, her father's smile and frown. Dorothy and George had given up the lease on their modern Maida Vale apartment and had moved to a modern semi-detached house in the suburbs of Bexley Heath, closer to the Kent airfields. It was owned by a former colleague of George, a wing commander posted to Malta who wouldn't be returning home anytime soon. George had urged her to give up her war work which she did, with a little reluctance and sadness. She was surprised to feel at least some relief and enjoyment when she did so. Emily had returned to live with her parents now the worst of the bombing seemed to have passed. Shipping losses and war production meant that there was always rationing, but there was enough to eat, however dull and monotonous the diet. With small children, Dorothy was even able to get little luxuries like orange juice occasionally, but such items were rare. Despite the hardships, life held a rhythm and a security both Dorothy and George had not known before.

'We should go to Cornwall soon. It's been too long and I'm dying for Granny to meet Anna,' she said one evening after the children had finally gone to sleep. George had just come in from the garden having mended the wheel on a wheelbarrow.

'Do you really think so?' George replied. 'After last time?'

'That will all have been forgotten about. No one liked Billy Mallett anyway.'

'Was he ever found?'

'No. Probably hiding somewhere like Plymouth. Who knows what happened to him – maybe he was called up. I don't really care.' They made tentative plans to go the next time George had some extended leave. George adjusted the blackout curtain and looked at the drizzling rain.

'You look tired,' she said.

'I don't think I'm tired, but I think I'm weary.' Dorothy looked perplexed. 'What I mean is, I feel I'm letting the side down. Like I should still be flying – not sitting behind a desk pushing pens.'

'You did your bit, my love.'

'Did I? I'm not so sure. You know, at first, when I was flying, I used to think we fliers had it so easy. The best food, best pay, best training – everything. Sometimes, especially early on in France, I would look down at those poor souls on the beaches or retreating. Their battle lasted day in, day out. I would be up there for an hour, maybe less sometimes, then home and in the pub or to my own bed. I felt disconnected like it was unreal.'

'You sound like you feel guilty about that.'

'I think I do.'

Listen to me, George.' She knelt in front of him and took both his hands. 'You are scared sometimes and you feel compassion. These are normal things – not something to be ashamed of.' Air raid sirens moaned hauntingly across the city.

'We should get to the shelter,' he said.

'It's probably a test or a false alarm. Come on – we are both tired. I need to sleep before Anna wants another feed.'

On hearing the sirens, Londoners trudged obediently to shelters, tube stations or took cover where they could. However, many chose not to bother. The heavy Blitz raids of the previous two years were in the past and people were not so terrified anymore. But only a few hundred feet above the Thames, two fast, low-flying German bombers had evaded their enemy. They were aiming for a specific target to the west of Tower Bridge. As the planes were adjusting course to make a run on their target, they were attacked by a pair of Spitfires. The British aircraft were faster and more agile. One quickly honed in on its prey and sent a burst of bullets into the bomber's port engine. The German plane began belching a trail of black smoke and slowly broke off, falling away. The Spitfire harried it, firing more rounds until both engines were on fire. The bomber almost glided to earth, one of its crew jumping and parachuting from the burning craft. Only at the last moment did it explode as fuel and ammunition ignited, sending debris over south London. The second attacker had taken evasive action, dumping its bombload and turning for home. It gained speed and height. Soon it was just a black dot in the sky.

When the high explosives fell, they woke a sleeping neighbourhood. A warden suggested there had been a gas explosion. Only when police and fire crew arrived did the real picture emerge. Two bombs had landed close together in a quiet suburban street. On one side of the road a house lay demolished, the front exposed. A family's furniture, clothes and personal things, all revealed and exposed, pathetically and without privacy. A chest of drawers balanced precariously on broken, splintered floorboards. There was relief when a neighbour informed the rescue parties that the inhabitants were away and staying with relatives in the country. The rescuers moved across the road to inspect the damage to a second property. Spits of rain flecked the dawn light and a crowd of onlooking neighbours gathered.

'It doesn't look so bad here,' said an air raid patrol warden. A bomb had landed at the corner of the street. There was a crater in the asphalt and a hole in the garden hedge. The house looked unscathed. A lawn mower was wedged in a downstairs window, thrown there by the blast.

'Windows have all gone. Better have a look inside,' said a policeman. The house was at first quiet and dark. Blackout curtains had been drawn dutifully; brown paper attached to a skylight. It was then that the policeman heard whimpering and crying. He went upstairs, his torchlight guided by the noises. On the landing of the first floor, he entered a bedroom. A child of no more than eighteen months old was sitting in a cot, crying, confused and frightened. The policeman called for some assistance and was joined by a fellow officer who comforted the child. Opposite this room, the door to another was closed. The first officer turned the handle. A hole, a few feet square, had been created by the explosion, blast and shrapnel. Through it poured daylight. Beside the hole was a bed. Two adults lay still, as if fast asleep. Small clots of blood had formed in their ears and at the sides of their mouths. They had been killed by the blast. At the other side of the room, the small voice of a baby gurgled, breathing weakly.

*

'Who's that at the door? The postman has been, hasn't he? Go and see who it is, would you, love.' Bob opened the door to the cottage. A boy, sixteen or seventeen probably, was standing solemnly in the porch. He handed Bob a telegram. Bob read it quickly.

'Is there a reply, Mr Chapman?' said the boy, his bottom lip trembling. Bob shook his head. 'I'm sorry, Mr Chapman, I'm sorry.' The boy hurried away.

'Who was it? Not that ruddy hawker from Newquay again?'

Bob walked into the kitchen and stood with the telegram in his hand. Gladys knew by the look on his face that something had happened to Dorothy. She snatched the note from his hand. The colour in her face drained. She sat at the table, grasping for its edges to keep her balance. And then she sat, unable to process what she had read, unable to stop time. Helpless, Bob sat beside her. She was silent and would remain so for days. But the sadness and sickness in her heart was only starting to grow, like drops of rain before a storm.

Dorothy and George were separated at death. At their insistence, George's body was brought home by his parents. He was buried in Surrey and was given a military funeral. At St Eval on a crisp autumn day, Dorothy was laid to rest. A fine and gentle mist drifted across the churchyard as her coffin was carried to the graveside. Restrained by the sadness that struck the community, the Reverend Dunning's service reflected on a young life, brave and spirited, taken by conflict. When it had finished, aged gravediggers were left to cover the coffin. A wake of sorts was held in the parish hall, but there were no words left to console Gladys; she had lost her son and her granddaughter in her lifetime, the natural order of things displaced by war.

'Will the children come to live with you, Gladys?' asked Vera softly as the afternoon sun melted through the panes.

'Yes, they will,' she replied quietly.

'They are with George's parents at the moment,' added Bob, 'but, we have agreed it is quieter for them here – not so near London.' Vera knew what he meant. Gladys was struggling. Tom Merriman and his wife caught Gladys's arm.

'If there is anything we can do, Gladys. Anything at all.'

'Thank you, Tom.' Bob took Gladys outside. 'I had a letter from George's mother. They are going to bring the girls here next week,' she told him.

'Better make sure we're ready for them,' Bob said gently with kind-hearted good humour.

'I don't think I can do this without you, Bob,' and she stared in the direction of the sea. He put his arm around her shoulders. Far distant was the outline of Trevose Head, powerful and immovable. Nearby, from a spray of hazel, a nuthatch stole a prize. It then wedged it in the bark of a tree and started to hammer the nutshell with all its might. Its work done, the bird flew away above some rosehips and the last of the elderberries. A farmer ploughed stubble in an adjacent field. The seasons were waving goodbye to one another.

The following week George's parents arrived from Surrey, not without considerable difficulty. Unused to travelling cross-country, let alone with two very small children, they were exhausted by the time Reddie Bland's informal taxi service dropped them at Penrose. Mrs Drake appeared especially disgruntled and disorientated when Gladys served a very late lunch at three o'clock. The atmosphere was strained and a little jangled.

'Have you thought about schooling at all?' Mrs Drake asked as they finished their meal.

'Bit early for that, isn't it?' said Gladys. 'Anna's not even one.'

'I think what my wife is trying to say is how we might agree to pay school fees,' Mr Drake said. Gladys was uncomfortable with the comment.

'Fees? Do I look like the sort of person who has money to pay school fees, Mrs Drake?' she said defensively.

'I didn't mean to offend you, Mrs Trewithen, I simply wanted to discuss the issue.' An awkward silence fell across the table.

'My wife and I would like to pay for the girls' education. George was our only son. The girls are all we have left of him.' On that, Gladys could agree – they were all she had of Dorothy.

'I'm sorry,' she said with uncharacteristic humbleness. 'I may have overreacted.'

'I am sure there are many good schools in Cornwall.' The formality of the conversation had thrown Gladys off balance, more so because she felt she had been cornered in her own home.

When Mr and Mrs Drake were satisfied the girls were in safe hands, they did not stay long. They handed Gladys a file containing various documents, names and addresses. Neither rude nor impolite, but efficient and practical, they quickly scurried back to Surrey, taking the last train out of the West Country. Later that evening, Gladys and Bob stood in the garden of Trescore. Above them, a vast canopy of stars, the palest of gold, sparkling in the deepest of blue.

'I wonder which one is my boy?' said Gladys.

'If he's anything like you, he'll have taken more than one.'

'And Dot and George? Maybe they're up there.' The night was hushed and perfectly still. 'You were there when they found him, weren't you, Bob? What was he like?'

'What do you mean?'

'Everyone said he looked at peace. Was that true? I couldn't bring myself to look.'

'Yes, it's true.'

'I don't know if I believe you. But they said Dot did too. But how can you be if you're killed by a bomb? Surely, surely...' But she couldn't take her thoughts forward; her imagination choked and resisted. She had no reference point, no images, no knowledge of what she was trying to visualise.

'Dot and George were killed by the blast. There was no pain,' he said, struggling for any words that could possibly describe what he meant.

'Nothing can happen to those girls, Bob, nothing.' Her eyes were wild and alive.

The following morning brought more fine autumn weather. An armada of slugs moved across the lawn leaving their wake like a convoy of ships in mid-ocean. A crow cried a loud, raucous screech as if complaining and went about its morning work. Bob was starting a leaf fire when the Reverend Dunning appeared, propping his enormous black bicycle against the hedge. His head bobbed along the beech like a puppet.

'How are the new arrivals settling in?' he said in an annoyingly jolly greeting. Dunning was well-meaning at the worst of times, but his boundless good humour was quite dull.

'Very well, thank you, Vicar,' Bob replied, raking chestnut leaves onto the smoking pile.

'Time for a christening before too long, I would imagine,' the clergyman continued with unwavering optimism.

'Something to discuss at a later date, I think,' Bob added diplomatically. But Dunning was obtuse and pressed further.

'Is Gladys at home?'

'Yes, she is.'

'May I?' Dunning asked rhetorically and moved keenly towards the cottage door. 'Mrs Trewithin,' he called, 'it's Reverend Dunning.' Gladys seemed to have heard most of the prior conversation. 'I was just doing my round and thought I would pop by to see how you were.'

'See if we are going to get the girls christened more like.' Gladys emerged from the porch, her slight frame armed with a rolling pin.

'I suppose I did wonder if, perhaps, you were thinking along those lines.'

'Not at the moment. My faith is a little fragile at present. Good day, Vicar.' Dunning hadn't time to remove his bicycle clips before he was retreating down the path back to his bike. With a wave of the hand, he was gone, wobbling down the lane and out of sight.

'He's got a bloody nerve,' Gladys scowled.

'He's only trying to do the right thing, love.'

'I don't believe in any of it anymore – if I ever did. Mumbo jumbo. No god would leave those two children without a mother or a father, just like it wouldn't have left Dot an orphan. They didn't want to bury my boy at St Eval, did they? Said he was a Methodist. He's better off where he is – with his pals.' The words were raw and too much. She went back inside the house and sank into a long, dark mood of despair – just one of a countless number that would descend like storm clouds in the months and years to come. Bob stoked the fire. The white smoke puffed upwards and was carried a little in the tiniest hint of wind. Somewhere in the heart of the fire, the leaves crackled and popped in the heat. Bob took a step back away from the smoke. Something made him look back and up at the cottage. In their bedroom window, Gladys was staring out over the trees in the hollow beyond the garden, her gaze fixed on some point in the mid-distance. There was an odd serenity to her expression. She looked young, he thought, but pale against those dark eyes. For the briefest of moments, he thought he saw Dorothy.

The days moved by quietly, with routine and without fuss. The make-do-and-mend stoicism was better suited to the tough Cornish, whose ancestors had known far worse, than to urban townsfolk, softened by the conveniences of modern life. Besides, they had the land, the woods and the sea; it is always possible to live from these things. Gladys gave nearly all her love to the children, or what there was left to give. But it was Bob who, a few weeks later, was troubled by family events.

'I'm going to sign up, Dad,' Eric said.

'What on earth for?' Bob replied. They were standing in the garden of Bob's cottage at Porthrowan. His son was smoking a hand-rolled cigarette.

'I'll get the call anyway and I'd rather have some say in it.' He extinguished the cigarette under his boot.

'Plenty in the last war who regretted it.'

'It's a different war, Dad.'

'They said that last time. Over by Christmas, they said. Just didn't say which Christmas.' Bob had finished digging over a vegetable bed. 'Beautiful soil that. Needs some manure on it.'

'Are you going to ask me what I'm going to join?'

'Why don't you tell me,' said Bob, holding back his disapproval.

'Minesweepers.'

'Minesweepers?'

'Or minelayers. I don't know. Both, I suppose. Lots of the lads in Padstow are going to do it as well. You don't need a medical.'

'Well, every cloud and all that,' added Bob sarcastically.

'Thought you might be pleased. Doing something useful – something patriotic.' Bob wasn't pleased, but proud in some inexpressible way.

'I just don't want to lose you, son, that's all.' He changed the conversation abruptly. 'Now give us a hand with those spuds, will you?' When they had heaved the sack into the shed, Eric rolled another thin cigarette with a tiny pinch of tobacco. He licked the paper and put it in his mouth, lighting it with a cupped match.

'I'm going to the pub for a quick drink. I'll see you later.' As he walked away, Bob called after him.

'Have you learned to swim yet?'

'I'll cross that bridge when I get to it.'

'You'll have to bloody paddle across,' muttered Bob under his breath and shaking his head.

Bob returned to Trescore in the early evening to discover Gladys sitting with Emily, feeding her stewed apple. Gladys wore a vacant look, almost trance-like. But for the ticking of the clock, the house was silent.

'Is everything alright?' he said, sensing concern. She didn't speak, but her eyes pointed to an unfolded letter on the table. Bob picked it up and started to read handwriting he recognised.

Dear Granny,

All is well here. We're in the new house. It's modern and spacious and I think you would approve! The girls are keeping me very busy, especially Emily. She reminds me of you the way she behaves sometimes.

We are hoping to visit very soon. George's leave is often cancelled without any warning, so things are difficult to plan. Maybe we will just turn up out of the blue. Would you be put out if we did that? Thought not!

It is quieter here – much more so than in town. It's really no different to Wadebridge – well, maybe a bit different. There are few raids. Sometimes we get the odd one, but most of the time they are just false alarms. The worst thing is the food. It's just not the same up here. What I would do for a decent home-cooked meal.

Anyway, I must dash. So much to do.

Give Bob a kiss from me. With all my love,
    Dot

It was a simple note written in that wild scrawl of hers. He stepped outside. The trees teased a gentle hush. A sprinkling of beech leaves fell and scattered, brown and thin. Bob breathed in deeply. Dot had become like a daughter to him. The thought of his son as another victim of this awful war was almost too much to bear. He thought about the conversation he had with Gladys the previous day. How did Dot and George die? Was it just a blast, or did the blast obliterate their bodies into thousands of pieces of flesh? He didn't know; neither he nor Gladys had formally identified the bodies. The Drakes had done this, and so he comforted himself with what they had told him. And there, he dammed the incoming tide of his imagination. What did it matter – flesh and blood and bones? He had all those memories – and as the second hand passes the moment, all anyone ever has.

Gladys joined him and pulled him inside by the arm. There was no need to exchange any words; they were all there between the lines of Dot's letter. Gladys made tea from fresh leaves, a rare treat. She cut two slices of apple cake. The girls were down and asleep.

'I think we will want a fire tomorrow,' Bob said finally. 'The nights are drawing in now.' Gladys agreed quietly, nodding approval. The clock ticked comfortingly above the fireplace.

'I haven't made any supper, I'm afraid,' she said apologetically.

'This cake is just fine,' he said.

When they had finished, Bob cleared the cups and plates. Gladys was reading Dot's letter again.

'Time to put that away now, love, don't you think?'

'Should I burn it?'

'No. Keep it. It's her voice in those words.' He was right, but she needed to hear it. Gladys put the letter in a drawer of the dresser along with all the others she had kept. All the images of her granddaughter, those she wanted and cherished, were forming like playful ghosts, gathering their cues and waiting in the wings of her memory. For the first time in many nights, Gladys would sleep with some peace.

Eight

London and North Cornwall - Summer, 1985

At nine-thirty on Friday evening, Sir Charles unlocked the floorplate in a city office which gave access to a ladder, which in turn descended into cellar rooms. From here, he was able to take a long and winding metal staircase to the abandoned tube station where he had been called to a meeting. When he reached the disused platform, only a few lights partially illuminated it.

'Pleased you could join us so promptly, Gifford.' It was the same calm voice, laced with tones of deep menace. 'We have some breaking news. Would you like to hear it?' Sir Charles could feel the blood pumping in his arteries. He was sweating profusely. 'There has been an incident in Auckland. A fishing trawler belonging to the New Dawn protest group has been raided by French special forces. At least two activists have been killed. Groves isn't one of them as far as we know.'

'That's what we want, isn't it?' said Sir Charles.

'We will see. The problem is this incident is attracting a lot of news coverage around the world – something we very much don't want.'

'I'm not sure I follow,' said Sir Charles uncomfortably. The voice from the darkness deepened and was sinister.

'The French are now under pressure from the international community to suspend testing.'

'I see.'

'Do you? All of this could have been avoided if your plan had been executed correctly. Your very expensive plan, Gifford. But we must be pragmatic. Can you update us on your clean-up operation?'

'O'Brien's body has been found. The case on the attack of the girl is closed.'

'And the old man?'

'Dealt with,' Sir Charles added.

'I do hope so. For your sake. And you will now disperse your squad. We will be in touch.' A few moments later, the tunnels were silent. A large rat scurried in and out of the darkness, its pale tail visible in the shadows. Sir Charles made his way back to the city streets. He was near the end of a failed mission. Overpowering gloom and melancholy fell upon him. His energy and spirit were sapped, but the evening was not over. Before the next chime of the city clock, he would be dining with Jonathan Popplewell.

When Sir Charles arrived, Popplewell was already ensconced at a table in the corner of his favourite restaurant. He was sipping fine French white wine and smoking a cigarette.

'What will you have, Charles?' Popplewell nodded to the sommelier.

'A large Cognac,' said Sir Charles; the wine waiter nodded, as if in disapproval.

'You seem to have lost your joie de vivre, Charles. The sea air not done you any good?'

'I think you could say we are both at an impasse.'

'Both?'

'Both, Jon. The bank is calling in the debts.' Popplewell's playful teasing vanished as the colour drained from his face. 'You had better catch up with Rouvier. It looks like the French are pulling out on all fronts. And you know what this means.' Popplewell was stunned. He quickly lit another cigarette. He staggered to his next sentence.

'You are clearly not up to speed, Jon. You'd better read tomorrow's papers.' Sir Charles ordered another large brandy. But Popplewell was lost in thought and shock. For what seemed like an age, there was no conversation between them until he spoke.

'I am done for, Charles.' He spat the words across the table in a furious whisper, tiny bullets of saliva peppering his dinner guest.

'You knew the stakes, Jon. We all did. The bank wins. We lose.'

Popplewell's food arrived. He pushed it aside.

'Well, if you're not eating, Jon...' Sir Charles helped himself to the abandoned plate.

'You insufferable pig. How dare you implicate me like this.'

'I haven't finished.' Sir Charles's tone veered maniacally. 'You still need to do one or two bits of tidying up, Jon.'

'What the hell do you mean?'

'Ward-Lock.'

'What about him?'

'He needs to be, how shall I put it, reassigned.'

'Reassigned? To what?'

'More to where. Somewhere very far away. I suggest Foreign Office work. Somewhere like the Central African Republic. His close relationship with the French Ambassador should stand him in good stead. He will do very well out there.'

'You cannot be serious?'

'Just get it done.' Sir Charles looked at Popplewell in a way that instilled terror in the politician. A nearby table looked up, sensing disagreement.

'And I suppose you have something lined up for Nicholas as well?' Popplewell was containing his rage with whispers.

'Nicholas is no fool. In fact, he is about the only one who will emerge unscathed. He's done the decent thing and resigned. Already taken a job in the City with a broker.'

'Fitzmaurice?'

'Very sad.' Popplewell looked at Sir Charles disbelievingly. 'Involved in a dramatic car crash last week. Really, Jon, do you not read the papers anymore?'

Sir Charles skewered another piece of fish with his fork. 'I think I will have some wine now.' He motioned to the waiter and ordered a different bottle to Popplewell. The waiter poured a little wine. Sir Charles smiled approvingly as he took a greedy swig, and the waiter filled his glass. 'I must say, Jon, this is really very good of you to take things so well.'

'I will have no choice but to resign.'

'That is, of course, your decision. But at least that way, what will be left of your reputation will remain intact.'

'You have ruined me.' His eyes were glazed.

'No. Your own ambition and greed ruined you. I merely helped you along the nasty little path and down the slippery slope.'

'And you – what becomes of you?'

'I am a soldier, Jon. I live to fight another day.' Popplewell threw down his napkin in disgust and drank the rest of his wine. Without saying another word, he got up and left the restaurant. Sir Charles finished his meal.

'Excellent. Very good, indeed,' he said as his plate was taken away. 'My friend had an urgent appointment.'

'Would you like anything else, sir, or just the bill?'

'Nothing else, thank you. Actually, perhaps a whisky – the forty-year-old Balvenie. But please add the bill to my friend's account, would you?'

'Of course, sir.' Sir Charles chuckled to himself. The colour was returning to his fat cheeks.

*

At Park Head, Ed Merriman parked his Land Rover with a skid, next to an old bothy. The two men knew these tracks and paths like nobody else. They had played here as children and worked the land as men; there wasn't an inch of this coast they couldn't traverse blindfolded. Eric followed Ed along the path that wound its way into the cove. The tide was high. Gulls dived and climbed above the teal water.

'Where now?' Eric said, looking to Ed for instruction.

'The caves,' Ed replied calmly, but loudly, as he competed against the strong breeze from the sea.

'We'll need to take Low Walk,' suggested Eric; it was a name they had used since childhood – just one of many they had given to the innumerable paths and shortcuts scribbled into the cliffs.

'Better grab that bit of rope.' They made their way across the cliff calling Anna's name, but the noise of the surf was almost deafening.

'We can't get any closer – it will be high tide in half an hour,' Eric said. And then, between the breaking waves, they heard a faint and distant calling.

'Did you hear that?' said Ed urgently.

'Yes. From over there.'

The water was now breaking over their ankles and knees, breaking and crashing against their faces. Anna was shivering, exhausted and her throat was hoarse. She thought of Charlotte, her playing with Mary Chapman, wondering when Mummy would pick her up. Next to her, Frank was tiring; he had lost a lot of blood. With the last of her failing strength, she screamed once more for help, the call reverberating from the grey, granite walls and then vaporising into the boiling sea. The waves were quicker now, the cave filling up with the Atlantic tide. Anna thought she heard a voice holler from outside, somewhere not far away, but her energy was spent and she was fading fast. Have I have done my best? she thought, and she spoke the words aloud, as if in prayer.

'Grab hold of my hand, Eric.' Ed lowered himself into the water. He slipped and nearly fell but kept his balance. He waded towards the mouth of the small cave from where the noise seemed to be coming.

'Anna,' he called, 'Anna, is that you?' At the entrance to the cave, he could see only black. There was little time, but he had no choice. The water was strong and one wave almost toppled him, but he waded into the blackness. The currents were pulling against his legs and his feet sank into the sand. Twice he staggered and fell. The light of the fading day was behind him and he tried to adjust his eyes to the darkness. He called her name again. Then, like a plea, he heard what was unmistakably Anna's voice.

'Ed – is that you?' He almost walked on top of them; they were almost submerged in the water. There was no time for explanation. Ed reached beneath the water. He tried to lift them both, but it was no use. 'Hurry, please, Ed,' Anna said as another wave pounded into the cave. Ed then took his knife from his belt. He felt for their tied hands and then pulled against the thin rope that bound them. With his blade, he made strong cuts against the fibres. The sea, almost merciful for a minute, was calm enough for Ed to cut through the rope. He tugged and it loosened. He pulled Anna to her feet, and she made her way to the entrance. Ed wrapped Frank's arm around his shoulder and followed Anna.

As they turned to wade towards the shore and the path, a monstrous wave broke, throwing them off balance and into the water. Their heads and eyes were full of salt and the sea. Anna helped Ed carry Frank forward until they saw Eric lying forward on the cliff path. He had secured the rope around a rock spur. They pulled Anna out of the water first. She collapsed on the path, her mouth dry and sore with salt.

'Throw down the rope, Eric,' called Ed. 'We'll get him up first.' Ed tied the rope around Frank while Eric hauled him from the sea. Ed didn't need the rope to get out of the water. He knew he had only a few moments, or his chances of getting out alive were slim.

When Ed appeared from the water, he saw Anna and Eric tending to Frank. It was clear Frank was in a bad way. His forehead and skull were bloody; his eyes sunken with pain.

'He needs a hospital and fast,' said Ed. Anna was past tiredness and pain now. Her thoughts were on her daughter and Frank. It was the last throes of twilight, and the cliff shapes were now only blank outlines in the murkiness. Anybody who didn't know these paths and tracks well would have foundered quickly. By design or sheer luck, they made quick progress back to the Land Rover on the headland.

'Anna – you get in the cab. Eric – you will have to keep him as comfortable as you can in the back. We'll get back to Pentire and call an ambulance.' The drive back to the farm was not long. Anna shivered uncontrollably. Ed's gaze fixed firmly on the road in front of him. They pulled up outside the farmhouse. Di Merriman quickly greeting them as she emerged from the orange glow of the kitchen. She was followed by Mary Chapman and Charlotte. Before the Land Rover had halted, Anna had opened the door and was running to her daughter.

'My love,' she said as she wrapped her arms around her.

'You're all wet, Mummy,' Charlotte complained. They went inside with Mary. Ed and Eric carried Frank, dragging him upright into the house. Sensing what had happened, Di fetched towels and blankets. Once inside, Frank began to groan with pain, as if shock and cold were wearing off like a fading anaesthetic.

*

At breakfast in Belgravia, Sir Charles was scanning Monday's morning papers. He had spent the weekend recuperating from his Cornish expedition, making a series of long telephone calls to a close group of guarded associates. The headlines made light entertainment to assuage the fractious excitement of the previous few days: 'Minister Resigns Amidst Personal Tragedy' – some horrid little drama hastily invented by the party press office, no doubt. Buried in the smaller stories was mention of changes in personnel at the French Embassy. He contented himself with the assumption that recent events were simply one lost battle in this theatre of war. Nuclear testing would resume, just as soon as the world had a newer and more fashionable crisis to worry about, and when that happened, he would be needed again to broker and close a deal or two. That's how it worked because it always had done.

A memorial service for Fitzmaurice was to be held in Chelsea later that morning, but there was still plenty of time to enjoy the comforts of fresh toast with Brittany butter before any further thought needed to be given to this. He took a slurp of coffee and selected a tabloid from the pile of dailies in front of him. It was neither the caffeine nor the bread which made him choke, but a headline in the news pages. 'Murder Thwarted in Cornish Cave'. As Sir Charles read on, he discovered Anna and Frank's rescue. More disturbingly, a suspect bearing his description was urgently wanted in connection with the crime. He picked up the phone and made yet another call to a trusted ally. During the next few minutes, he went to the garage and changed the number plates on the car with a spare set from the boot. He put a cover over the Mercedes, disconnecting the battery at the same time. Outside, summer rain started to fall on London. Sir Charles had drawn a little too much attention to himself. He was old and wily enough to retreat when he needed to. A dark blue, shabby Ford saloon arrived in the mews. Its driver got out and walked quickly away. With a suitcase on the passenger seat, Sir Charles got in and slithered into the watery streets.

*

Frank had been in Truro Hospital for nearly three days. The prognosis was neutral. Pumped full of rehydrating saline and pain relief, he was responding, but only just. Conscious, but weak and bleary, he cut a much older self than only a week or so ago.

'Do you have family we can call, Frank?' Anna was by his side, holding his hand and stroking it with her thumb. Frank shook his head, then closed his eyes and drifted into sleep.

'Come on, Anna,' Ed called. 'You have done all you can for now. We can visit again tomorrow.'

'But we can't just leave him, Ed. He's…' and she hesitated. Ed didn't prompt her but waited for her to finish her sentence. But she didn't. Letting go of Frank's hand, she took her bag from the floor and followed Ed out of the ward.

'You will call if anything happens, won't you?'

'Of course,' a kindly nurse replied. As they walked to the car park, Ed stopped and turned to face Anna.

'You were going to say something in there – something about Frank. What was it?' His words were gentle but curious. Anna looked up, her eyes awash and on the brink of tears.

'I don't know if I should tell you, Ed,' she said. 'If I am honest, this feels unreal – somewhere between a nightmare and a dream.' Grey cumulus clouds drifted in the sky above and the wind picked up a little.

'In some strange way, I think I know what you are going to say.' Anna was astonished.

'What do you mean?' she asked.

'I think we need a drink, don't you?'

*

'You said you thought you knew what I was going to say – what did you mean?' They had stopped at a pub in St Columb. It was a quiet, early evening and the only customers beside themselves were a couple of men drinking pints and smoking cigarettes at the bar.

'The man in the hospital – Frank – I am almost certain I know who he is.'

'Who?'

'You know that old story from Porthrowan about the German submarine in the war?' Anna nodded; everyone closely related to the village knew it. 'Well – it's a true story.'

'What do you mean? It was just an old tale they use to trot out at Halloween, wasn't it?'

'No, Anna, it wasn't.'

'How do you know?'

'Because I was in it.' Her eyes widened in disbelief. 'When we were about ten or eleven, Rosie and I took a dinghy out towards Quies.'

'Quies?' she exclaimed. 'You rowed out to Quies? Were you mad?'

'Well, Rosie has always been a bit mad. We got a way out, but there was a really thick fog. We got lost and the dinghy capsized. You know how the story goes.' Ed took a sip of his ale.

'Yes, but I didn't know who the children in the story were. That was all part of the mystery.'

'Well, it happened.'

'And you never told anyone?'

'We were sworn to secrecy. Mother threatened us and said we would be arrested and hanged as traitors if anybody found out.' Anna laughed and apologised.

'So, how does this relate to Frank?' As soon as her words were loose, the penny dropped like lead. Ed nodded.

'You see? I recognised the scar above his eye. His voice – I remember it, only it doesn't sound quite so foreign now.'

'My God.' They were lost for words and understanding.

'But you were going to tell me something?'

'Can I have another drink, please?' Ed brought another whisky back to the table and a glass bottle of Coca-Cola.

'Maybe make this one a bit longer?' he joked, placing the mixer alongside the spirit. She smiled and compromised by adding a slug of Coke to the glass.

'When we were in the cave, I really thought that was it. I couldn't see any way out. I don't know how you found us.'

'Instinct, I suppose. And you told Eric that's where you would go.' Anna ignored his comment, but not with any malice.

'Just before you got there, Frank told me something. That he had been to Trescore before – said he met a girl.'

'Did he say who it was?'

'My mother.'

'What? You're kidding me?'

'No. He called her by her name.' Ed sat back on the dark wooden chair and exhaled a long shot of breath. 'But there's something else – another part to this story that nobody knows. You have to promise me you won't say anything. Not at least until all of this is resolved.' Ed nodded. He was well-versed in keeping confidence. 'When Emily was twenty-one, my grandmother sat down with her and told her about her father. Gladys was very old by then – it could only have been a few years before she died. I remember it well because the door to the sitting room was closed. They were in there for what seemed like hours. When they had finished talking, Emily left and went out for the evening. Granny was just quiet – didn't say anything.'

'So, you are saying that Frank is Emily's father?' He paused. 'I don't know what to say.'

'I didn't find out until after Granny had died. Emily told me then. Nobody else knew – well, maybe Bob, but he wouldn't have betrayed Granny – he would have done anything for her.'

They sat in still silence some more. One of the men at the bar shuffled off his bar stool and left the pub. His companion lit another cigarette and chatted to the landlord.

'Are you going to tell Emily?'

'Yes. I think so. I don't know. Would it do any good? She's in America anyway. We don't even know if Frank will get through this.'

'You have to tell her,' Ed had cut in sharply. 'I'm sorry, Anna. I didn't mean to startle you, but you have no choice. She would never forgive you if you didn't tell her.' Anna finished her drink. The pub was silent.

'Yes – you're right. Thank you, Ed. I needed to hear that.' She paused and looked at her watch. 'Do you think

Charlotte and I could stay at Pentire tonight? I just don't think I am strong enough to go back to Trescore today.'

'Of course. Di practically ordered me to invite you anyway. We'd better go. Supper will be on the table soon. I'll tell her it was your fault we were late.' They walked arm-in-arm to the car like brother and sister. Despite her best intentions, Anna was still undecided as to what she should do.

*

In deepest Sussex, the battered blue Ford saloon pulled up outside a large Victorian villa. Wisteria and ivy clung to the skin of the house like veins. Sir Charles was greeted at the door by a welcoming and trusted woman of long-standing acquaintance. Ushered inside, he was quickly seated in a comfortable chair overlooking a striped lawn bordered with summer blooms.

'A spot of bother, Charles?' the woman said as she handed him a large gin and tonic. The mixer fizzed tiny bubbles across the skin of the lime in the glass.

'You read me too well, Veronica.'

'What is it this time? Foreign Office capers or something a little darker?' Her voice was a gravelly mix of received pronunciation and dormitory mischief. She sat down beside him in an adjacent chair.

'For once, I might have paddled out a bit too far.' He took a huge slurp and gulp. 'Bit out of my depth, perhaps.'

'Out of your depth? My God, Charles, what have you been up to?' Her mirth receded.

'Let's say I played some very high stakes. Time to leave the table, my dear.'

'For how long?'

'I don't know, but I will need your help – yours and Alan's of course.'

'You mean leave the country for a bit and lie doggo?'

'Exactly.'

'How long do we have?'

'Not long. The papers are putting out descriptions.'

'Descriptions? This is serious, Charles. I will call Alan now.' She got up and walked into the house. Sir Charles sat, sipping his drink, still with an uncharacteristic calm. He looked into a border full of dahlias and sea thistle. Behind the flowers was a freshly cut yew hedge, dark and menacing. All was silent and above the sky was cloudless. A house fly buzzed and rested on the table. The serenity of it all was deeply sinister.

Veronica returned after a few minutes, seemingly with refreshed composure.

'Alan is leaving town now. He should be here in an hour or two.'

'Thank you, Veronica.' There were tears, real or otherwise, forming in his eyes. She put her hand on his leg and squeezed it gently.

'Well, you were one of my favourites, Charles. So dashing in uniform all those years ago.'

'You mean Cyprus?'

'Cyprus? I was thinking Monaco.' Sir Charles couldn't remember Monaco, or Cyprus for that matter.

'Great days,' he said vaguely.

'Even better nights,' she replied impishly. The sun was still hot but beginning to dip westwards. 'I think we should have another large drink, Charlie. Alan won't be here for a while.' She went inside again to prepare more gin and tonic. Sir Charles relaxed in his chair. He caught sight of a woodpecker on a distant prunus tree. The bird was hungry for insects. Sir Charles raised what was left of his gin and drank a toast to the lonely bird.

*

At Pentire, Di Merriman had cooked a sumptuous meal from her farmhouse kitchen. She and Anna had cleared the table, but Di had sent her out of the kitchen, insisting that she talk to Ed. Anna thanked her, but was a little suspicious that Ed had said something to betray her confidence. When she walked into the sitting room, Ed was sitting in an armchair, as if expecting her.

'Have you said something to Di?'

'Of course I haven't, but she is perceptive enough to know we need to finish a conversation, Anna.' He sounded a little frustrated.

'Is there a conversation to finish?' Anna said only partly with irony. Ed didn't respond and just stared at her patiently. 'Okay, I will call her.' He half smiled expectantly, but still said nothing. 'Okay, okay. I will do it now. Can I use the phone?'

Anna came back about a quarter of an hour later. She had been crying but looked strong. Di had joined them and had brought coffee. Everything in the house was familiar and secure. Furniture that hadn't moved for decades and wouldn't do so anytime soon. The ticking wall clock struck nine.

'Are you okay, Anna?' Di said.

'Yes.'

'And Emily?' Di scolded Ed with a look.

'Funny – she said she knew it was me calling before the phone rang, and she said she knew it was something to do with our mother.'

'You were always so close as children, Anna, that it doesn't surprise me she said that,' Ed said as tenderly as he could. Anna was too deep in thoughts to hear him.

'She's flying to London as quickly as she can.'

'You have done the right thing,' Di said. Anna nodded and cradled her coffee. 'And Ed will go and collect her from the airport.' Di looked at her husband with a well-worn expression of deep affection and command.

'Thank you,' Anna said. 'I think I might go to bed now.' When she had gone, Di sat next to Ed.

'And how do you feel now?' she said. Ed spoke his reply like the words had been waiting to be spoken for years.

'Like a fog has lifted,' he said. Beyond the house and the yard outside, the ocean heaved and roared.

*

Alan Mottram arrived home in the early evening. With a clatter of keys and a yell to his wife, he was greeted by Sir Charles who barely rose from a seat in the drawing room.

'Where the hell is Veronica?' he said irritably.

'Taking a shower, old boy,' replied Sir Charles casually.

'Always in the bloody shower, that woman.'

'Well, at least you know where she is, Alan.' Sir Charles winked to his inner self.

'Yes. Anyway – what is this business you have got yourself into, Charles? Sounds murky from what V has said.' He helped himself to a large Scotch from a table at the side of the room.

'I need to get out of the country, Alan. Soon.'

'How soon?'

'Tonight.'

'Tonight? You're going to have to do better than that, Charles.'

'Government business. Things got a bit out of hand.'

'For God's sake. How out of hand? DIS? SIS?'

'Above that.'

'No. I'm not getting involved. You can forget we ever had this conversation, Charles.'

'No – I can't do that, Alan. Anyway, you are involved now.' Sir Charles refilled his whisky glass. 'You have always wanted to be involved, haven't you, Alan?' Mottram's face fell like a child from a fence. He was beaten all ends up. Given he had enjoyed his wife's very intimate company only an hour before, Sir Charles nearly felt sympathy for his old friend, but the desire to survive was spurring him on.

'I will make some calls,' Mottram sighed. He firmly placed his glass on a table and scuttled away to the telephone. He must have passed his wife in the hall because Veronica arrived a few seconds later, clearly relaxed and refreshed from her interminable shower.

'Went the date well?' she laughed unforgivingly, and lit a long, thin cigarette with a silver lighter.

'Like a midnight in Moscow,' Sir Charles replied somewhat obscurely. Veronica laughed, but neither of them knew what he had meant.

'I think we need something to eat,' she said. 'We have all worked up quite an appetite.' She giggled and glided out of the room.

'I need a drink.' Mottram had returned to the drawing room. He poured more amber into a fresh glass and then picked up a framed photograph, looked at it absently and replaced it on the table. 'Whatever this is, Charles, it had better be worth it.'

'Thank you, Alan,' his guest replied with warmth and gratitude, and perhaps even affection. 'The nights are getting chilly.' Sir Charles was staring into some mid-distance beyond the walls of the house, no doubt caught between the high jinks of the past and the future, never in the here and now.

'Two of Irving's men will arrive this evening,' said Mottram, intent on spelling out the rubrics of a hastily concocted plan.

'Irving?' interjected Sir Charles.

'Irving,' affirmed Mottram. 'You don't need to know, Charles. In fact, better if you didn't hear that name. Rest assured we have used him before.' Sir Charles had no choice but to surrender and follow orders. 'When they get here, you will leave with them and do as they say. You have your passport, I presume?' Sir Charles nodded. 'Not that you will need it.'

'Then I had better make myself look beautiful,' Sir Charles joked.

'This won't be cheap, Charles.'

'I will have the money ready for Irving in a few days.'

'I hope for your sake you do.'

It was almost ten o'clock when a dark-coloured van pulled up on the gravel outside the Mottrams' house. The air was still but cool with the first breath of autumn, and a faint summer mist drifted in front of a bank of yew trees bordering the property. Two men got out of the van and walked quickly into the house, the door closing behind them, extinguishing a smudge of orange light as it did so. Mottram led the two men to a dining room adjacent to the hallway. Here they were joined by Sir Charles and his suitcase.

'Good evening, gentlemen,' he said, disguising any apprehension with well-rehearsed nonchalance. There were no introductions, merely exchanges of functional talk.

'We are ready when you are,' said one of the men, his words as undistinguished as his appearance.

'May I ask where it is we are going?'

'Just do as you're told, Charles,' urged Mottram with nervous quiet. The other man opened the dining room door with a gloved hand by way of invitation to leave. Three men walked into the night and two of them into the van. The third got into the old Ford saloon. Within moments, red taillights faded and Sir Charles Gifford had vanished.

Nine

North Cornwall and Berlin –
Spring, 1945

The sea, the colour of dead lavender, pounded the foreshore at Porthrowan. Emily and Anna played in the wet sand, engrossed in some wondrous childlike game that adults soon forget how to play. Gladys and Bob, proud grandparents and tired parents both, sat on a comfortable ledge of rock at the side of the bay. There were few reminders of conflict here, as war's endgame closed on the ruined wastelands of Germany. Above the ocean, some miles out, a Royal Air Force spotter plane buzzed about its business.

'Eric said there was a huge explosion last week – out there,' Bob said, looking to the horizon beyond the Quies rocks.

'A boat?' asked Gladys.

'No, they don't think so. Maybe a mine or something. Came from the water.'

'Is Eric okay?'

'Yes – he wasn't there. Talk of the town apparently.'

'A mystery from the depths.' They laughed and their attention rested with the little girls on the beach.

'Emily will be starting school soon,' Bob said.

'Not for months – next year, even,' replied Gladys a little wistfully. The girls were running towards them, waving their arms like windmill sails. Emily explained they had found something washed up and entangled with seaweed. Arousing something like excitement mixed with fatigue, the grandparents followed their eager beachcombers to the edge of a rock pool near the water's edge.

'Whatever is it?' Gladys exclaimed. Bob bent down and retrieved the flotsam.

'It's a lifejacket,' he said. 'German, I would guess,' pointing to words on the canvas.

'Poor souls.' The girls had lost interest and were immersed once again in their play.

'Better theirs than ours,' Bob retorted with uncharacteristic callousness.

'It'll all be over soon. What does it matter?'

'Until they find something else to fight about.' Gladys said nothing, but a colder world-weariness had fallen about Bob in recent months. They gathered their things and the girls and trudged slowly back towards Penrose.

*

Under flaming skies, Berlin was all but defeated and in the hands of Soviet forces. The city centre was encircled; Hitler was dead. Only madmen, fanatics and the unlucky still stood scrapping out a fight which was lost long ago. Amidst the rubble and chaos, Germany's once vast armies were now reduced to old men, schoolboys and a motley collection of ragged servicemen – led by maniacal Nazis who still believed in some miraculous final victory for the Fatherland. Hans Kramer thought differently. Attached to an anti-tank unit in the southern suburbs, he knew the war would end in days, if not hours. He also did not want to be captured by Russians, wild and intent on revenge. News of the Führer's death was whispering through the lines. Kramer stood inside a roofless shell of what must have been some sort of office building or apartment block. He and a few others warmed themselves around a modest fire. The night wasn't cold, but the damp cold of the north was still lingering in the spring air.

'It is over,' said an unblinking face in the flickering shadows. The soldier wore the uniform of a Luftwaffe mechanic.

'You are right,' agreed Kramer, his face gaunt and haggard with war.

'You say that with relish,' added the voice, but there was no judgement in its tone.

'Look around you,' continued Kramer. 'What is it we are fighting for?' There was a brief pause for reflection in the conversation.

'Our families, perhaps.'

'Maybe for you.'

'You have no family?'

'I did. All killed in the Hamburg inferno.' There was a longer silence now. The raids on Hamburg were well known for their hideous tragedies. Some of the others who were gathered by the fire drifted into the darkness, to smoke, sleep and wait. Only Kramer and the mechanic remained.

'So, what now? Fight or surrender?' Kramer looked up, his turn now to stare without blinking.

'Escape,' he said. He lit the scrap of a cigarette. The man by his side gazed into the dying flames, neither the betrayer nor the accomplice.

Kramer lifted his greatcoat collar around his neck and pulled the peak of his field cap over his face. Not far away, rattles of gunfire and shell bursts peppered the air. Occasionally, flares illuminated the sky, but for a little while at least there was a lull in the fighting. Sensing there were only hours of war left to burn, Kramer gambled: stay, be killed or surrender to a life of brutal Soviet captivity, or slip into the deathly shadows of night? Either way, the odds in favour of survival were long. But while there was a last chance to throw the dice, what else was there to do? Kramer had gambled before and won. He would do so again. There was little to live for in the ruins and dust of his homeland, but there was another life to be had and his thoughts melted into Cornish mist.

A rasping cough hacked from a huddle of dozing soldiers a few metres from where Kramer stood. A boy of no more than fifteen years of age was dying from an infected shrapnel wound, malnutrition and pneumonia.

He would die alone, far from his mother, far from his home and far from any great sense of compassion. The war had been responsible for millions of bitterly lonely deaths, unmarked in their passing or their final resting place. Such are the noble causes man fights for. Kramer took his chance. As the boy roared with a fit of bronchial failure, Kramer stepped back into the shadows of the bombsite building. Nobody it seemed noticed his disappearance. He looked upwards. There were no ceilings or roofs remaining, just an open, framed canopy of sky. Kramer edged forward carefully through rubble, broken furniture and chaos. More than once, he nearly fell.

The streets were fractured shadow shapes, jagged edges of masonry, and pitted with craters deep and shallow. Gunfire pounded the sky at intervals, both far and terrifyingly near. An occasional flare briefly revealed a photo negative portrait of the city's Armageddon. Kramer breathed in the cold of the last April evening and the inescapable dust of 60,000 bombs. Bent almost double above a mound of collapsed building shuffled a figure of indeterminable age, foraging like an animal for fuel and, more hopelessly, food. She was a rubble woman. Briefly, a flare's arc illuminated her thin body's outline like Old Father Time and the woman paused for a moment, still like a freakish statue. Only then did Kramer see that the woman had a baby tied to her back in a makeshift sling. A mother, a grandmother? It was impossible to tell. But Kramer marvelled at the woman's strength and stoicism as she picked through the bombsite for scraps. If anybody was to get out of this inferno, it would be the likes of her.

Like distant thunder and lightning, the sky shuddered and flashed with shell fire. The rubble woman sensed Kramer's presence, furtively looked to his direction, and then like a hunted rat scurried into the night.

Dawn would not be long in coming. A better opportunity to get to the relative safety of the American lines, thought Kramer. But how? His plan was simple: go north-west to the Charlottenbrücke and get across the river, and then somehow to Spandau and the Yankees beyond. The rain started to fall, and a wind swept in from the east. Kramer heard a dog howling in an alleyway, surprised only that it hadn't been slaughtered for meat. Kramer made his way through what was left of the Hansaviertel; he reached an intersection; the city was edging into the suburbs. He would need to be careful. Russian patrols and snipers were never far away. Glancing left and right, Kramer sprinted to the other side of the street. He was close to the river now. Resting for breath in a copse of birch trees, Kramer lay back on damp grass and closed his eyes. Exhaustion overcame him and sleep came fast and heavy.

Kramer slept in Dorothy's arms. The bed in the little Cornish cottage was soft and warm. When he woke, the morning was young and a wood pigeon was calling peacefully. Dorothy stood at the window clasping a cup of tea. She turned to him, half smiling, half sighing. He sat up and held out his arms to her. Her smile broke into a grin as she placed the cup on the window seat and stepped towards him, her knee gently nudging his thigh as she did so. Kramer experienced a rush of desire. He felt another touch to his leg, only this time harder and less playful.

He stretched and opened his eyes. Standing above him was a fat German of pensionable age, only half dressed in uniform, wielding an ancient rifle. Kramer's countryman spoke in a thick Berliner accent.

'Why are you not at the front, soldier?' he said threateningly. Kramer was addled and annoyed at having been awoken from his paradisiacal dream.

'And where is the front exactly?' Kramer replied through squinting eyes.

'Get up,' ordered the man. Kramer obeyed, trying to work out his escape route as he did so. 'You are clearly a deserter. You will follow me. Raise your hands above your head.' Again, Kramer complied; there would be plenty of opportunity to overcome this zealous idiot, he thought. The man led Kramer through a path of undergrowth and trees.

'Thousands of young boys and old men are laying down their lives for the Führer and the Fatherland and you would rather hide? You are a coward. Where is your regiment?'

'Most of them are at the bottom of the Atlantic Ocean,' Kramer said bluntly and without sarcasm.

'What do you mean?' For the first time, the man was confused.

'I mean they are dead.'

'At sea?'

'I am a submariner, not a soldier.'

'Your uniform would suggest otherwise.' Kramer did not answer. Too much time was being expended talking to the deluded fool. 'Germany will win this war. Even if we have to win it with the Americans. Our Führer will guide us through.'

'The war is lost, old man. The Führer is dead, or he has escaped, or both.' Kramer's clear words were too much for his keeper. The man thrust his rifle butt into Kramer's back. Kramer lurched forward in pain and half stumbled across the path. As he did so, he twisted and kicked out at the gun barrel pointing at him. The rifle slipped from the man's grip, twisting his right index finger to breaking point. The old man yelped in pain and surprise. Kramer quickly rolled and got to his feet. It was now an unequal fight. Kramer towered above his opponent. The man sprang to retrieve his gun, but Kramer threw a huge punch into his cheekbone and he fell instantly, his jaw fractured. Kramer lifted the man by his lapels and slammed his back into a tree. The man collapsed, bewildered, defeated and bloodied. Kramer winded him with a second punch to the solar plexus. The network of nerves behind the man's stomach were traumatised. His eyes were glazed and terrorised. Kramer repeated his words.

'The Führer is dead. Long live Germany.' Kramer picked up the man's rifle and left him, crippled and immobile under the wet birch tree.

Morning light was gathering now. The murky air might conceal Kramer's escape. There would be no light on the dark rivers from the flaming buildings to illuminate his crossing. As Kramer approached the bridge, he could see he was not alone. A crowd of soldiers and civilians was beginning to converge on the riverbank. Chaos reigned. He could make out a few junior officers trying to marshal some kind of order, as they pointed and waved their pistols frantically. Kramer watched. Suddenly, machine guns opened fire towards a position to the east. As they did, a group of twenty or thirty people ran across the bridge. Return fire from a Russian gun tore down all but a few who made it to the other side. Kramer heard screams from the bridge. A young girl was walking in circles around a dead body. More gunfire quickly cut her down. Kramer had seen enough. He would try his luck downstream.

Westwards the river stretched, flanked by Spandau's old town to the north, the parks and suburbs of the city to the south. There were only thin strips and corridors, small gaps to get through to avoid Russian capture. But Kramer knew the city well enough. Unlike his comrades who spent their leave collapsing in beer halls, Kramer liked to explore the city early in the morning by bicycle. It had surprised him how green Berlin was with its lakes, forests and parklands. He liked the city but had not warmed to its people. Resourceful and tough maybe, tolerant of outsiders he wasn't so sure. His thoughts wandered with tiredness until he glimpsed an iron footbridge across the Havel several hundred metres to the west of Charlottenbrücke. Kramer approached carefully. Surely this was too good to be true? The bridge was intact. It was eerily quiet. Why was nobody else here? Perhaps those upstream felt safe in numbers, protected by their soldiers. Kramer's heart pounded in his chest. He threw the werewolf's rifle to one side. The morning light was lifting above the Spandau skyline. The river was grey and cold. It was now or never. Kramer sprinted across the iron footplates. The noise was deafening, he thought. He was almost at the other side when the sound of a rebounding object ricocheted from the bridge's handrails. Sniper. Kramer dived for cover in a walled alleyway as he reached the northern bank. While he considered his limited options, a second shot pinged against the wall in front of him, a splinter of brick clipping and piercing his cheek. Kramer wiped a little blood from the superficial wound. He was ambushed and cornered. The game was up. He sighed deeply. And then a marble rolled between his legs. Kramer picked it up and frowned. He then tentatively stuck out a leg from behind the wall. Another shot whizzed its way towards him but missed. The marksman had lost his aim.

Kramer appeared from the alley. Squatting ahead of him about twenty metres away was a boy of nine or ten years of age. In his hands was a catapult. The boy stared long and hard at him, then turned to run.

'Wait!' Kramer called. The boy didn't stop. 'Stop or I will shoot.' The boy turned and Kramer beckoned him towards the bridge. He approached nervously at first, but then, when he seemed to recognise the uniform, he quickened his pace and dived beside Kramer for shelter. Protectively, Kramer's brain retuned to that of a soldier, no longer a fugitive.

'What is your name?' Kramer spoke with the gentle authority of a kindly father.

'Dieter,' the boy replied quietly.

'And what are you doing out here, Dieter?' The boy didn't answer and simply stared into the mid-distance. Kramer could easily fill in the blanks. Parents killed in an air raid, by shells, by a lynch mob. It didn't really matter. Whatever the boy had seen, he wasn't going to relive it by telling his story now. 'We must leave the river and get to that church over there. Can you see it?' The boy nodded. 'Okay. I will go first. Stay by my side. If we are attacked, do as I say. Do you understand?' The boy nodded again – his bravado and catapult to one side for the moment.

The gunmetal river was almost still as they left it behind and made their way along the alleyway and stealthily into open ground. Expecting a Russian patrol or a sniper's bullet at any moment, it was spookily quiet. The silence was pure as if the war had stopped, but Kramer knew not to trust these lulls and flickers of peace in battle. Years beneath the waves had taught him that. Despite everything the combined Allied forces had thrown at Die Hauptstadt, not all the city was a wasteland. Here, spring shoots and blossoms had not surrendered to the Armageddon. A bumblebee looped its way towards flowering brambles. A wood pigeon called rhythmically. Nature, as it always does, was winning the final battle.

'I'm hungry,' the little voice complained, no longer the boy-soldier. Kramer felt inside an inside pocket and handed the boy a scrap of black bread. He devoured it like the scrawny animal he was, sunken, moving cheekbones beneath dirty skin that was lined and grey before its time. When he had finished, a little vigour had come to the boy's face, his voice a little calmer in pitch. 'Can we stay here?' he said.

'Not if you want more bread,' Kramer replied, half in jest, half in threat. He grabbed Dieter firmly by the arm.

They moved, stooped and furtive with every step. Their predators would be active now, prowling the suburbs, seeking out the last pustules of resistance. Kramer estimated they were no more than a few hundred metres from what little was left of his country's last stand. In front of them was a green space of overgrown parkland, chestnut and maple trees. The sun was casting a little warmth, but the air was chilled with easterly bite. Beyond the parkland was a church. Its square tower looked undamaged and almost like a fortress under siege. Kramer urged the boy onwards, yet he felt unease. The shaded side of the street was cold. They exited the park through collapsed iron gates and emerged on a deserted suburban road. The church was not far now. They turned a corner. Kramer's chest pounded; he couldn't swallow. The boy held his arm with both hands, his head turned away. In front of them, idling and threatening, was a Russian armoured car.

Instinctively, Kramer raised his hands in surrender. He was unarmed and with a child. There really was no other option. Two soldiers dismounted from their improvised seats on the wheel arches of the vehicle, their rifles poised for action. They stood wide of their enemy's approach. The commander lifted himself from the turret hatch and called out. Kramer and the boy edged uneasily forward, hunched and bending at the shoulders. The commander looked surprisingly relaxed, half smiling with curiosity.

'The pride of the German army,' declared the Russian in his own language. His comrades laughed heartily in agreement. 'Weapons?' he added, this time in heavily accented German.

'We have no weapons,' Kramer replied.

'No secret rockets?' The soldiers laughed again, enjoying themselves. Kramer tried to keep his composure, at least for the boy's sake. Then, with a sudden movement, the boy broke away from Kramer's hold. He slid to his knees and in the same movement fired his slingshot. Something pinged and ricocheted off the armoured plating of the car. The boy sank into the road and curled into a ball. Kramer's eyes flashed. There was no getaway. But the Soviets looked on, unperturbed, undisturbed.

'Cigarettes?' the commander asked. Kramer pulled a pack from inside his tunic, under the careful watch of the Russians. He handed it to the nearest soldier who took one and passed the rest among the men. They took turns to light them. The commander inhaled deeply, then exhaled approvingly, pinching a strand of loose tobacco that had stuck to his tongue. He flicked it away, then took a flask from his jacket and offered it to Kramer.

'Vodka,' he said. Kramer took a swig. The vodka was strong and rough, and tainted with the taste of oil and filth. But it was good. He was about to take another gulp but thought better of it and handed the alcohol back to its owner.

'Go!' called the commander as if issuing an order. He sensed Kramer's confusion. 'We don't kill children in cold blood where we come from,' he added, emphasising the pronoun. Kramer didn't need to be told twice. He grabbed Dieter and, half dragging him, turned and made for the church.

An old woman sat alone on a bench, softly rocking back and forward. Her cheekbones sunken, sallow and sharp. Whether eaten by hunger, disease or loss, Kramer didn't know. But she would probably die there within hours, of cold, hunger or both. Or because she did not want to go on. A blast-broken terrace of town houses partially blocked the approach to the church which was situated in a small square lined with lime trees. If Kramer was expecting a last stand of heroic resistance, it wasn't here. Inside its brown Gothic brick walls, the church was gloomy and quiet. A scattered mix of worshippers shivered in silent thoughts and prayer. In the murky shadows of the choir transepts, a thin priest moved quietly about his work. Seated were mainly older women and children. Kramer looked around him. There was little point staying here. The Russians would surely roll in before noon. As he turned to leave, the priest appeared, and bowed as if to greet them both.

'Is this your son?' The priest spoke softly, with kindness and concern.

'No,' Kramer replied plainly. Dieter gazed at Kramer with wide brown eyes, disappointed perhaps.

'Then leave him with us,' said the priest taking Dieter's hand. The boy shook his head in faint protest. 'It is your duty to carry on the fight.' There was a plaintive pause disturbed only by the bronchial coughing of a weary Berliner. 'He will be safe here.' The priest spoke with the ecclesiastical assurance that might convince the most battle-weary of men. Kramer knelt on one knee and looked at a weeping Dieter. A tear fell from the boy's left eye and slid like a falling hand slipping down a rock face. Kramer squeezed Dieter's cheek and skull.

'Be brave, little man,' he said and smiled like a father to a son.

As Kramer exited the nave of the church, the noise of battle grew louder. It was difficult to tell where the enemy was. Maybe the area was already encircled. From somewhere in the direction of the U-Bahn station guns fired towards the streets where Kramer was standing. Suddenly, like a violent stroke of thunder, a barrage of shells exploded. The church was hit and masonry fell in clouds of appalling smoke and breaking stone. The churchgoers spilled from the chaos. Children screamed for their mothers. An elderly man collapsed, his arm torn from his body. A young mother stumbled clutching a large patch of red on her stomach, before falling still in the dust. Last to leave, the priest, arms buckling under the weight of a dying boy. Kramer couldn't stay to see anymore. He pulled the peak of his field cap over his brow and retreated further into the streets of the old town. Behind him, those who weren't dead and dying would soon meet an enemy who would spare them little mercy and fewer bullets.

Disorientated, hungry and exhausted, Kramer walked and ran to wherever offered relief from the noise of war. At least once he heard somebody shout at him – maybe an order, maybe an insult, probably a threat. But he didn't respond. He buried his face deeper inside his greatcoat and scurried among the shadows. A bullet, if intended for him, missed by metres. Was it an enemy sniper? Was it his own countrymen? He no longer cared; his was the raw will to survive – nothing more. He heard children's voices laughing. Child soldiers whose lives would be wasted and terminated in the last hours of battle. He saw a pretty teenage girl being dragged semi-naked by her hair into a cellar by Russian soldiers; her fate was sealed. For a mad moment, Kramer thought to try to rescue her, but what could he do? Give up his own life so she could live for a few minutes more? A stiff wind gathered and blew along the street-line, dust and sand spitting in his eyes. The morning made noon. Kramer paused, almost breathless at a street corner, panting, hands on his knees, bent double. From a nearby doorway, someone hissed and beckoned. Gaunt, sunken cheekbones and a pair of wild eyes hung as if suspended in air. They stared imploringly. Invisible lips hissed again, a mad whisper. Kramer had nothing to lose. He ran to the voice, through the entrance. The door closed quietly, its blistered paint flaking in the wind.

Kramer found himself standing in a dim corridor. There was no lighting, and Kramer assumed correctly that, like just about everywhere else in the city, electricity was unavailable or banned for domestic use by order of the Führer. What light there was seeped through open wounds in the building's walls and roof. The wide, wild eyes looked up. They belonged to a small, gnarled woman whose age had been accelerated by years of deprivation and hunger. She wore creases and lines like a mask, her clothes black, shabby and loose. A skeletal cat trotted through the hallway and disappeared through a hole in the wall. The old woman ushered Kramer wordlessly, deeper into the block and down some stairs to a basement apartment. Somehow, Kramer felt safe and protected, if only from the merciless east wind.

'Come,' the woman said finally with gentle inflexions in her voice. 'Sit.' She lit the stub of a cigarette with a strip of folded newspaper ignited from simmering embers in the hearth. Exhaling blue smoke from the side of her mouth, she looked keenly at Kramer. 'Deserter?' she said without judgement. She turned and started to prepare coffee with a small metal pot. Kramer said nothing. When she had finished making the coffee, the old woman poured it into two small ceramic cups. She handed one of them to her guest. Kramer sipped gratefully. The coffee was excellent. He wondered where a frail old woman like this would acquire good coffee at a time like this. Reciprocating the kindness, Kramer offered the woman a cigarette from a pack hidden in his coat. She accepted it as if it were gold. Kramer offered her a flame with an American lighter. He clicked it shut after lighting his own. Both inhaled deeply, the nicotine spinning their brains gorgeously. Kramer felt the smoke hit his chest and the flavour of the tobacco moisten his mouth.

'The Führer wouldn't approve,' Kramer said at last, exhaling a perfect tunnel of smoke. They both laughed mischievously.

'Good,' said the old woman. 'To the Führer,' she said in a mock toast, and raised her coffee cup half-heartedly.

'Here,' said Kramer, 'have these.' He pushed the pack of cigarettes across the table to the old woman.

'Thanks,' she said, counting how many were inside. There was an easy pause. The old woman refilled Kramer's cup.

'So why did you call to me?' he said. The woman stubbed her half-smoked cigarette out on the hot plate of the hearth and placed it carefully in a makeshift ashtray on a shelf above.

'If you'd have walked across the road in front of you, you would have been killed,' she replied coolly. Kramer's expression prompted her to explain some more. 'There are many Russians just around the corner – there is a roadblock.' As Kramer still seemed unconvinced, she continued. 'I saw five civilians killed there this morning – two of them children.'

'Is the city surrounded?' Kramer asked.

'Almost,' said the old woman. 'The rumour is the Americans have stopped at the Elbe. They don't want to upset Uncle Joe.'

'Or sacrifice their own men when the Russians can do it for them,' added Kramer.

'And who can blame them?'

'True,' Kramer agreed. He lit another cigarette.

'Would you like something to eat?' The voice didn't belong to the old woman. Kramer turned in his seat. Standing at the door of an adjacent room was a very beautiful girl who Kramer guessed was probably sixteen or seventeen years old.

'My granddaughter, Marta,' the old woman said by way of introduction. The girl stood nervously, playing with her fingers that hung above her waistline. She cast a sad glance to the floor.

'That would be lovely,' Kramer said warmly. 'Thank you.' The old woman smiled.

'And I am Elsa.' Marta worked quietly and industriously in the kitchen. She prepared a small, but exceptional meal of bread, sausage, cheese and jars of preserved vegetables and fruit. Kramer was astounded – where did these women find food like this in such impossible times?

When Kramer had greedily devoured the feast, he sat back in his chair and pulled another pack of cigarettes from his pocket. He offered one to Marta, but she declined. Elsa took one for her and smoked it.

'How will you escape?'

'I don't know if I can,' replied Kramer. 'If what you say is true, then we will be captured or killed by the Russians.'

'And we know what they do to our women and children.'

'Not all of them. And no more than we did to theirs,' answered Kramer. Elsa didn't comment but looked at her granddaughter. 'I cannot protect her, Kapitän.' Kramer was surprised by her mode of address. Elsa paused before adding, 'But you can.' For the first time, Elsa looked at him pleadingly and with some helplessness; her war-broken face somehow radiated a beauty and resolve. Kramer's logical brain kicked in and he spoke bluntly.

'And how do you propose I do that?' he said. Elsa shuffled to a chest of mahogany drawers in the corner of the kitchen, her cigarette burning from her mouth. She tugged at the stiff middle drawer of three and took out a folded piece of paper. She handed it to Kramer. He looked up questioningly.

'An escape plan,' she said without any irony. Kramer dubiously unfolded the paper. What was revealed was unexpected. Written in minuscule hand, but finely detailed, was a map. Kramer studied it carefully. When he had finished, he looked at Elsa in awe. She anticipated his next question. 'I have lived here in this district all my life,' she said. 'There isn't one scrap of it I don't know like the back of my hand.'

'You think it can work?' Kramer asked hopefully.

'Maybe. But it has to be worth the trying.'

'I agree. But why did you choose me?'

'I didn't,' Elsa said knowingly. 'You chose us.' Kramer struggled to interpret her logic but was prepared to go along with it all the same.

'Then I suggest we leave as soon as we can,' Kramer suggested.

'Not before nightfall,' instructed Elsa. 'You must change. I have clothes. And of course, you will need these.' She looked to Marta who had reappeared, guarding two heavy black bicycles. 'Your transport, Kapitän.' And her smile broke into a mischievous but nervous laugh.

Ten

Cornwall - Summer, 1985

Emily Kasprowicz walked through Heathrow Airport's Terminal 3 shortly after eight o'clock on Saturday evening. Exhausted and bewildered, she was greeted by Ed Merriman in the arrivals hall. They hadn't seen each other in twenty-five years, but they recognised each other almost immediately. Ed quickly disposed of his hastily misspelled pick-up sign.

'Spelling was never your strongpoint,' Emily teased and threw her arms around her chaperone.

'How are you, Em?' Ed said heartily. 'You must be exhausted.'

'Surprisingly, I feel pretty good,' she replied breezily. Ed noticed a stateside twang had sun-kissed her lazy double consonants. Emily had organised her journey almost as soon as her sister had put down the phone. Three airports and almost twenty-four hours later, she was sitting in Di Merriman's small hatchback on a motorway heading south-west. She turned to look at Ed, who was concentrating on the road, and giggled.

'You still have that look of worried concentration,' she said.

'Well, it's these bloody motorways, Em. I'm not used to them. Give me a Cornish country lane any day.' Ed's strong hands gripped the steering wheel, knuckles clenched white. She found it amusing that this strong, rugged farmer was unsettled by cities, airports and people. The traffic thinned as Surrey became Hampshire.

'How bad is he?' Emily asked.

'Not good, I'm afraid,' Ed replied uneasily. 'But he's strong.'

'Does he know?'

'Know what?' Ed was distracted by an overtaking police car.

'About me.'

'Sorry. No. Well, at least I don't think so,' Ed said. Emily breathed in deeply through her mouth. 'Are you okay?'

'Yes,' she replied. 'Just a little tired and feeling emotional, I guess.' Inside, she was beginning to feel turmoil, excitement and a deep sense of worry. The enormity of the situation was now rolling in towards her like a freak wave in winter.

They arrived at Pentire in the early hours of Sunday morning. Watchful and gentle, Di was waiting for them, tea and toast to hand. Ed carried Emily's cases into the house. A sleepy collie sighed in its basket, seemingly unperturbed by a visitor in the middle of the night.

'Hello, Di,' Emily said. They hugged briefly and Di offered Emily tea. Ed sat down, weary, if not a little shell-shocked.

'Anna must be sleeping,' he said.

'Sleeping?' spoke a cheery voice from the bottom of the stairs. 'How could I sleep?' The sisters fell into each other's arms, buried in laughter and tears. A few minutes passed before they disentangled themselves from their embrace.

'When can I see him?'

'Tomorrow, Em.'

'And he doesn't know?' The question was vague and ambiguous.

'He doesn't know,' Anna replied with sisterly intuition.

'We should all sleep. Charlotte will no doubt wake us all at dawn.' Di Merriman then cleared the table of mugs and plates. 'There's a bed made for you, Em. And there's a towel in the room.'

'Come on, Em – I will show you.' The sisters went to bed. The dog sighed and the kitchen clock struck three.

'What have I done?' said Ed to his wife with a look of wide-eyed concern. She took both of his hands in hers.

'The right thing,' she said and held his head on her shoulder.

*

In a remote and abandoned stone house somewhere in north Dorset, Sir Charles Gifford was trying to get his bearings. He sat in a sparsely furnished room at a plain cottage table.

'I would like a cigarette and a drink,' he requested rather half-heartedly and self-pityingly, and feeling rather morose. A large man with a soldier's build lit a cigarette and passed it to his charge. 'And the drink?' The man didn't respond. 'Can we at least have some bloody light in here?' The man adjusted a door shutter slightly and a thin and blinding slit of light sliced the window space. Dust danced in the sunbeam. It didn't serve to improve Sir Charles's moribund mood. Sir Charles smoked without pleasure, coughing as he exhaled. He was now an occasional smoker, and these were inferior cigarettes. But the curling blue smoke sent his imagination to happier times past. He thought of North Africa, the bars of Cairo and Alexandria, his pals, buddies and brothers-in-arms, and most of all the dark-eyed women and desert nights.

A few dreary minutes passed. Only the call of a solitary wood pigeon hinted of a world outside. As Sir Charles stubbed out his cigarette on a breakfast plate, the door handle turned. Two men walked in.

'I trust you are comfortable.' The smaller of the two spoke without any noticeable whiff of irony.

'Fabulous,' said Sir Charles with unrestrained sarcasm.

'Well, you leave in half an hour.'

'And may I enquire as to the destination?'

'You may not.' The man paused, removed the tortoiseshell spectacles he was wearing and fogged the lenses with his exhaled breath. He cleaned them with a cloth and without looking up added, 'Have a pleasant flight.' Both men left the room, closing the door quietly as they did so. Sir Charles grunted disapprovingly. The lack of control was causing him distress he was trying to hide with bravado. The attending watchman looked on indifferent and unmoved. Sir Charles got up and motioned towards the adjacent lavatory. He urinated weakly. A small window above him offered a chance to reverse his plans. He heaved himself on to the bowl and reached for the window catch. It was a tricky manoeuvre and its success would require the dexterity of a young and agile cat burglar. Sir Charles's whisky-sodden limbs were struggling. He leant out just a little bit further hoping to unstick the rusted window. As he did so, his left leg slipped and he crashed downwards with a thumping splash. The commotion had aroused attention. The door opened. Sir Charles stood as if posing as an ancient statue, one leg submerged in the lavatory bowl, the other turned ninety degrees, bent and bowed. For the first time, the watchman revealed emotion and laughed at the failed escapee.

The small Piper Cherokee aircraft rose from the grass strip. Sir Charles sat back in his seat. He looked out over southern England. How green it still was in midsummer. And for all the cities, towns and villages down there, how few buildings there seemed to be. There was nothing he could do now. He was even relieved to have let go of whatever decisions he had left to make. His destiny was unknown and uncontrollable. It didn't really matter. Exciting perhaps in a way. Still the hero of his story. The plane climbed a little more before levelling and settling into its flightpath. It was heading south, that much Sir

Charles could work out. France maybe. There were three other men in the plane. Nobody uttered a word.

Land soon became sea. Sir Charles succumbed to sleep. He woke periodically, half dreaming he was falling from the plane. The afternoon sun was lowering now, westward and golden. The Cherokee began its descent. The two men sitting at the controls briefly glanced at a paper map, each pointing to something on it. The pilot then nodded as if agreeing with a suggestion. Quickly, the land below rose to meet them and they landed uncomfortably, but safely, in a large field surrounded by dense thorn and hedgerow. Slightly dizzy and nauseous, Sir Charles stepped off the wing and staggered onto the grass strip. Two men dressed plainly in casual clothes formed an informal welcoming party. They conversed briefly with two of the three men who had exited the aircraft and exchanged envelopes. Then, the little Piper was gone, climbing like a gnat in fading daylight. Sir Charles was standing somewhere in the diagonal of emptiness, the lonely, rural lands of France. This time tomorrow he would be in Switzerland.

*

Anna and Emily drove themselves to the hospital in Truro. Ed had insisted, but the girls wanted and needed to do this on their own. There was much to talk about, lots to catch up with, to understate it hugely. Emily knew much of Anna's life in London. She had studied there briefly after all. It was a world she could relate to. She was eager to learn more about Charlotte and every moment of her journey. Of course, she spoke to her sister on the telephone and they exchanged long letters, but real physical time with her own flesh and blood was so precious and so, so rare. Anna, on the other hand, could not grasp her sister's life in the Salinas Valley. To her it was only the landscape described by Steinbeck, somewhere sun-drenched, but raw and huge. She envied her sister's life in many ways – the childlessness, the money, the sun, the career in a Californian university. But the mild jealousies were held only fleetingly. Charlotte had only to gaze at her in need or want or curiosity, and she was whole again and complete as she could be.

From the passenger seat, Emily looked out on a rugged landscape of moorland. Despite the August days, the Cornish weather could turn quickly, hundreds of feet above the sea. She tucked a strand of blonde hair behind her ear.

'Do you think he will be able to see me? To hear?'

'I don't know, Em. He was so weak when we saw him last.' The road climbed the moorland highway. In recent years Emily had given up all hope of finding her father. The scant information Granny Trewithen had given her all those years ago at Trescore had offered no clues to his identity. She had often wondered whether he had re-joined his regiment somewhere in England, was killed in the war or survived. Either way, he couldn't have abandoned what he had never known. Her thoughts overlapped like a wind-blown tide; she changed the subject with a question.

'And how is Alex?' Emily said without removing her gaze from the landscape.

'You mean how are Alex and me?'

'I guess so. I mean, he is thousands of miles away fighting western democracy. Are you not worried about him?'

'If I'm honest, no.'

'Because you know he will be alright?'

'No.'

'What then?' Emily probed, a mixture of concern and knowing glint in her eye.

'No, I don't worry as in I haven't really thought about him. In all the time he has been away, I haven't thought about him. Since he's been gone, my life story has started so many chapters. And what's sad, and what's exciting too, is that he doesn't know any of it.'

'But you will tell him, right?'

'Maybe. But only after I have told him I am leaving him.' Anna's words came as no surprise to Emily. She hadn't needed them to explain her sister's intentions. 'His world is his world. It always has been and it always will be.'

'But he loves you and Charlotte.'

'Yes, I think he probably does,' Anna said. 'But it's difficult to love somebody back when they put world peace before their marriage. I can't compete with that.' They both fell into laughter before Anna had a chance to cry.

They parked and walked to the hospital entrance. A confusing map made of all good intention only served to confuse and delay their visit. Within the maze of corridors, they found Treyarnon Ward.

'Ready?' Anna said, squeezing her sister's arm.

'No,' Emily replied with a nervous smile.

It was still, quiet and there were only a few visitors. An orderly was busily changing bedclothes. For a moment Emily looked pale, but Anna reassured her and pointed further along the ward. They moved through the beds. A man near death was curled like a sleeping cat, silent, sunken and nearly not human. Another stared like a shell-shocked soldier, all bulging, mad eyes. A nurse drew the cubicle curtain around its ceiling track. The man vanished like a movie ending that cuts to black.

'Snow falling faintly through the universe and faintly falling.'

'What was that?' Anna asked.

'Just a line from a story,' Emily replied dreamily.

'Here,' Anna said and gently tugged at Emily's hand.

In the last bed of the ward in front of a window that opened on to a sloping grass bank he slept quietly, head and chin propped on chest. Anna thought he looked smaller and frailer. Perhaps he was, but Frank was still strong, still handsome somehow. The sisters stopped, almost daring to go no further in case the moment's peace was disturbed by cold awakenings. Decisively, Anna breathed in deeply through her mouth, stepped forward and sat in the ugly bedside chair. She didn't have to wait long. Frank stirred, sensing her presence. His blues eyes, the hue of an Easter ocean, opened, as young and alive as they'd always been.

'Anna,' he whispered with a voice as dry as sand.

'Yes, Frank, it's me,' she said gently. He smiled at her, almost paternally. 'Frank, please listen to me. I have brought somebody to see you.' He seemed to understand. The muscles in his face relaxed and softened, his stare widened, then narrowed. Instinctively, he lifted his gaze above Anna's shoulders. With blonde hair like his own, but with eyes he thought he would never see, there she was, his daughter.

Emily moved closer to him – nervously, not knowing how at first. She couldn't speak. But she didn't need to. Words were needless now. Frank raised his arms weakly, outstretched, imploring her to step forward towards him. And as she did so, his tears began to fall. One by one like first drops of rain, and then they poured. He hugged her and held on tight to the moment, daring not to let go in case it slipped away. Emily eased her hold; she pulled herself away and sat back to look at her father properly for the first time. Tenderly, she stroked tears from his face.

'Dad,' she said, 'Dad, I am Emily.'

'Emily,' he repeated. 'My Emily.' They both smiled and he laughed. Their smiles were similar, mouths a little downturned as if coy of the mirth.

A nurse arrived at the bedside, urgent and concerned.

'Mr Fox, is everything alright?'

'We are fine,' Emily said reassuringly. The nurse frowned a little and returned to her work elsewhere. A stillness fell calmly on the early afternoon. The sun was already tiring, despite the heat and light outside. Summer yes, but autumn whistling in the distance. Anna sat close by. She left her sister and Frank to talk. She caught a stray word, the fragment of a phrase, a laugh, a sigh, but the narrative was unheard. Occasionally, she thought she recognised a similar intonation or inflexion, rises and falls alike in pitch. Maybe she was listening for them, imagining them, wanting them to be there. Maybe they were.

The eager nurse returned half an hour later with an intensified frown. Anna suggested to Emily they leave.

'I will see you tomorrow?' Emily asked.

'I would like that very much,' Frank replied in a hoarse, dry whisper. 'Very much.' He smiled, with his blue eyes as much as his thin lips. He blew her a kiss. She caught it and put it in her pocket. The sisters turned and left the ward. Quietness returned. Somewhere not far away a patient coughed with the lungs of a dying man. Frank rested his head to one side and looked out of the window into the mid-distance. The trees were heavy, and their green was darkening. A small black and yellow-feathered bird perched on a bench seat. Frank could just hear its trills and tweets. It stayed a few seconds more, then flew quietly away.

*

It was a long drive east. More than 300 kilometres. The last hundred had been excruciating. Sir Charles was slumped in the back seat of a car, flanked by a silent chaperone with the personality of poison and the face of an anvil. There was no escape. He was at the mercy of his escorts, the hired help of Alan Mottram, if his friend even knew who these people were. These things never used to frighten Sir Charles – it was simply the wear, tear and collateral of the job. But this assignment had taken its toll. Sir Charles was an old man now, his stamina and spirit almost spent.

He looked outside the passenger window at the huge landscapes around him. Even in the depths of summer, specks of snow sparkled on the highest peaks. Like Moriarty or Holmes at the Reichenbach Falls, was this the last stand? It was a problem to solve, perhaps the final one.

The car swerved off the mountain road and made its way up a steep, inclining track that snaked for a few kilometres more, before stopping carefully outside an old chalet made of stone and wood. Nearby there were some sheds – mazots. Finally, the man next to Sir Charles spoke.

'You will stay here. It is quiet and it is comfortable.'

'For how long?'

'Until things are quieter for you in England.' The man got out of the car and walked around the back of it to open his passenger's door. Sir Charles was hollow inside and feeble outside. His legs almost buckled beneath him as he walked to the chalet. As he did so, he glimpsed a holstered handgun inside the man's jacket.

'This is Madame Brunner. She is your host. Now please, make yourself comfortable.' The man nodded to Madame Brunner, turned and got into the car. It left thin clouds of summer dust and left the mountainside. The housekeeper smiled and said nothing. She simply extended a beguiling arm. Sir Charles stepped wearily into the darkness of the chalet.

Silently Madame Brunner brought some cheeses, meats and bread to the table, with wine and water. She was a calm woman, with strong and broad hips. Her face was weather-beaten, but young-looking. Sir Charles guessed she was perhaps sixty years old.

'Thank you,' he said with genuine kindness. He ate slowly and gratefully. All the time, Madame Brunner half watched him from somewhere in the room. When he had finished eating, she cleared his plate and then instinctively led him to a bedroom. As she closed the door, Sir Charles fell backwards on the bed. Within seconds he was asleep, dreaming of different mountains in different times. In London, he was a wanted man.

*

Over a fine summer supper at Pentire, Anna and Emily talked into the evening. They recounted stories of a childhood that ran towards them faster and closer with every anecdote shared. Only every now and then did Emily pause quietly, lost in the emotion of the day.

'They only spent one night together? Really, it seems so unbelievable.' Anna's face was a picture of childlike surprise.

'I think it's beautifully romantic,' Emily said in a whimsical voice uncharacteristic of her. 'But it troubles me. It troubles me.'

'What do you mean?' said Anna expressing noticeable concern, but the question remained unanswered as Ed walked into the sitting room.

'Strange things happened in the war,' he said.

'You can say that again,' said Anna.

'I mean, in a weird way, I am responsible for your being here, Emily.' The girls laughed before Ed got the joke. 'No, I mean if I hadn't have fallen into the water, then none of it would have happened. Your parents meeting that is. And then...' but before he could finish the sentence, Di squeezed his shoulder and Ed stopped talking.

'Like I said, very romantic,' Emily concluded quietly, but with a repeated tone of concern. A not uncomfortable silence offered a brief pause to the talk. Emily got up from the sofa and walked to the window which looked out on to a field which rose slightly, then curved as it made its way to the cliffs' edge.

'Do you think he will pull through this?' She wasn't asking the question to anyone in particular. Anna glanced anxiously at Ed and Di.

'I don't think so, Em,' Ed said with plain kindness. Emily didn't reply. Anna joined her sister at the window and put her arms around her. Emily rested her head on Anna's shoulder. They stood in the stillness of the room and the clock struck nine.

*

In the mountain hideout, Sir Charles awoke from a hideous nightmare in which he had been interrogated and tortured by the secret service on a theatre stage, while his family was watching from the stalls, an enthralled mass. Sir Charles found it most humiliating that his great-nieces and nephews were devouring huge buckets of popcorn. As an agent was about to drill a hole through his knuckle bones, he had also seen the ghost of Neil O'Brien smirking in a box. The dream was almost at an end when Sir Charles was made to dance naked about the apron of the stage to the soundtrack of the Nutcracker Suite. Half-hearted clapping and derisory whistling had thence provided his alarm call.

As if watching on some monitor screen, Madame Brunner appeared with a plate of eggs and some coffee. Sir Charles was struggling to know what time of day it was. Perhaps it was breakfast. What he did know was that he disliked the way that Madame Brunner didn't knock when she came into the room. 'Impertinent woman,' he muttered under his breath. Madame simply smiled at him, without like or contempt, but with a look of knowing that she had seen the likes of him and this before. A housefly landed on the plate. Sir Charles watched it closely. Not visible to his naked eye, the fly regurgitated its saliva on the food, liquifying the eggs, sucking the vomitous meal through a trunk-like nose. With a sweep of his hand, Sir Charles caught the insect and closed his palm. The fly buzzed frantically in his closed, cupped hand. Sir Charles threw the fly against the wall. With a popping sound, it fell to the floor, spinning wildly. He pinched it by a wing and held it in front of his nose. He paused and then, like a lizard, crushed it between his teeth. A car pulled up outside the chalet. Sir Charles spat what remained of the fly on the plate and pushed it aside. He drank some of the tepid coffee and winced. A beam of dust-dancing sunlight shone a beam through the window shutters. Low voices murmured outside.

'It is time to move.' A tall, broad-shouldered man stood above where Sir Charles was sitting. He wore a black polo-neck sweater and a grimace struck on an anvil. The man extinguished an untipped cigarette on the meal plate and picked a shred of tobacco from his lips.

'We have only just arrived.' Sir Charles frowned weakly. Another man entered the room. Uglier than the first, shorter and sporting a professional scowl, he brought more menace to the gathering.

'You must leave now.' The tall man fixed unblinking, deep-set eyes on Sir Charles. 'Unless of course you want to be found, Mr Gifford?' Sir Charles was affronted more at his captor's mode of address than the order to move out forthwith.

'If you please,' invited the second man, more warmly and softly than Sir Charles expected.

'And may I ask where we are going?' The men didn't answer. The car pulled quietly away. Glancing briefly behind him, Sir Charles saw Madame Brunner standing at the doorway dressed in black and a thin, thin, inscrutable smile.

A sinking sun cast the mountainsides in oranges and pinks like embers aglow. Sir Charles stared in wonder at the beauty of the vast country. The borders of his own empire were fading – surrendering, retreating, and the scraps of power that remained were hundreds of miles from the Alpine backroad he was on. The shorter man leaned across the front passenger seat and offered Sir Charles a cigarette.

'No thank you.'

'About two hours more,' the man said quietly. 'I suggest you rest.' The car began to descend the mountain roads, cruising steadily into the valleys below. The grasses were lush and green here, glossy meadows full of buttercups.

'I need to stop,' said Sir Charles abruptly. Neither of the men responded. Sir Charles repeated his request. 'Unless you want me to defecate in this warm car?'

'What is he saying?' the driver demanded. The car stopped near a waterfall in a ravine. 'Two minutes, then we go.' The friendlier passenger accompanied Sir Charles. The two men walked just beyond the car's eyeline.

'Such a beautiful evening. Like a Turner sketchbook.'

'I'm sorry, but I don't understand,' said the man with the odd scowl.

'Never mind, old boy. Could I trouble you for that cigarette now? Helps me get going, if you see what I mean.' Sir Charles squatted as if he was about to use the lavatory. The man grinned benignly. Sir Charles accepted the cigarette and put it between his lips. He then patted his chest to suggest he didn't have a flame to light it. With a rather friendly half-smile, the man took back the cigarette and pulled a lighter from his pocket. He tipped his head slightly forward and out of the breeze, cupping his hands around the flame. Sir Charles moved. Instantly, he took a handkerchief and lunged at the man's face. With his free hand, he flicked a windproof lighter at the cloth which set alight with a thump of flame. The man lurched backwards in agony. His hair, clothes and skin were catching fire. He writhed on the floor as if blind. Sir Charles quickly manoeuvred behind the man. He grabbed his head by the hair, yanking it upwards, then slammed the man's skull on to a rock partially sunken in the earth. With cold-blooded efficiency, he repeated the attack thrice more. The man's head was split, his pink, blistering face lifeless in a pool of darkening blood.

Sir Charles searched the dead man's pockets. He took his wallet and a silver pocket pistol. Feigning an old man's footsteps, he made his way back to the idling saloon.

'That's better.'

'Where is Vincent?'

'Admiring the view. Here he is. Just over there.' The driver looked away from the rear-view mirror with his forged grimace pinned on the low ridge above.

'Stay there.' He turned the engine off and got out of the car. Sir Charles could see a little panic and agitation in the man's movements as he strode towards the incline. Seizing a few stray seconds, Sir Charles opened the rear passenger door and took a kneeling position behind the trunk. With cool, cold aim, he fired a single shot into the man's back, the bullet penetrating his heart. Briefly, the man's arm raised as if in gesture of goodbye and then his corpse lay still in the silent twilight. His killer rushed to check his dead pulse and retrieved the key to the car. Almost before the last echoes of the gunshot had reverberated around the valley, Sir Charles was motoring north-west on a course for the Jutland Peninsula.

*

Emily woke the minute before dawn. The house was quietly busy. In the yard, Ed Merriman was preparing to start the barley harvest. He and a younger man were checking various rotating mechanisms. Emily marvelled at the speed and skill of their work. The great yellow hulk stood silhouetted against the appearing light, an ugly, clever thing. In her sister's dressing gown, she walked with a mug of tea to the yard.

'How on earth do you understand how it all works?' she asked the younger man, a muscular, fair-haired youth, not more than twenty years of age.

'I don't,' he joked, 'I just copy Ed.'

'I wouldn't do that, Joe, if I were you. That'll end in disaster.' Ed tapped the cutter blade with a huge spanner.

'Are you cutting it all today?' Emily asked.

'We'll see.' He was in no mood for small talk.

'We'll probably go to the hospital,' she said.

'You'll have to drive yourselves. I'll be busy here.' Emily left the men to their machine. The day's lesser crises, she thought, lighten life's drama.

The sisters left Pentire shortly after breakfast. The morning was blustery and fine. Out on the ocean, the sea was a mass of teal and white breakers. By the time they had reached Truro, they could have been in a different country. The weather here was still like the hospital wards. Treyarnon Ward's reception desk was deserted.

'Should we wait?' Emily nudged her sister.

'We've no time to lose, don't you think?'

'We can't just walk in, can we?'

'This is Cornwall, Em, not Orange County.' Emily pulled a childish face at her sister's sarcasm. They walked quickly with light feet along the polished floors. A bed that was occupied yesterday was empty now. At the end of the ward by the window the curtain had been pulled around Frank's bed. Emily let out a gasp in shock.

'It's fine, Em. They're probably cleaning him or something.' An orderly pulled the curtain around the rail and removed a box of cleaning materials. The bed was empty.

'Where is he?' Emily blurted.

'I beg your pardon?' replied a well-spoken, black voice.

'I'm so sorry. I didn't mean to be rude. I thought my father was here?' The orderly shrugged and continued with their duties. The sisters hurried to the ward desk; it was staffed now.

'Excuse me. I am looking for Mr Fox. Frank Fox. He was in this ward yesterday.' The nurse receptionist checked her notes.

'Are you family?'

'Yes,' the sisters said in unison.

'Mr Fox was moved to Harlyn Ward earlier this morning. From Treyarnon.'

'Harlyn Ward?'

'Just as a precaution.' Emily's face changed to a deepening shade of red. 'To monitor his breathing.' The nurse patiently explained the way to reach the new ward.

Anna led Emily through the maze of sterilised corridors, passing a hurrying doctor as they did so. A nurse carrying a clipboard of notes beat them to the doors of the ward.

'Please can you help us?' Emily pleaded. The nurse turned to them with a gentle smile. 'My father was transferred here this morning. His name is Frank Fox. I

am his daughter. I have flown from California to see him.'
Emily was talking in torrents, but the nurse interrupted
her.

'Let me check my notes,' she said. 'There's nothing
here. Let me ask the ward sister.' The nurse left them for a
few minutes before returning with a calm expression. 'I'm
afraid we have no record of a Mr Fox. Are you sure you
have the right ward?'

'Yes. Harlyn,' said Anna.

'I'm sorry. You will have to check with Treyarnon, was
it? Now, if you'll excuse me.' Emily shuddered with disbelief.
Anna felt it too. Something wasn't right. They checked
Treyarnon Ward again. Calls were made to the central
records team. Nothing. Only a porter could remember
seeing someone of Frank's description wheeled out of the
ward earlier that morning. By two medics. A small, old
doctor and a younger man with a permanent smile. Both
had Mediterranean faces, the porter had guessed. Emily's
face turned ghostly white. She felt a squeezing of her skull
and a storm of sickness in her stomach. A sudden, heavy
gust of new rain lashed the window. Frank Fox had left the
building.

Eleven

Germany and Cornwall - May, 1945

In the east of Moscow, Stalin returned to his dacha following the exertions of the May Day parade. There, he made repeated demands that he barked at his generals on the telephone, usually with the same theme: where is Hitler's body? Then he tended his watermelons and strolled beside the birch trees. In Berlin, Marta Scholl and Hans Kramer crept into the night. They were lucky. They passed exhausted and drunken Soviet soldiers sleeping in the streets. There were checkpoints and patrols, but Kramer was alert and these were avoided. Only once did they meet a Soviet soldier, half entangled in the arms of a woman under the arch of a broken bridge. He quickly disappeared. A thin column of uniformed prisoners, haggard and bowed, shuffled towards their fate, watched closely by Red Army guardsmen. Some captors of this far corner of Germany's capital were sleeping off a May Day hangover, and some were preparing to attack the Citadel of Spandau and greet German white flags. The defeated, meanwhile, were about to flood their underground stations. The apocalyptic grotesque played its last scenes; Marta and Kramer were beyond the city making their way to the Havel and the Elbe beyond.

'Are you not worried for your mother?' Kramer whispered in the night. The likelihood of there being any Russian soldiers in such a remote Brandenburg woodland were slim, but Kramer retained all the stealth of a submarine commander.

'Yes and no,' Marta replied in a clear, untempered voice.

'What do you mean?' Kramer seemed genuinely confused.

'Our destiny is in your hands – always.' It was a cryptic response.

'I am not sure I understand.' The forest path was only visible by faint skylight through the thick tree canopy.

'I mean that Mother will not worry if I am safe. My safety is in your hands.'

'Is that all you mean?'

'Of course not. But you know that, I think.'

'So?' Kramer pressed curiously.

'We are just the women of this war. Mothers, sisters, daughters. Victims of male brutality. Victims of men's crimes. When your peace comes, you will continue to fight your battles in different ways. What will be left for us?

Our scars will never fade.' Marta pedalled harder, her head thrust forward over the handlebars. Kramer followed, silenced by her wisdom. She was right, of course. And there were no words to comfort, console or contradict her.

They had been cycling for hours and dawn was near rising. The forest was beginning to thin.

'We must stop soon and rest,' said Kramer. 'It will soon be light and we must hide during the day.' Marta did not object. Fatigue was overcoming them both. Kramer found a dense patch of woodland beyond the forest path. 'Here,' he said. 'We stop here.' They ate a little food. Inside his coat, Kramer illuminated Elsa's map with his American lighter, careful not to expose the light.

'Do you know where we are?'

'Yes,' Kramer lied.

'Good. Then wake me when it is time to leave.' Marta curled into a foetal position and was silent. Kramer lay awake trying to work out where they were. He knew they had travelled west, but too far north perhaps? The great rivers couldn't be far away now – maybe they could reach the American lines in a couple of days, if they were lucky, very lucky. But Kramer owed his life to this girl and her mother. If it was too late to save his own family, surely there was just enough time left to save them. Somewhere in the trees young tawny owls were calling. Not far away, roosting buzzards listened.

Kramer opened a flask of tepid coffee and offered it to Marta. The day was starting to close.

'Can you swim?' Kramer asked.

'Yes.'

'Well?'

'Yes.'

'Good. Because we may have to,' said Kramer. A wind picked up and shook the trees. The sky above was beginning to thicken with grey clouds. After a few minutes, Marta began to talk.

'I learned to swim at the Olympic Stadium at Grunewald. My father used to take me every week. I swam and he would sit and watch. Afterwards he would sometimes take me for ice-cream – chocolate ice-cream. We sat in the park and we would talk about our dreams for the future. I said I wanted to be a diver, or an ice-skater. He always encouraged me to follow these dreams.' Kramer listened intently.

'And what were his dreams?'

'His dreams were my dreams, I think. But he said once that he wanted to travel to Canada to see the Great Lakes.'

'And did he ever go there?' Martha was silent for a few seconds before replying.

'No. He died. Just as the war started.' For the first time in their company, her voice wobbled.

'I'm sorry.'

'Please don't be. Everybody does, don't they?' And she laughed dismissively, betraying her late-adolescent causticness.

'Did he die in the war?'

'No. He was killed by a tram. And you? What of your family, Kapitänleutnant?' Kramer was taken aback by her use of his rank.

'They live in Hamburg,' he said vaguely.

'Your wife, children?'

'Yes.' Kramer was making a habit of telling untruths to this young woman.

'What are their names?'

'My wife is called Clara.'

'And your...?'

'Daughter.'

'Your daughter?' she asked. Kramer paused.

'Dorothea,' he replied. Marta looked at Kramer with a softness he had not seen before. She brushed him lightly along his coat sleeve.

'We should leave soon?'

'Yes,' said Kramer, his attention snapping to. 'This will be a dangerous journey and we must be extremely careful. Whatever happens, we stay together unless I say otherwise. We stick to your mother's story. You are my niece and we are trying to get back to Tangerhütte.'

'I understand, Uncle,' she joked. Kramer shook his head with a smile. They edged their bicycles towards the path and headed south-west.

*

'Unite and unite and let us all unite, for summer is acome unto day, and whither we are going we will all unite, in the merry morning of May,' sang Bob Chapman at the side of the road.

'Feels more like winter in this bloody rain and wind,' moaned Rowe from beneath the bonnet. Bob continued singing and whistling his jolly tune.

'Your musical interlude isn't going to fix my van,' said Reddie Bland. 'We're never going to make the 'Obby at this rate.'

'You the Teaser and all,' teased Bob. 'Well, I've got my accordion and my whites.'

'Right, try her now, Reddie,' instructed Rowe. Reddie Bland turned the ignition key and depressed the starter with his foot, slowly pulling on the choke stick as he did so. The little van coughed into life.

'You're a genius, Rowe. Ugly as a bull, but a genius nonetheless.'

'This genius is owed a pint of dark and mild.' The three Cornishmen squeezed into the van and chugged away towards Padstow.

Padstow had many reasons to celebrate the 'Obby 'Oss Festival. The war would soon be over, the boats able to return to calmer seas, as long as the mines were cleared. And those few who'd escaped to war would demob and come home, or at least most of them would. The town's steep, winding, narrow lanes, its shopfronts and snug harbourside were decked with greenery and flowers. Bob Chapman harnessed his accordion and winked at his companions.

'It's all in the bellows, lads.' They laughed and joined the crowds in Lanadwell Street. Gladys saw Bob first. She was standing near the Golden Lion Inn.

'You just keep singing and playing, Bob Chapman, and keep your hands off those maidens!' The Penrose men were just in time to follow the Old 'Oss through the town. A flustered Reddie Bland, the Teaser man, tried to force his way to the front, but was jeered and pushed as he did so. Two young girls screamed as the 'Oss tried to catch them, while a catapult shot rebounded from the horse's mask – fired from some unknown quarter. Soon, the town was in song. Somewhere a few streets away a similar scene was taking place, if a little more abstemiously, as the Blue Ribbon 'Oss trotted along the Quay.

'Come here, Bob Chapman. You look spent.' Gladys pulled Bob from the procession.

'You can say that again, love,' he panted. They withdrew and sat on a bench by the harbour. 'I'm getting too old for this.'

'And too old to take care of the girls?'

'Who said anything about that?'

'I don't want them going to a fancy boarding school miles from home. It's not what they need. For what? To be raised by strangers? So they can talk like they're not from Cornwall?'

'It's not about that though, is it, Glad.'

'What is it about, then? You tell me.'

'It's opportunities for them. What are they going to do if they stay here? Work in a shop, on a farm? Marry the likes of Billy Mallett?' The Old 'Oss parade was fading towards another part of the town. A young seagull stared at his feet on the harbour wall.

'I still can't bear the thought of it.'

'Maybe there's a compromise to be had.'

'What do you mean?'

'They could board at Truro during the week and come home every weekend. Every weekend would be like a holiday.' Bob could see Gladys's look of reflection turning to a quiet satisfaction.

'I'll think about it,' she said. And Bob knew this meant she had.

Arm in arm, they walked from the harbour to the coast path to a bench overlooking the estuary and the Doom Bar. The sea breeze picked up and some early sun broke through the grey sky.

'Times will change here, Glad,' Bob mused with a wistful tone.

'For better or worse?' Gladys replied. Bob finished a mouthful of sandwich.

'Both,' he added quietly.

'Time to vote for it soon.'

'Change, you mean. Horabin will get in again, I'm sure.'

'Let's hope so. I've had enough of Winnie and his cigar.' But neither of them were talking about politics. The war had brought them so much loss and pain, yet it had offered purpose and a direction to follow. The war's end would provide a temporary joy. Thereafter, many would get lost – demobilised and immobilised as they handed back their uniforms and walked uneasily to Civvy Street. Far and wide across the British Isles, the old ways were breaking up like a tired old tramp steamer on the rocks. Along the shoreline waited salvors and beachcombers.

'Let's go home,' Gladys said affectionately.

'Good idea. I want to plant beetroot and those marrows tomorrow.'

'I fancy a cup of tea and some of that fruit cake.'

'I'll get Reddie to take us back.'

'Where will he be? You won't find him in that crowd.'

'I know exactly where he'll be.'

'The Lion?'

'Or the London.'

'Shipwright's?' they said in unison and laughed heartily. The walk back to the town was a gentle one. The estuary and the bay, wide and sweeping to the west, were gathering the incoming tide. Gladys paused on the approach to Quay Parade. 'They will be okay, won't they?' she asked.

Bob nodded. 'Of course they will, my love.' And he looked into her sparkling eyes. 'We'll give to our children all the happy days you have given to me.'

They were back in Penrose by early evening. Reddie Bland and Rowe were snoring in the back of the van. The 'Obby 'Osses would soon be back in their stables for another year. Some of the early blossoms were fallen, scattered by the wind.

'How many marrows are you planting?' said Gladys.

'About a dozen,' replied Bob.

'How many marrows will that be, then?'

'Fifty or sixty,' Bob reckoned.

'What are we going to do with sixty marrows?'

'Make wine,' said Bob. Gladys shook her head disapprovingly and muttered under her breath as she went back inside the cottage.

'And you a Methodist, Bob Chapman.'

'We can take our very own Communion here.' But Gladys was already upstairs, tidying, pottering, worrying.

Bob sensed she had was regaining her strength. With her curmudgeonliness came peace and purpose.

Morning came with a loud thwack on the door. It was Vera Craddock. She was smoking a pipe with excited and wild puffs. She wore her gum boots on the wrong feet.

'What on earth do you want, Vera?'

'Have you not heard?' she bellowed.

'Heard what?' said Gladys.

'Hitler's dead. The Nazi murderer is kaput.'

'So does that mean it's the end of the war?'

Bob appeared, lifting the first cup of tea of the day to his lips. The women looked to him for some sort of confirmation.

'I should think so,' he said hesitantly. 'It must mean they've taken Berlin.'

'I need to tell Annie Rowe. I will see you presently, Glad.' And Vera Craddock trotted off to Quarry's Turn at a pace she'd not displayed since the last war.

'It'll mean Eric can come home,' Gladys said.

'I'm not so sure. I think he's caught the sea fever. Anyway, the whole Channel's full of mines. It'll be years before they scoop up all those things.'

'Maybe it's the direction he's been looking for.'

'Maybe.'

'Opportunity and all that?' In the lane, Stump walked past and greeted them with a hat tip. Bob reciprocated by lifting his teacup.

'Seems like the whole village is up early today,' he said grumpily, and he went back inside.

'Don't forget your marrows,' Gladys called mischievously.

*

Kramer could smell the river. The treeline stopped a few metres from the bank. Only faint moonlight silhouetted the water.

'You said you could swim?' he asked in a whisper.

'We could cycle,' Marta answered, only half-jokingly.

'If you would like to meet some Russians,' warned Kramer.

'We leave them here?'

'Yes.'

'Where are we?'

'I think this is The Havel.'

'You think?'

'We swim to the western bank. There, we move quickly until we find somewhere to hide during daylight.' Kramer was plotting his course with the precision of a military officer. He hid the bicycles in nearby undergrowth. When he returned, Marta had already made preparations for their crossing.

'Tie your pack around your forehead. Like this – okay?' Kramer couldn't prevent a chuckle. She was a genius, if not ridiculous.

'Spring collection for the Potsdamer Platz?' His poor joke was met with another instruction.

'And keep the map dry – if you know how to use it.' Kramer acceded and folded the map into his cigarette tin. They removed their shoes and tied them to the packs.

'Ready?' They spoke at the same time.

They edged over the shallow bank, holding the

exposed roots of an alder tree. The water was cold – ten degrees at most. Marta cut across the current powerfully. Kramer laboured with the weight of his clothing and pack. The width of the river was little more than thirty metres, but its current was strong. Kramer started to drift. He called to Marta. She swam back to him.

'Keep going,' she urged. Kramer felt himself sinking lower in the water. He began to swallow water and coughed. The shock of the cold was beginning to take effect. Again, Marta returned and caught hold of his arm. 'Swim, damn you.' And she spat the words at him with wild eyes. The current eased as they approached the bank. Marta lunged for an overhanging branch and rested to regain her strength. With relative ease she lifted herself onto the bank. Kramer followed her. She helped him from the water. He was shaking with cold.

'You must rest. Drink this.' She handed him what remained of the coffee and a piece of chocolate.

'Thank you.' His voice was a shivering whisper. The chocolate tasted like heaven. Not for the first time he wondered where she got these things.

'To those trees?' she said, pointing to the black outline of a nearby copse.

'Yes,' Kramer replied. The woods were thick and impenetrable in places. They collapsed in a small clearing. Somewhere to the west the sound of gunfire rumbled like distant thunder.

'I think I can see lights,' Marta whispered urgently. 'Look!' Kramer lifted himself onto an elbow and squinted through the woods. Indeed, there was something out there. 'What is it?' she continued.

'The Americans if we're lucky. The Russians if we're not.'

'Or ours?'

'We're Czechs, remember. German-speaking Czechs.'

'I'm scared, Hans.'

'Me too. Whoever it is, we will find out tomorrow one way or another. Get some rest, Marta. We leave tomorrow at dusk.' Kramer did not sleep. He was too cold and too tired. He looked at the lights once more through the trees. He knew where they were. Approximately thirty-five kilometres to the Elbe.

'We must be near the American line,' Kramer said. The land around them was flat river plain. Scattered with copse and low undulations, it could have been almost anywhere in northern Europe.

'How do you know?' Marta asked.

'Because those lights are getting brighter.' Their food and water were almost gone. Beneath a small oak in the corner of a field they ate the last of the bread and dried sausage, and savoured the last few drops of coffee.

'Listen!' instructed Kramer. Voices sang drunkenly in the next field. Marta gripped Kramer's arm, her nails biting his skin. Kramer crawled leopard-like to a cluster of small thorn trees and peered through a gap. He could make out the outline of a group of men. They were walking, arms linked, swaying and singing. Russians. It was time to find better cover. He turned around, but as he did so his boot broke a piece of rotten branch. The noise disturbed the inebriated chorus; they staggered towards him.

'Der iwan kommt,' called one of the soldiers with cartoon menace in his voice. Kramer lay flat, his face pressed to the damp earth.

'There's nobody here,' said another. Kramer guessed there were three of them.

'Let's have a closer look, shall we?' the first voice said in a sinister tone.

Kramer kept silent and still. He waited for the men to pass. He could smell vodka and sweat and stale smoke. And then he was gripped by sudden panic. The men were walking towards Marta. Lifting his head slightly, he could see they were standing above her.

'What do we have here?' The voice spoke in a southern Russian accent.

'A German peasant whore.'

'Who must get on her knees for her Fatherland.' The men laughed aggressively. One took a slug of alcohol from a bottle and passed it to his comrade. The third man walked behind Marta and grabbed her by the hair. The other two unbuckled their trousers and stood in front of her. Kramer had no time to think. He ran to the nearest of the three soldiers, wrapped his right arm around the man's neck, tightened his lock, and with a swift execution, broke his neck. The heavy, drunken corpse collapsed into the field. Kramer now faced two swaying brutes intent on bloody revenge. The first, armed with his bottle, stared at Kramer. With a wide, flat face and eyes spaced wide apart, he could have been no more than twenty years old. The anarchy of war had made him behave like a beast twice his age.

'The war is over and still you want to fight?' The Russian charged, swinging the bottle at Kramer's head. Kramer blocked his opponent's attack with his left forearm and swept his legs from under him with a strong kick to the calf. Instinctively, Kramer picked up the bottle and almost in the same movement crashed it into the soldier's face. He screamed in agony, his nose pulped and oozing blood. Terror had seized the third Russian.

'Leave or I will kill her,' he said weakly.

'I don't understand you,' Kramer replied, but his enemy understood. He let go of Marta and backed away with arms raised, tripping and losing his side cap as he did so.

'Come on,' Kramer instructed Marta as he retrieved the Russian's hat. 'Time to leave this little get-together.' They grabbed their packs and ran into the night.

It wasn't long before they stumbled onto a road. Kramer could make out the shape of a vehicle parked close by.

'Stay here,' Kramer warned Marta.

'I think I will join you this time, if that's okay?' Kramer was impressed by her humour given the circumstances. As they came closer, Kramer found an empty Kübelwagen. On closer inspection, he could see a Soviet red star had been painted on its doors.

'Care for a ride?' asked Kramer. They got in and slowly pulled away. 'They'll have a long walk home. Or at least two of them will.'

'What were they doing there?'

'I have no idea, but we must keep going. Here, wear this.' He gave the Soviet cap to Marta. He glanced at her briefly. 'It suits you. Better than your last effort.'

'Do I look like a Hollywood movie star?' she said and flicked her head to the side coquettishly. 'Like Ingrid Bergman.'

'How do you know about Ingrid Bergman?'

'Everyone knows about her. Have you not seen Casablanca?'

'Nobody has seen Casablanca. It's banned.' Kramer was partly astonished, partly amused by the girl's story.

'Everyone has seen Casablanca. At least they have where I come from. Chocolate?' She passed him a small block.

'And who gave you this? Humphrey Bogart?' Marta giggled, her mouth stuffed full of candy.

They had driven for about ten kilometres when they reached a long, wooded bend in the road which veered south-west. The first shade of dawn revealed the black treelines beneath charcoal-blue skies.

'My God! What is that?' Marta saw it first. Kramer pulled to the side of the road. The noisy German-built jeep idled throatily.

'People,' Kramer replied simply. No more than fifty metres away, a column of hundreds of prisoners trudged pathetically, silhouetted just by the thin headlight beams of the Kübelwagen.

'They look like animals.' Marta's recent bravado receded in shock.

'They are women. They are prisoners from a camp for women,' Kramer added.

'Germans?'

'Jews probably. Or opponents of the regime.'

'Prisoners of ours or theirs?'

Kramer looked at her squarely. 'Is there ours and theirs anymore? We must get off the road. It's too dangerous here.' They abandoned the car and climbed the low verge at the side of the road and crept into the adjoining woodland.

The prisoner column moved past. Women of all ages reduced to scraps of human rags, eyes vacantly fixed on the mid-distance ahead of them. Shepherding them were a handful of young Red Army soldiers, rifles slung nonchalantly over their shoulders. The silent, macabre procession shuffled past the stationary Kübelwagen. A gaunt figure, ageless and bent at the waist, collapsed and grabbed for the spare wheel mounted on the sloping bonnet. As she tried to hold on, her eyes penetrated the undergrowth and she seemed to stare fixedly through Marta and Kramer.

'Keep very still,' whispered Kramer urgently. The woman slipped and fell to the roadside. A guard rushed to her and lifted her to her feet. But she sank again and was still. The soldier called to a comrade; they both conducted a cursory search of the jeep with flashlights. Nobody else stopped and within minutes the road was silent again.

Kramer climbed back to the road. He checked the woman's pulse. It was faint, expiring. Momentarily, she opened her eyes. Kramer held her hand. With all her dying strength, the woman opened her other hand to Kramer. In her palm was a worn photograph and a plain, simple cross on a chain. 'Mój syn. Mój święty synu.' Her voice was no more than a breath. Kramer stroked her brow, wiping the thin, matted hair from her skeletal forehead. The woman's eyes closed. A peace came to her face. A wind picked up and the birch trees sobbed. She was gone.

'She didn't die alone,' Marta said. 'And with a little dignity at least.' Kramer didn't answer. He unfurled the photograph and it revealed a Polish soldier, fresh-faced and smiling somewhat bashfully at the camera. Where he was now Kramer could only imagine – a camp, a grave, some bleak wilderness on plains to the east. Kramer tucked the photograph back inside the dead woman's coat. Far down the road he could hear shouting like a drunken argument. They didn't wait to find out what it was; Marta and Kramer were creeping through the trees.

With daybreak came a chill wind. Marta and Kramer hesitantly emerged from the safety of the wood. In front of them a vast flat river basin and the great, grey Elbe. They sat and surveyed the landscape of fields and sparsely scattered willows. Running parallel to the river was a track full of people – refugees, soldiers, wounded.

'What are they all doing?' Marta asked.

'They're trying to find a way to cross the river. To get to the west bank and the Americans. Before the Russians arrive.'

'But the Russians are here, aren't they?'

'Well, we met some.' Kramer's tone was in no way sarcastic, but matter of fact.

'And what do we do?'

'Get across the river.'

'Swim?'

'I don't think so. We will join them. If your mother's right, there's a bridge a little way to the north at

Tangermünde. It's risky, but we could try for it.' Marta nodded in agreement. 'But don't forget our story.'

They walked steadily across the open field and filtered into the human chain dragging itself beside the water. It was a desperate and sorry scene. Women and children, dirty and dishevelled, shuffled along dragging cases and makeshift trolleys. War-beaten soldiers limped beside them, some bandaged and broken. They had barely walked a few metres when a young woman tore through the line and jumped into the river. She managed a few strokes and then started to struggle, birling in the current, coughing and gasping. Marta stepped forward as if to attempt a rescue, but Kramer pulled her back with a fierce tug of her arm. He shook his head. They continued in the silence; few were in any mood to talk. After less than an hour's walking, a townscape appeared in the distance, less damaged than one would have imagined. The red brick tower of St Stephen's and the town hall stood impressively above the Elbe.

The crowds of people were becoming thicker and more chaotic now. Civilians and soldiers merged in a bewildered mass of dull colours. Spanning the river was the twisted wreck of a railway bridge. At its base hundreds of people waited to clamber across what was left of it. Marta watched a little girl and boy wander helplessly, all the time calling for their mother. A body lay face down in the river mud. Curled in a foetal ball beneath the concrete abutment an SS officer was ripping the insignia from his uniform. A proud, ruthless nation now just animals ensnared in ruin of its own making. An old woman pulled at Marta's sleeve;

she pointed madly and repeatedly to the west bank of the river, not once speaking a word. Kramer motioned Marta forward.

'We will cross the bridge,' Kramer said plainly. They moved towards the queuing line. Kramer felt something jab his ribs.

'Get back,' the voice said aggressively. Kramer turned to see a giant soldier pressing a rifle to his side. His face meant trouble. This was clearly somebody for whom the war was not over. Kramer calmly studied the man, his Aryan features and Hitlerian schooled demeanour. 'Wermacht first, my friend,' he continued sarcastically. Kramer looked closely at his lapel badges.

'But you're not Wermacht, are you?' Kramer held his nerve. The soldier grunted dismissively. 'You're SS.'

'And what difference does that make?'

'To me, none, but to you – on the other side of that river, I imagine they will be pleased to meet you.' The soldier turned his chin downwards and looked at his uniform. 'So, I suggest you freshen up, my friend, and maybe go see a dressmaker about your clothes.' Snarling, the soldier barged past Kramer and walked somewhere into the crowd.

'Nicely done, Uncle,' Marta joked. Kramer lit a stub of cigarette plucked from a pouch. His hands were shaking as he lit it. He inhaled deeply; the coarse tobacco smoke burned his throat. 'Here,' she said, and passed him a peppermint. Kramer raised his eyebrows, not for the first time. 'Wermacht field rations. All perfectly legal.' She turned back to the line which shuffled a few paces onwards.

The morning sun was rising to meet midday. The twisted mass of metal was barely passable. As they reached the apex, a scream tore through the air. Ahead of them a young woman had lost her footing and fallen through the bridgework. Her body smashed against the structure, and she plunged into the currents below. The onlookers gazed only for seconds and then continued in their tentative footsteps. Whining, buzzing sounds swarmed somewhere to the north-east, rising and falling like flies.

'Quick!' shouted Kramer. 'Take cover.' He grabbed Marta and wrapped his arms around her and pulled them both into a buckled shield of plating. Moments later three aircraft flew low over the bridge. Each let out a stream of deafening gunfire, strafing whatever there was to kill. Ricocheting bullets exploded. More hapless people fell. Kramer held on. Seconds later it was over. For now, anyway.

They were now metres from the centre of the bridge. Panic had gripped the horde. A hatless soldier tried to restore order and fired a rifle into the air. Marta looked to the other side of the river. She could see soldiers, vehicles and hundreds of people.

'Look,' she called. 'Americans?'

'Yes,' replied Kramer. 'Just focus on getting across, Marta.' The far side of the bridge was less damaged although still in poor shape. They were now minutes from the western bank of the Elbe. Kramer helped a wounded civilian with the last few steps. As he let go of their hand, he looked up into the eyes of an American GI.

'Keep moving,' he ordered with a chewing mouth full of gum. Marta and Kramer joined another line of refugees.

This time they were herded towards a crudely assembled checkpoint. Finally, they were standing in front of a table, behind which sat two American servicemen. The first was young, wore black-rimmed spectacles and neatly side-parted, brown hair. He held a pen and guarded a stack of neatly organised paperwork. The second, superior in rank, was much older, balding, fat and chewed tobacco.

'Identity papers.' The soldier spoke in German. Marta handed her card to the studious pen-wielding corporal.

'Your name, Fräulein?'

'Marta Laszlow.'

'You are German?'

'Czech,' she said, as per the script.

'But you speak German?'

'Yes,' said Marta and she offered no further information. The corporal consulted with his colleague.

'Where are you travelling?'

'Tangerhütte,' Marta answered, 'to my family. My mother's family.' Marta added a wistful plea to her tone. The Americans were falling for it. Or for her good looks at least.

'How are you going to get there?'

'Walk.' The older man laughed.

'Well, sweetheart, I'm sure someone back there will be willing to give you a ride.' Marta ignored the innuendo.

'Thank you,' she said innocently.

'On your way,' the sergeant said in English.

'Excuse me?' asked Marta in German.

'Go,' said the younger man. Marta walked a few metres beyond the checkpoint. 'Next.'

Kramer moved forward in the line. Elsa hadn't given him new identity papers. He placed his card on the table.

'Kapitänleutnant Kramer?'

'Yes.'

'Kriegsmarine?'

'Yes.'

'You must wait over there.'

'I am the girl's uncle,' Kramer replied confusingly.

'Which girl?' enquired the corporal. He wrote something down on a piece of paper and placed it on a pile, tidying fastidiously as he did so.

'That girl. The girl before me.'

'Really? Where is she from?'

Kramer was thrown off balance; he hadn't prepared for this scenario. 'Prague,' he said hopefully.

'No. She is from Pilsen. Over there.' The corporal pointed with his pen towards a small compound full of German prisoners. Kramer looked at Marta. He could just make out the expressions of her face. For no more than a second or two they looked at each other. Marta stepped forward as if to come back, but Kramer shook his head. Once more she looked at him, then lifted her hand just above her waist by way of gesturing farewell. Then, she turned and melted into the migrant column heading west. Kramer walked into the prisoner compound. He looked incongruous in his drab civilian clothes. But he wasn't the only one. He looked at his fellow countrymen. Some were talking, some smoking, some just sitting or standing, relieved perhaps that they had made it to the end in one piece. But most chilling were those who sat alone, haunted and inscrutable, already buried men, six feet in secrets and terror. Kramer felt deep in his pockets for cigarettes, but he was out of luck. He felt a scrap of paper and took it out. He unfolded a note. On it, in almost childlike writing, was a message, presumably from Marta: 'Thank you. Here's looking at you, Uncle. Isla.' It would be a long time before Kramer understood these cryptic words.

Twelve

London, North Cornwall and Europe
- Summer, 1985

'Thank you, both,' Frank said quietly.

'It is a pleasure, my friend,' replied Carlo. 'We can't have you dying in that hospital, can we?' They laughed together. Rico smiled and shook his head; he didn't always understand his own family's humour.

'I am not sure these clothes fit, but I think you did well with the stethoscope,' Frank joked.

'You're lucky I didn't bring the suppositories,' Carlo retorted. They were all sharing the humour now.

'There is somewhere I must go before we leave.' Frank's voice was now serious, if not sombre.

Rico parked close to the cottage.

'Can you help me? I won't be long.' The two friends

lifted Frank's failing body through the little gate for the last time. Not very much had changed here in over forty years. He breathed in the scents of the summer garden. There were flowers on the beans. The first blackberries were turning from green to red. Did Anna make wine like her grandmother? A cabbage white rose above the potato beds. Frank gasped for air when they reached the porch and the small, almost sunken door. With a shaking hand, he reached inside a pocket and took out an envelope. It was addressed to Emily. He put it through the letterbox.

'I must sit down,' Frank said. He heaved his languid frame forward and sat on the garden bench, his breathing heavy, his skin sallow and waxen. But his blue eyes shone, and his thin lips smiled. Carlo and Rico were almost carrying him to the car, his slippered feet dragging behind him. An ancient woman in a wheelchair passed them, her gaze fixed on Frank.

'I've seen those eyes before,' she said.

'Which eyes?' asked her carer.

'That old man. His eyes.'

'What do you mean?'

'I'm telling you, I've seen those eyes before,' she insisted. The carer pushed hard against the slope. 'Where's my pipe?'

'You stopped smoking years ago, Mrs Craddock.'

'No I didn't.'

'Come on, it's nearly time for a cup of tea.' They disappeared in gentle argument behind the curve of the lane.

'Home, sir?' Rico offered cheerily.

'Home, my son.' Carlo answered for his friend. Frank slumped into the back seat. Within minutes, he was asleep.

*

'Can we stop at the cottage before we go back to Pentire? I need to get something for Charlotte.' They passed the old lady in her chair. 'You'll never guess who that is, Em.'

'Who?'

'Vera Craddock.'

'Is she still alive? She must be about 500 years old.'

'One hundred and two to be precise. Just a minute – I won't be a moment.' Anna dashed into the cottage. Emily felt her stomach churn with nerves. Where was he and what had happened? Surely some mistake had taken place at the hospital; they would get back to the farm and Di would be waiting with the news that everything was alright. But something deep inside her knew something else. It wasn't her imagination conjuring a filial bond. It wasn't unrestrainable fear. It wasn't hopeless guesswork. The human spirit is like the sea, she thought, pushing and pulling, every day and every night, in storm and calm. Beneath the moon.

Anna handed an envelope to Emily. 'It's for you,' she said. Emily held it and was motionless.

'You're not going to open it?' Emily did not answer. Anna reached for the letter but thought better of it.

'Please, Anna – just drive to the farm.'

Di Merriman laid a simple lunch on the dining room

table. 'You must eat something. Both of you.' Her words were soft, but firm. As she slowly carved a slice of rich gammon ham, Emily held the envelope in front of her at a distance. Her name was written in the sloping, compact strokes of a shaking pen. Anna studied her, then turned to help Di. Emily took a butter knife and sliced the folded seal. She pulled out the paper and as she did so, a small metal object fell onto the table. Squeezing it between her thumb and forefinger, Emily lifted it to the light and then held it for Anna to see.

'A piskey?' Anna said, putting down mugs of tea.

'Yes,' answered Emily. She read the letter. Meine liebste Emily, it began in German, before continuing in precise and elegant English. He told his story – his early life in Hamburg, a brief account of how he and his men had plucked Rosie and Eddie from Quies, his escape from Berlin and his life in England after the war. But it was the passage in the middle that Emily read over and over again. How he had never forgotten her mother. How Dorothy had rescued him, saved and sheltered him. How he had longed to see her again. As the letter finished, he described seeing Emily for the first time – those same blue eyes, the same smile: his only child. Frank had finished his letter with an apology. That he had never known her grow up. That he had left without saying goodbye. And that, now, finally, he had to go home.

Emily's eyes were full of tears, filled to the brim, but not spilling. 'I have to find him,' she said.

'I will help you.' Ed's Cornish lilt spoke through the room.

'But where? In London? He never told me where he lives,' Anna said.

'Perhaps the hospital will have the address. As next of kin, you could request that, I'm sure,' Di added.

'No, he won't be there.' Emily was sure of this. 'The letter says that he wants to see plants and flowers one last time.'

'Plants and flowers? Where, Em?'

'Hamburg,' she replied certainly. The room paused.

'Then I'd better get my passport,' Ed said.

*

North of Lake Geneva, the Opel saloon cruised anonymously through the night. Sir Charles stopped for fuel and a small bottle of vodka. It was a little careless of his hired assassins to keep so much cash in the glove box, but very good of them all the same. More usefully, he found his new passport. Reginald Hook. How very English, he mused with a cunning smile. He took a swig of the vodka, and it satisfyingly burned his throat. A driver climbed out of his truck and walked towards the service station. The neon glowed depressingly in the mid-evening twilight. Sir Charles studied the tattered road map. He calculated the journey. Allowing for a light sleep at the mid-way point, he could be in Hamburg by lunchtime tomorrow. There he would visit an old friend, an adversary, an ally, a good man to know in bad circumstances.

He accelerated slowly from the forecourt. A little girl ran out in front of him; her mother shrieked and called her name. Every inch the gentleman, he braked and got out of the car.

'Je suis vraiment très désolé, madame,' he apologised.

'Pas de problème, monsieur,' the mother replied. She scolded her child and dragged her away.

'Les dés sont jetés,' he said to himself. The serpentine confidence had returned. Tomorrow Hamburg. And there we will have our revenge. It is my duty to bring these criminals to trial. The fantasies began to play out in the homemade movie of his imagination. He wound the window down and sang in a voice like sand, 'Lazily the brook like a silvery stream, ripples in the light of the moon, and a song afar fades as in a dream.'

*

Evening television chattered blandly, filling the small flat with nothing better than white noise. Alex Groves turned it off. He was tired and angry. Were the news stories not carrying everything that happened on the other side of the world? A boat lay a half-sunken wreck in an Auckland harbour, a victim of government sabotage. Didn't anybody care? He poured himself wine and placed a copy of Dark Side of the Moon on the turntable. David Gilmour sang 'Breathe in the Air'. Had she not even left a note to say where she and Charlotte had gone? He knew that anyway. Cornwall. He drank more wine. Then the door opened.

'Anna?' he asked nervously. She walked into the flat carrying Charlotte, followed by Emily and Ed.

'How was your trip?' she said with obvious disinterest.

'It was difficult. Very difficult.' He paused. 'You've seen the news? Read the papers?'

'No. No, I haven't' she repeated. 'And to be honest, I don't give a bollocks, Alex.' He was taken aback by her language. 'But you can do something for me.'

'I'm sorry?' He spoke querulously.

'Look after Charlotte. Keep her safe. I am going away for a few days.' She left the room to put Charlotte to bed, fetch her passport and some clothes. Alex then recognised Emily.

'Emily. How are you?' It was hardly a composed salutation.

'Fine, Alex, thank you. Please trust her. She will explain everything when she gets back.'

'Gets back? But she's only just arrived?'

'And how long have you been gone?'

'Shall we wait in the car?' Ed was uncomfortable. He loathed London and he wasn't enjoying the impromptu visit to Anna's home.

'Okay, let's go.' Anna closed the passenger door. In the lit doorframe, Alex waved weakly, downcast and miserable. 'Idiot,' Anna mumbled. Emily caught her sister's eyes in the rear-view mirror; something in them said she didn't mean it. A curtain twitched in the neighbour's flat. They rolled into the city's evening streets, busy still, but it all seemed calmer, soothing almost, as they stopped and started between traffic lights. Some Japanese tourists looked lost and were peering into the lit plate glass of an estate agent's office. A huddle of the homeless loitered, squatting on cardboard only metres from the Thames and a little upstream from the Palace of Westminster. She wanted to stop, to help, but what could she do? Two young lovers embraced and kissed by the water. Anna thought about Alex and how they seemed to be so happy when they met; he so full of ideals and zest for life. Why was their world not enough for him anymore? She had never known her parents. Charlotte had the right to know hers.

'To Harwich, then,' Ed said, breaking the heavy silence.

'Dover,' replied Anna.

'Dover?'

'It will be quicker, and we stand a chance of getting a boat, Ed. Trust me.'

'Are you sure?'

'I'm sure. There have been one or two benefits of living with a travel nerd for all eternity.' They were beyond Blackheath now and its wide open common, almost like the countryside, almost.

'I'm afraid I have something to say,' Ed announced. His tone sounded both guilty and formal. 'Something to tell you.'

'Okay,' Emily said, again catching her sister's eyes in the mirror.

'It involves Frank. Hans. Your father, Em.' Neither sister answered and they waited for him to continue. 'And your mother too.'

'What is it?' Anna asked as patiently as she could.

'When your mother died, your grandmother found a letter among her things – it was addressed to Frank. Before Gladys died, she gave it to my mother who then gave it to me. I don't know why.'

'Why didn't you give it to me – to us?' Emily said. Somehow, she didn't seem surprised, or hurt.

'My mother told me that it should only be passed to Frank – if he ever appeared.'

'That doesn't really answer the question, Ed,' Emily said, pressing him a little.

'I don't know. Perhaps your grandmother was protecting you. Perhaps it was Dorothy's wish. I really don't know anymore.'

'And why now are you choosing to tell us?' Anna added. Ed stared into the carriageway ahead, concentrating on the movement of a braking vehicle.

'Because I have it with me,' he replied. They drove on through a light evening rain towards the port and nobody said anything.

*

Sir Charles walked into the Reeperbahn via a wooden barrier covered in stickers and graffiti. No place for children or the faint-hearted. Inside die sündigste meile, he walked past the cafés and sex clubs. But Sir Charles wasn't here for light entertainment. The evening air was thick with cigarette smoke and the occasional waft of frying meat. On the south side of the street, he turned into Herbertstraße. Behind tall glass windows sex workers displayed their wares. Sir Charles remembered the brothels of North Africa all those years ago. Such young girls, beautiful and plentiful. Somebody's daughters, he mused. But not his. He now stood in front of a blistered, weathered door. He buzzed the intercom. A gravelly voice spoke hello. With a well-used password, Sir Charles stepped inside. He took the basement stairs and knocked twice on a door in a dark passageway, illuminated only by dim blue light.

'Sir Charles Gifford, how good to see you again.' The voice was welcoming with a hint of ugliness.

'Indeed, a pleasure,' replied Sir Charles, 'and in such opulent abode,' he continued jokingly.

'Needs must, I'm afraid. We can't all wine and dine in SW1 these days. However, I think your circumstances may have changed?' There was almost a hint of German accent in the man's voice.

'Temporarily, Stephen.' The other man merely half smiled, only half believing his friend. He led Sir Charles out of the entrance hall into an open-plan arrangement of kitchen and sitting room.

'Whisky?' Stephen Carter had served in khaki with Sir Charles in Algeria in 1942. These days he wore a little crimson lipstick and a purple silk kimono.

'I thought you would be drinking schnaps these days.' Carter poured two large drinks from a decanter into fat tumblers. 'A Laphroaig. Very good.'

'So, what can I do for you, Charles?' Carter smoothed a scarred cheek with his fingertips and settled his wiry frame into a comfortable chair. Every now and then, he twitched, his head flicking itself upwards. Sir Charles stood and leaned against a bookcase built into the wall.

'It has been a time of unbelievable coincidence, or not,' Sir Charles began cryptically. He finished his whisky and placed the glass in front of his friend. 'Our plan to trade goods with the French has been sabotaged. They are suspending testing. You heard about the boat in New Zealand, I assume?' Carter nodded and Gifford resumed. 'Our entire plan was scuppered from the off, Stephen. I have reasoned it is not coincidence. Our attempt to frighten off the rainbow warriors was thwarted at the first hurdle. Their intelligence must only have come from the inside.'

'Who do you think it is?'

'Difficult to say, old boy, but we've lost some good people – unnecessarily.' Carter had refilled the tumbler and handed it back to Sir Charles. 'But there is a curious twist.'

'Go on,' Carter said, his interest piqued.

'An ex-Nazi – probably SS or stormtrooper – is involved.'

'With environmental campaigners? Seems a little unlikely.'

'You would have thought. But in some way, he is linked to this lot.'

'Get rid of him, then. Shouldn't be too difficult.'

'Believe me, we've tried, but he is…' Sir Charles paused, a misty look to his red eyes, 'he is indestructible.'

'Where is he?'

'God knows, but it is my conviction that he is or soon will be in Hamburg.'

'Why?' Carter sipped his whisky, gripped by the story.

'Because everyone tries to crawl home to die.' Sir Charles placed his tumbler on the low table with a sharp crack. 'You know this city, Stephen, and I need to get this rat before it sinks the ship.'

'I am almost retired, Charles,' Carter said with little conviction.

'Then consider this a bonus for your pension.'

'You'd better tell me what you know.'

'We are looking for a man called Kramer. Hans Kramer.' Sir Charles skilfully changed pronouns.

'Address?'

'No. But I think we will find him in the Hammerbrook and Rothenburgsort districts. Do you know them?'

'What's left of them,' Carver replied. 'They were virtually wiped out in the war.'

'I see,' Gifford said, somewhat gloomily.

'But I have some useful local sources. It may take a little while, Charles.'

'Take whatever you need, Stephen. However, time is of the essence.'

'And you are sure he is here in Hamburg?'

'Most certain. If not now, then soon.'

'Very well. Then call again in a couple of days.' Sir Charles left the apartment and walked into the late-night streets, seeking solace and a little company. All allowable expenses, naturally, he thought.

*

Ed was exhausted as they breakfasted in a small café west of the Außenalster. The morning sun was bright and the sky a northerly blue.

'I need sleep,' Ed complained, 'and more sleep.' A young waitress with cropped, dark hair brought their food to the table. Anna divided some apple pancakes to share with her sister. Emily poured strong coffee from a metal pot.

'Cream, Ed?'

'Isn't there any tea?'

'Probably. Would you like to order some?' Ed declined and reluctantly sipped his coffee, wincing at its bitterness. 'What about your food?' Ed had ordered a farmer's breakfast thinking his carnivore appetite would be satiated.

'There doesn't seem to be any meat,' he said, a little miserably.

'Perhaps German farmers don't eat pig for breakfast, Ed,' Anna joked. She tied her hair and ate quickly. Ed silently and slowly chewed his eggs and potatoes.

'We're here. What do we do now, Em?'

'Get a shower. Get some sleep. Find my father.'

'Did the letter say anything about his home? Any clue, details?'

'Nothing. Only that he had to go home.'

'But isn't London his home?'

'No. I don't think so,' Emily reasoned, 'this is his home.'

'If there's nothing in his note, then I can't see how we can find him. It's not like he's going to be in any directory or public register.' Anna took an anxious, deep breath.

'Perhaps this might offer a clue?' Ed spoke firmly; he held Dorothy's letter between thumb and forefinger, elbow bent on the table. He and Anna waited for Emily's response. She took the letter from Ed.

'It might contain something. It's worth a try, right?' Emily was hesitant, needing reassurance.

'Can it really do any harm?' Anna offered.

'But breaking Mother's wish? I don't know.' Anna pushed her plate away.

'Look, Em, does that really matter now? We don't have any options. This all might just be fantasy. A wild goose chase. I mean, what are the chances really?' Anna held her sister's hand and squeezed it comfortingly.

'Okay,' she said and broke the envelope's seal. The paper inside was thin, the ink a faded violet blue. She carefully unfolded the letter being careful not to damage it. Anna and Ed watched intently.

'Well?' Anna couldn't contain her curiosity. Emily lowered her reading glasses.

'It's in German,' she said.

'German!' Ed exclaimed. 'Dorothy spoke German?'

'Or at least wrote it,' Emily added.

Anna called to the waitress. 'Please can you help us?' The young woman spoke in a heavily accented, high voice; her English was unconfident, but good. 'We have a letter. Please would you read it and tell us if there is an address or a location in it?' The waitress took the letter. As she read it, her eyes gave away surprise. Whatever narrative was contained in Dorothy's lines, it began to hook its reader. The waitress followed the faint handwriting with her finger, rereading the words.

'This is very interesting. Is it old?' she asked quietly.

'Yes, yes it is,' Emily replied.

'There is one location,' the waitress concluded, 'Planten un Blomen. It is a park. Plants and Flowers.'

'Plants and flowers? Where is this park?' Emily spoke quickly. The waitress thought carefully about her reply.

'The writer says that she wanted to visit it with... this person.' Her English faltered.

'Is it near?' Anna interrupted.

'Yes. Less than a kilometre.' The waitress pointed across the busy road.

'Thank you. Thank you. You really don't know how much this means,' Emily said. The waitress gave back the letter and cleared the table. They quickly gathered their things and made for the door. Ed hurriedly left some Deutschmarks and pfennigs on the table. The waitress shook her head with a smile.

The bright heat swept them towards the park, sticky in lead-filled air. Inside, an oasis of heavy green trees, flowers, ponds and lakes. A parkkeeper was picking litter from a herb garden. His back was bent and hunched, and his hair brown-grey like pig iron.

'You think this is what he means by home?' Anna's voice was unsure. Emily looked to the lake and the flashes of silver light on the water.

'Yes,' she answered, 'this is what he means by home.' They sat on a bench. Behind them some young birch trees whispered in the light breeze.

'And now we wait?' said Ed, 'this is a crazy idea. I have barley to harvest.'

'In shifts,' Emily said sternly, 'we wait in shifts. Three hours on and three hours off.'

'All day and all night,' Ed replied sarcastically.

'He's got a point, Em,' Anna said. The parkkeeper plodded past with his wheelbarrow, cigarette hanging from his lips.

'I will wait here. Go and find somewhere for us to stay. Please. At least for tonight. I know it's madness, but...' Her voice trailed off faintly. Anna and Ed did not respond, but left Emily in the park, and went to find a hotel.

*

Less than two kilometres to the south-west, Sir Charles breakfasted with a vast plate of cold meats, cheeses and a sex worker who lay sleeping silently on the bed of his cheap hotel room, a stone's throw from the church of St Joseph's. He had picked the girl for her North African looks, another reminder of his long-ago youth. The poor woman had spent a long night constricted in Sir Charles's lecherous embrace, listening to his rambling monologues about the Eighth Army and espionage in Alexandria; he had fallen asleep shortly after finishing a bottle of cheap whisky, much to her relief. A vehicle horn blared angrily in the street below. The young woman stirred, woke and reached for her clothes. Sir Charles continued eating. He watched her casually and then pointed to a pile of bank notes on a table. She took the money and left without uttering a word. 'Whore,' Sir Charles barked as the door closed behind her. He slurped more coffee like a greedy animal at the trough, then went to the bathroom and urinated spasmodically into the sink basin. Within half an hour, he was at Stephen Carter's Herbertstraße apartment.

'What have you got?' Sir Charles was in buoyant mood. Carter was arranging sunflowers in a tall vase. Classical piano music played from a cheap hi-fi system.

'Schumann,' Carter said.

'Very romantic,' Gifford replied impatiently. Carter took a step backwards to admire his arrangement.

'His was a very tragic life,' continued Carter, without looking at Sir Charles. 'Dead in his forties. Eight children. A broken hand. Yet, perhaps the finest Romantic composer of them all.'

'Fascinating,' said Sir Charles with undisguised sarcasm.

'Oh, it is. You see, Schumann experienced auditory hallucinations. Probably caused by mercury poisoning or tinnitus. He heard the note of A continuously – like a drone. One could say like the endless piping of a queen bee.' Carter finally turned to his friend. 'Coffee?' Carter returned from the dark kitchen area with a pot of coffee and a jug of cream. Apfelkuchen?' He unveiled a small apple pie. 'Courtesy of Frau Weckerin.' Sir Charles took a slice of the cake in his fat, clumsy fingers.

'Do you have any more information?' Sir Charles affected a humbler tone.

'Clara. His wife,' said Carter with a full mouthful of pastry and apple.

'Kramer or Schumann?'

'Both,' smiled Carter. He put his plate down on the low table between them. 'Kramer was married to Clara. They lived in a small apartment in Adenauerallee near the Außenalster. It is still there. One of the very few buildings that survived the inferno in 1943.'

'And is Clara alive? Does Kramer still live there? What was he doing in England?' Gifford's questions were urgent.

'Nobody has seen Kramer for years. Clara died years ago. There was a daughter, but she moved to Bremen. More cake?' Sir Charles shook his head.

'Kramer was living in England.'

'Yes, it would seem so.'

'Can you show me his apartment?'

'Of course, it isn't far. We can take the U-Bahn.'

'Thank you, Stephen. Speedy work, I must say.' Sir Charles handed Carter an envelope. Carter checked its contents.

'Very generous, Charles.' Carter put the envelope in a small safe inside a cupboard in the corner of the room. 'Shall we go?' he invited cheerily.

'I think a taxi, Stephen. We're not underground just yet.' Carter ignored the cheap wordplay.

The Adenauerallee stood at the side of busy roads in the St Georg district of Germany's second city. The architecture was mostly new, functional, square and depressing. But remarkably, the apartment Kramer had once occupied was a relic of a pre-war age. Its white façade rose above trees that screened it from the thoroughfare.

'Our boys must have missed this one.' Gifford's boast was a comment on the near annihilation of the city.

'Forty thousand civilians died, Charles. Nearly as many in a few raids as all those killed in Britain throughout the war.'

'You're going soft in your old age.' Carter didn't reply. 'I want to have a look inside.' They reached the apartment entrance hallway, courtesy of a doddering dogwalker who was too engrossed in conversation with her animals to notice the intrusion. Sir Charles looked around the foyer. He was trying to sense Kramer's presence. He felt inside his light summer coat; the gun was sleeping in its shoulder holster.

'A Walter PPK with ivory handgrips?' asked Carter.

'Of course, what else?' replied Gifford slyly.

'It's funny, Charles – you carry a German firearm.'

'I also drive a Mercedes Benz. Nobody said the krauts aren't fine engineers.' Carter was becoming fidgety.

'Can I help you?' A voice from the far side of the hall called to them in German. Carter tugged Gifford's arm as if to silence him.

'Perhaps,' Sir Charles replied in English, ignoring Carter's warning. 'I am looking for a gentleman by the name of Kramer. Hans Kramer.' The approaching voice belonged to a tall man in his early sixties pulling a golf trolley. 'He was a colleague of mine many years ago.'

'I am sorry,' the man replied in hesitant English, 'I do not think anybody of that name lives here.' The man paused as if to form his next sentence. 'How did you get in here? This is private property.'

'I'm so sorry,' interjected Carter, reverting to German. 'We are sorry to have troubled you.' The man opened the door of the entrance hall that led onto the street, extending his wrist as he stretched for the door handle. Gifford caught sight of a five-digit number crudely tattooed on his forearm. For a moment he felt pity, even shame. But as the late morning sun blinded him for a second, he couldn't work out who he despised more – Kramer or the golfer.

*

They ate a simple dinner in a restaurant not far from the university. The street was wide and grey with only the occasional tree to punctuate the drabness. Muffled rock music escaped from the Club Logo on Grindelallee.

'I'm sorry,' Emily repeated, 'tomorrow we'll go home. It was a stupid idea to come.'

'No. You needed to do it.' Anna's words were kind and timely. Emily tucked some of her blonde bob behind her ear. Her sister noticed a subtle streak of light auburn in it – something she'd never seen before.

'Tomorrow we'll go,' Emily continued. Ed tried to get the waiter's attention with a half-hearted raise of his hand.

'I say we spend the day in the park tomorrow. One more night in the hotel and then we can make our way home. Ed?'

'I suppose that makes sense,' he said with as much disguised reluctance as he could manage. Anna could see him making mental calculations to work out when he would be safely back in the cab of his combine harvester. 'At least we've had sleep, showers and something half decent to eat.' The waiter finally responded to Ed's call. 'Just thought I would try a bit more of that matrofish stuff.'

'Matrosenfleisch,' Emily corrected. 'I'm not sure you can just help yourself to seconds.'

'No harm in trying,' Ed smiled. Presently, the waiter returned with another plate of sailor meat – ragout of beef and pork with vegetables.

'Do you think he ever knew?' Emily said, breaking the pause in conversation.

'About you, Em?' Anna replied.

'I guess so.'

'Whatever he knew or didn't know, there was obviously a strong connection with Mother and with Cornwall. Does it matter?'

'I just want to see him one last time,' Emily continued, 'just to let him know.'

'Let him know?'

'That I will always be his daughter, whatever happens.'

'He knows that,' Anna said. 'It was clear in the letter. Perhaps that was the only way he could say goodbye.'

'Do you think we will find him?'

'Given everything that's happened so far, it wouldn't surprise me.'

Ed broke in with a mouth stuffed full of meat. 'There's only one way to find out. Tomorrow will be a day in the park. Maybe a very long day,' he added with a little humour.

'I agree,' Anna said. 'We can all be there in spirit, if nothing else.' Emily nodded and sipped some more of her wine. Outside, the long day was beginning to close. Headlights, shopfronts and neon half lit the streets, and an occasional car horn sounded the air. The iron-haired parkkeeper strolled past the restaurant with a small dog on a lead; he paused and looked in at the diners with a still expression on his weathered face, then moved on, cigarette burning, into the night.

*

The late summer morning was overcast. Low pressure and low stratocumulus making for a heavy sky. A sweating Rico wheeled Frank in a chair courtesy of Truro Hospital.

'We were 300 metres deep for hours. The hull should have crushed, but somehow, we survived.'

'And you were attacked by destroyers?'

'Porpoises,' Frank replied. 'One of my lookouts – Hütter was his name – was very nervous. It was his first patrol. He convinced everyone that he had seen torpedo trails in the water. So, we dived and waited, and waited some more. When we finally surfaced, we had no battery, but it was the best fresh air I have ever tasted. I even saw a porpoise, or was it a dolphin?'

'What happened to Hütter?' asked Rico through laughter.

'I think he became a cyclist,' said Frank.

'Yes, there were many nervous soldiers in the war. I remember a major in our battalion. Fossati was his name. He spent most of his time composing light opera or refining his family recipe for Crudaiola all'Arturo. One morning, a friend of mine was told to deliver a message to him which said that the British were likely to attack soon. Do you know what he said? He said he didn't know we were at war with Britain.'

'It is no surprise you needed our help,' Frank joked.

'We wished you all stayed at home. Then we could have all surrendered.' Carlo winked at his nephew.

'This is it,' said Frank and he pointed to the entrance. They left St Petersburger Strasse and walked through the park gates. Frank's eyes were alive and wide. He gazed intently at an arborist sculpting a long row of voluminous shrubs. Several times he asked Rico to stop at flower borders. Like a child seeing things new, he wondered at sea thistles, tobacco plants, Michaelmas daisies, irises and lupins. Blues, purples and whites. The morning sun tried to break through the cloud. Short bursts of warmth, followed by moving blankets of cold shade. Rico tried to find sunlight.

'Now you are older, do you miss Italy?' Frank asked his friend.

'No. I did at first – when we were captured. Then I realised that we were better fed as prisoners than as soldiers. The English were good to us. And some of the English girls too. Well, most of them. But I wouldn't know Italy now. It was such a poor place back then. Always fighting between the politicians. Il Duce. What a joke.'

'Your family? Your home?' Rico asked. It seemed he had never spoken to his uncle about these things before.

'Home is where your family is,' Carlo replied, 'for me, it's as simple as that. I have enjoyed a good life surrounded by the people I love. Everything else you can...' he struggled temporarily for the right word, 'import. Foods, traditions, culture. All of these things you can carry with you, but a life without family? I wouldn't want it.' They stopped at a bench seat. Rico went in search of refreshments.

'Do you think about death, Frank?' Carlo's voice was soft, even serene.

'I think about life. Regrets. Things I should have done.'

'What is your biggest regret?'

Frank turned to look at Carlo. 'That I will leave this earth holding nobody's hand.' Rico was walking back to the bench, desperately trying not to spill three polystyrene cups. His tongue poked through his closed mouth, his eyes fixed on the coffee.

'Family,' said Carlo wryly and they both laughed.

Thirteen

Germany and Cornwall - May, 1945

The long grey column shuffled through the countryside west of the Elbe. Thousands of exhausted, hungry, broken men. Some no more than boys and old men. The remnants of Hitler's feared, terrifying Wermacht. Disarmed and displaced they trudged solemnly for miles towards Wolfsburg. Kramer had pulled a field cap over his eyes, taken from the corpse at the roadside. An American jeep crawled beside the prisoners, accelerating occasionally to inspect further on up the line. A nonchalant GI loosely held a rifle over his lap, his legs sprawled in the back of the vehicle. He flicked a half-smoked cigarette into the road. Kramer got to it first.

'Let me have a drag,' a voice pleaded beside him. Beyond them, the jeep bounced over uneven ground; the GI looked at his flock unconcernedly.

'No,' said Kramer, 'find your own.'

'Please,' the repeated plea was even more pathetic this time. Kramer turned to his right to see a small, dark-haired, bespectacled infantryman. Kramer guessed him to be no more than eighteen years old.

'Where are you from?' asked Kramer indifferently. And he inhaled another deep, long drag before blowing it in the young man's face.

'Oxford,' he replied.

'Oxford in England?' Kramer replied, with amused bafflement.

'Yes.'

'Why in hell on earth are you here?'

'Give me the rest of that cigarette and I'll tell you.' Kramer smiled and handed it over.

'My father is English. He is a fellow at the university. My mother is from Heidelberg. We lived in England, but just before war broke out, my mother insisted she and I move back to Germany.'

'Because she thought we would win?' Kramer added intuitively.

'I suppose so,' the boy said glumly. He coughed on the cigarette smoke.

'And where is she now?'

'I don't know. Heidelberg, I think. But she will try to get to England if she can.'

'And you intend to join her?' The boy didn't need to answer; his situation was so clearly hopeless. The jeep came back down the side of the road. Kramer signalled to it. The GI jumped out of the back and came to talk to

Kramer. They exchanged brief words and two items. The jeep drove away. Kramer jogged back to his place in the line.

'What were you doing?' the boy asked him sheepishly.

'Just getting some cigarettes,' Kramer replied coolly. His companion plucked one from the full carton offered to him. Kramer lit their fresh cigarettes with the stub of the old one. Somebody behind them picked it up off the road. 'What is your name?'

'Ralph Webber. Or Ralf Weber.'

'Well, Private Weber, we must see if we can get Mr Webber home.' Kramer patted Webber on the back. The young man smiled and hastened his pace. Kramer stared at the road, but he was thinking of the sea.

*

At 3pm on 8 May, Winston Churchill broadcast to the nation to officially announce the end of the war with Germany. Many from Penrose, Porthrowan and Padstow had journeyed to Bodmin to join in the bigger celebrations. Spontaneous street parties danced into the night beneath the clock tower and Turret House. 'Britons never shall be slaves' sang a noisy, merry horde. The following morning, children were given the day off school. Streets filled with decoration and tables full of food. The parish bells rang throughout the late afternoon and early evening, and the town band played 'The Floral Dance' all the way to Mount Folly, stopping only for the King's speech. As night fell, fireworks flared in the peaceful sky.

In the cottage garden at Penrose, the girls were playing in the garden, running between the fruit trees. A milder south-west breeze shook the hissing leaves.

'I wish the weather would warm up a bit,' complained Gladys, wrapped up tightly in a woollen cardigan. 'There was a frost last night.'

'The coming of the Ice Saints,' said Bob mysteriously.

'Who are they?' Gladys barked.

'Saints' days in some parts of the Continent. When the last frosts come.'

'Like a blackthorn winter, then.'

'Exactly,' agreed Bob, sensing Gladys's ill-humour. Emily chased her sister, caught her with arms wrapped. Anna complained to her grandmother but received no more than a shoo away for her protest. 'Eric's going to be posted to the east,' Bob continued.

'But the war's over,' said Gladys.

'Not in Japan. They won't surrender until the last man's copped it.'

'Will it be dangerous?'

'Terrible battles are going on over there. Probably be safer at sea.'

'You're worried, Bob.'

'Who wouldn't be? Bloody fool could have stayed here on a Padstow boat.' Bob reached for Gladys's hand.

'Doesn't mean he would be in any less danger. Plenty of boats never come back.' She looked at him for a moment. His black hair was greying and the lines on his face were deepening, but his eyes were still set like Cornish sapphire.

'Crumbles,' he said, and she held his hand tighter. A low-flying aircraft roared overhead, on its way back to St Eval. The girls looked skywards tracing the plane's path.

'Do you think they remember them?' Gladys spoke quietly. The light caught her high cheekbones as she turned to Bob.

'They will ask you a lot of questions one day,' he said, not answering her.

The garden gate clicked. Two men dressed in dark suits and tan gabardine overcoats walked purposefully across the path.

'Mrs Trewithen?' asked the taller of the two.

'Yes?' answered Gladys nervously.

'I am Chief Inspector Croft from the county police.' The man displayed some formal identification. 'And this is Mr Wallingford from the Directorate of Military Intelligence.'

'Where?' questioned Bob bluntly.

'The Security Service, sir,' replied the shorter man politely. 'May we ask you a few questions?' Gladys looked to the children who were oblivious to the intrusion. 'Separately, if you don't mind. May we?' The man gestured to the house. Gladys rose unsteadily to her feet. Though short and somewhat slight, she was still a strong woman, even if her aching limbs were trying to tell her otherwise. She led the men into the cottage and reluctantly offered them tea.

'Gladys Trewithen – Mrs Gladys Trewithen?' Croft took notes as he asked questions. Gladys nodded as she stirred the pot. 'I will come straight to the point, Mrs Trewithen. There have been rumours in the county that a German submarine crew landed on the beaches in this area of Cornwall. Some time in 1940. Do you know anything about this story?'

'Everybody's heard that story, Inspector.' Gladys passed the cups of tea to her unwelcome visitors. 'Sugar?'

'No thank you,' replied Wallingford.

'Only that...' Croft attempted to continue.

'Biscuit?' Gladys interrupted.

'Thank you,' said Croft taking a homemade shortbread. 'Mrs Trewithin, we received an anonymous tip-off that you or your daughter may have, somehow, had something to do with this.'

'My colleague is trying to say that you met with them, Mrs Trewithen,' Wallingford said, dipping the biscuit into his tea. His voice was deep and reared near the Thames.

'My daughter is dead, Mr Wallingford.'

'I know, Mrs Trewithen. I am sorry. But that doesn't really answer my question. You see, fraternisation with the enemy is a very serious offence. One might say treasonable.' The security agent spoke with a smug and sinister side smile. Croft looked uncomfortable; he perfunctorily asked Gladys some questions about dates and times, which she answered vaguely with a sense of memory loss.

'You do realise the seriousness of this, Mrs Trewithen?' persisted Wallingford. 'If you have been giving us false information, or if you are simply lying, you will feel the full force of the law, should things become a little clearer to us, or shall I say, a little less foggy in your memory.' He put down his teacup and saucer firmly, betraying his vexation. A little tea spilled onto the table.

'Thank you for your time, Mrs Trewithen,' said Croft. He touched the brim of his hat and turned for the door. Bob walked in and blocked their leaving.

'What's all this about anyway?' he asked.

'They think we were involved with that German submarine story.' Gladys cut in before the men had a chance to respond.

'In cahoots with the Kriegsmarine, eh?' Bob laughed.

'A serious offence, Mr Trewithen,' Wallingford added.

'Mr Chapman, actually,' Bob corrected. 'Well, we're not known as Nazi sympathisers down here, even if we do seem a bit strange to you London folk.'

'We will be on our way,' said Croft. 'We have other inquiries to make and people to speak to.'

'The Duke of Windsor, perhaps?' called Bob as they walked along the lane towards Penrose.

*

'They've arrested Albert Rowe,' announced Vera Craddock. She was struggling to light her pipe through sheer excitement.

'Who has?' replied Gladys, feigning surprise.

'The police. Came for him this afternoon just after dinner.'

'Why?'

'No idea. Stolen goods I would imagine. Who knows what he's got stashed away in that workshop. And he's never short of a few quid. Not that he ever spends any of it.' Vera was enjoying her narrative and was now sucking on her smoke. Bob glanced anxiously at Gladys, before addressing Vera.

'Were there any plain clothes officers there, Vera?'

'What do you mean?' Vera pulled at a long, lone hair on her chin.

'Any men dressed not in uniform? In overcoats perhaps?'

'Come to think of it, yes, there were. Two of them. One tall, one small. How did you know?'

'I think I saw them in the village,' Bob improvised quickly.

'Who were they, then? Detectives?' asked Vera.

'Possibly,' said Bob without any conviction. He looked at Gladys again. She closed her eyes.

'Are you alright, Glad?' Vera was quick to notice her expression.

'Just exhausted. The children have worn me out, Vera.' The lie did its job.

'Well, I must get back and find out the next instalment. Perhaps they'll want to talk to us next?' Vera left in a puff of tobacco smoke, scented with a whiff of vanilla.

'My God, what have we done?' Gladys broke down and sobbed into her sleeves. 'What will they do? They could take the children away. Bob, what is going to happen?'

'Glad, are you listening? I am going to speak to Stump. I will be back soon.' She nodded. 'If they come back, don't change your story. Do you understand?' Bob left quickly, pulling on his flat cap as he closed the gate.

*

Just before sunset, the prisoner column stopped in woods just east of Wolfsburg. The land was flat and undramatic. Kramer craved the salt winds of the north-western ports and the grey seas beyond. Young Weber longed for the wooded valleys of his mother's hometown. The wind had dropped to low murmurs.

'Are we stopping here for the night?' Weber asked. His nerves were shredding fast.

'It looks like it,' answered Kramer. The Americans were handing out chunks of tinned meat, and packs of hard biscuits.

'A feast,' said Weber, gratefully accepting the food. Two GIs stood nearby, casually standing and keeping watch.

'What are they talking about?' Kramer was trying to understand the strange English intonations and expressions. 'I don't understand anything they're saying.' Weber raised his thick eyebrows.

'That's because they have strong New York accents,' he said. 'They are talking about clearing minefields. Soon they will take some of us for this task.'

'Why are they laughing?'

'Because they think it's a suicide mission.'

'Where are the mines?' Weber listened for a few minutes. 'Near Stuttgart. Weinsberg.'

'Weinsberg is in Württemberg.' The penny was starting to drop.

'You cannot be serious, Kramer?'

'Kapitänleutnant Kramer, Private. Tell them we volunteer.'

'No. It's madness.' The boy's face was white like quick lime powder. Kramer ignored him.

'Please,' Kramer called in English to the American soldiers. They turned around, still in mid-conversation.

'Tell them,' Kramer ordered in furious whisper, 'or I will tell them you are SS.'

'What?' snarled one of the soldiers, chewing gum with wide open mouth.

'We wish to volunteer,' Weber said in perfectly formed English received pronunciation.

'For what?' growled the second GI.

'Mine duty,' replied Weber. The Americans looked at each other in mildly stunned bewilderment. One of them called along the line.

'Hey, Sarge, come over here, would you?' Moments later, a burly sergeant appeared. 'Looks like we've found ourselves two willing minesweepers. In fact, Harold Lloyd here speaks like the King of England, so you can ask him yourself.'

'Well?' the sergeant uttered.

'We wish to do our duty as Germans. It is right that we clear the mines so innocent people are not harmed.' The Americans were caught somewhere between amusement and incredulity.

'And you?' The sergeant stared at Kramer.

'Yes,' said Kramer making the most of his limited English vocabulary. The sergeant took a fresh stick of chewing gum from a pack.

'Corporal, get these two over to the trucks. These Germans are crazy sons of bitches. I get the feeling they enjoy getting themselves killed.' The corporal motioned Kramer and Weber to get to their feet with his firearm.

'Thank you,' said Weber as they were marched towards a group of Jimmies lined up on the edge of a woodland track. The sergeant shook his head in disbelief.

'Why did you make me do that?' Weber was on the brink of tears.

'You want to get to Heidelberg, right?' Weber stared groundward with a sallow frown. He tugged his field cap low over his forehead and kicked the dust in front of him. 'Then how else do you propose we cover 500 kilometres?'

'And what do we do when we get there? Run through the minefield into the arms of my mother on the other side? You are mad, Kramer. Why couldn't we have just bided our time?'

'You think they were going to let us lie there and bathe in the sun, and bring us a meal three times a day? If you do, then you're the one that's mad. This war may be over, Private, but there's still a lot of dirty work to do. And I can tell you that it won't be the Amis and the Tommies. Take your chances – you want to go to Heidelberg or wait to see if the Iwans need to borrow some labour?'

'Or be blown to pieces.'

'Well, at least you won't know a thing about it if you are.' They climbed into the back of a Jimmy. Kramer was surprised to see it was nearly full. He gave Weber a cigarette and slapped him on the back. 'I hope your mother is a fine cook, Private.' Four more prisoners squeezed into the truck before its engine started and it slowly moved away.

It was the middle of the night before the engine pulled out of the station. Kramer sat in a battered carriage, but it was a passenger coach, nonetheless. He had expected to be herded into a cattle wagon. The train rolled south, the flatlands giving way to the undulating beauty of Swabian lakes, valleys and ancient towns. Weber cut a lonesome figure as he sat by the window gazing into the blue and black landscape, as if for the last time. But for the rhythmic percussion of the train on the tracks, the car was silent, punctuated only by the coughing of a dozing soldier.

'Why was a submariner retreating across the middle of Germany?' Weber asked.

'Wasn't everyone an infantryman by the end?' replied Kramer, rhetorically.

'I don't follow.' Weber's war had been mercifully brief.

'The first phase of the war was a different time. I enjoyed my work. Can you believe that?' Kramer began to tell his story. 'Yes, we sank ships, but we did it with at least a semblance of good conduct.'

'What do you mean?'

'If we sank a lone ship, we often waited for its crew to get into their lifeboats first. We would give them food. Once, when we were in Norwegian waters, there was a heavy swell. Conditions were terrible. We surfaced and approached this old steamer – an ancient thing. We flashed lights at it and fired our deck gun across its bows. Slowly it stopped. I called to the captain. He knew the game was up and they all got into the boat. We opened fire and this old thing was gone in two minutes – full of iron ore. Sank like a stone.'

'And what happened to the crew?'

'We towed them until they could see land, then waved goodbye.' Weber looked amazed. 'You seem shocked, Weber. But even Hitler abided by international rules in the early days. We were winning the war. We called it Die Glückliche Zeit.'

'What changed?'

'The war got dirtier. Dönitz wanted blood. Anything that moved was fair game.'

'But that doesn't explain why you're here.' The train waited at a signal junction. Above a whistle and a burst of steam, Kramer continued.

'It was late in '41. It was certainly the end of the happy time. We weren't sinking anything. We had very few boats at sea, and we had lost a lot of good men. We were on patrol south-east of Iceland. The waters there are desperately cold and wild. We spotted a straggler that was miles astern of its convoy – it could only have been doing five knots. We came in close and attacked with three torpedoes. One of them hit and the boat quickly settled in the water.'

'And you rescued the survivors?' Weber was gripped.

'Yes.' Kramer stopped talking.

'But?'

'We picked up the dozen or so who were left. Wrapped them in blankets and confined them to the officers' quarters.'

'But there's something else,' guessed Weber.

Kramer was committed to finishing his story. 'When we got back to Lorient, one of my junior officers, Lange – a loyal Nazi – complained to my superiors that I had endangered the lives of my crew by bringing survivors on board. I was hauled in the front of the Grand Admiral himself and narrowly escaped a court martial.'

'They were going to shoot you?'

'Shoot a U-boat captain who'd received the Knight's Cross? No, they wouldn't do that. I got worse than a firing squad.' The comment startled Weber. 'They sent me to a desk in Heligoland.' Kramer laughed drolly and lit a cigarette.

'What happened to your boat?'

'Lange took command. Sank with all hands on his first patrol.' It was Kramer's turn to stare mournfully out into the night. He thought of Stuckmeier, Emmerman, Witte, Forstner, but most of all, Mertens, his wife and six children. 'There was one survivor,' concluded Kramer with a wry aside. 'A Capitano Cossato – an Italian officer who was on loan to us from their navy.'

'What happened to him?'

'He overslept. Entwined with a French girl in a Port Louis villa. They left without him.' The train heaved into Stuttgart at the edge of dawn.

*

Stump Trelawney was attending to his runner beans. Curiously growing on a slope, Stump was winding stalks between a temple of precarious, south-facing sticks. His iron hair was covered by a brown cloth cap. Like many a gardener in a valley, he seemed to walk on legs of different lengths.

'Morning, Stump,' Bob called cheerfully. They knew each other well enough for Bob to stroll into Stump's patch.

'I imagine you have come to talk about this police business,' replied Stump matter-of-factly and without a sharp edge to his words.

'Yes,' Bob confirmed gloomily. 'Do you know anything about it, Stump?' Bob plunged his hands into his corduroy pockets.

'They are questioning Rowe. They think he knows something about our visit all those years ago.'

'And does he?' Bob asked ambiguously.

'I think he won't. Rowe might be a bit of a bully, but he's a mewling baby at heart.' Stump's runner bean improvements were completed, and he sat down on a splitting block.

'Where do you think they got their information?'

'I'm surprised it's taken them so long. The story's the stuff of legend. Especially if Mallett got talking after a few drinks.'

'Where is Mallett?'

'Nobody's seen him. Wouldn't surprise me if he's dodging his call-up.'

'Dinky Young?' Bob threw a stray log on to a pile stacked beside the block.

'He's somewhere in France, I believe,' Stump said with a watery smile.

'That only leaves Tom and the children.' Neither needed to say anything. It was inconceivable Tom Merriman would have done anything to put Rosie or Eddie in danger.

Later that evening, Albert Rowe returned to the village, a gaunt and haunted man. For days he didn't leave his home and workshop. Only Vera Craddock was able to prise information from Rowe's long-suffering wife. 'They think he knows something,' she kept saying. 'The shame of it, the shame of it.' On the fourth day, Doctor Bosanko arrived with grim news and a black bag. He wanted Rowe to go to hospital, but Rowe refused. While the police continued to ask questions to anybody who would listen to them, Rowe caught some strange fever like it had blown in from the sea. In the long, dark hours of night, the day after the doctor's visit, Rowe's heart faltered and broke. By dawn, he was dead and the next day as cold as moorland stone. Doctor Bosanko had no cure for fear.

Reverend Dunning sat alone at a table in the village hall. Despite it being mid-morning, the room was dark and only a little natural daylight brightened the room.

'You are saying you know nothing about this incident, Reverend?' Chief Inspector Croft asked him in a voice tired by days of fruitless investigation.

'I have told you several times, Inspector, I have no idea what you are talking about. Do you really think Germans landed on this coastline? Do you know the sea here? It's wild and unforgiving.'

'Reverend Dunning,' Wallingford addressed the clergyman in sombre tones, 'it's not if they landed as much as whether your parishioners know if it happened.' The politely laid cups of tea sat untouched.

'I am a man of God, Mr Wallingford. Your impertinence is an affront to our Lord and Master. 'You are familiar with

Psalm twenty-four, I presume?'

'The Lord is my shepherd; I shall not want. He maketh me to lie down in green pastures: he leadeth me beside the still waters,' replied Wallingford with smug satisfaction.

'Quite wrong,' said Dunning, 'that is Psalm twenty-three. Psalm twenty-four says, "the earth is the Lord's, and the fulness thereof; the world, and they that dwell therein. For he hath founded it upon the seas."' For a moment, Croft and Wallingford looked blank and bewildered. Croft feigned to write something down in his notebook.

'I'm not sure I follow,' Croft said at last.

'Then I suggest you pray to the Lord our Father, Inspector. His word is final. And it's his guidance you need.'

'Thank you, Reverend,' Croft replied. 'We will bear that in mind.' Wallingford shook his head and sat back in his chair.

'Good morning, gentlemen. Now, if you will excuse me, I must visit a grieving widow.' Dunning's comment was barbed and pointed. He left muttering Christian expletives under his breath.

At four o'clock that afternoon, the last police car motored out of the village along the coast road. Nothing had been gleaned or gained from the investigation. The Security Service in London received Wallingford's meticulous report which contained nothing worthy of further pursuit. Resources were stretched. Wallingford was recalled to SW1. There was plenty of work for him to burrow into there. Mosley and his Blackshirts were already plotting a post-war fascist revival, and double agents needed rounding up.

'Something happened here, Croft,' Wallingford mused as the car drove towards Truro, the moor above them vast and ominous.

'I just don't believe it, sir,' Croft replied respectfully. 'A submarine in eight fathoms, less than a mile offshore – how would it have got through a minefield?' There was a brief quiet above the straining engine of the Humber Hawk, before he added, 'What kind of captain would bring his boat that close to land? Near an RAF station?'

'Unless they were lost, Croft. Lost in the fog.' Rain began to spit at the windows. The conversation had ended. Wallingford filled his pipe with Hugh Campbell's Shag and struck a match, just as the car disappeared beyond Indian Queens.

*

'How is she?' Dunning met Vera Craddock at the front of Mrs Rowe's house.

'Relieved, I think,' said Vera. Dunning looked surprised.

'Because they have all left?' he asked tentatively. A wren perched on the saddle of his bicycle.

'No. Because the old man's gone.' Dunning recoiled. 'Don't look so shocked, Vicar. He was a bully. Years she's cooked, cleaned, washed and waited on him hand and foot. What did she get in return? Yelled at day in, day out, and a black eye at Christmas.'

'But even so, Vera…' Dunning was interrupted curtly.

'There won't be many sad to see him passing.'

'But Mrs Rowe will want to see me about the service?'

'She might. Or she might just stick him on the bonfire with all the other dead rot. Cheerio, Vicar.' Vera left in a puff of blue smoke. The little bird flew to its low nest. Dunning's bike collapsed from its resting place by a wall. He spent a long time picking it up.

*

'I hope that's the end of it,' Gladys said. The evening was cooling, and the hour struck nine.

'I would certainly think so,' Bob replied surely.

'The girls don't deserve this.'

'They'll be alright. They've got us. There's plenty who will have lost fathers and mothers in this war.'

'Cursed, it is.'

'What is, Glad?'

'Trevose. Deathly place it is. That foghorn – it's like the moan of a dying man in the night.' Bob listened, but he didn't know what to say. 'I never want to go there again. Do you hear me? Never.' Gladys gathered her needles and wool, threw them on the table and went upstairs. The cottage was silent, but for the ticking clock. Upstairs the girls slept soundly. Bob drew the curtains. It was still light outside, just.

*

Kramer and Weber joined a work party at Weinsberg. Nearly a hundred German prisoners stood beneath the ruins of a castle on a hill, and beneath it what looked like decayed vineyards. The town itself lay in a worse state than the castle – one of the last towns to be pulverised by Allied bombing in the war. An American officer greeted them in poor German.

'Today, you will clear the mess your comrades have made,' announced the American. In between bursts of orders, he consulted a colonel standing next to him. 'You will collect your comrades from the field.' The confused prisoners were given heavy bags and marched to a starting point at the edge of a narrow road.

'I have a very bad feeling about this,' said Weber. A light, grey rain started to fall.

'I have a plan, Weber. We must wait for the opportunity,' Kramer replied. At gunpoint, the Germans were made to stand in a horizontal line, no more than a shoulder's width apart from one another. The American guardsmen stood behind them at a safe distance wearing protective uniform. The Germans were ordered to walk slowly across the field. Suddenly, Weber was startled by a man to his left who was retching vomit.

'Oh my God,' Weber screeched. The man had trodden in decomposing human remains.

'Pick it up!' yelled an American who was watching closely. The man fell to his knees and began to scrape human flesh and bones into a bag.

'You'd have thought they'd give us gloves.' Weber couldn't tell whether Kramer was joking. They continued to walk for another 200 metres and were then ordered to halt and turn around.

When they arrived at the side of the road, the prisoners were slowly led to a small compound in which some unfortunate souls had been tasked with the job of sorting the remains of the dead. Next to them was a small and scruffy American corporal, puffing on a half-smoked cheroot. Kramer watched him fixedly. Every now and then, the American would spot something of interest to him and take it from the corpse.

'Look at him,' whispered Kramer. 'He's stealing from the dead.' They shuffled closer.

'So much for the Geneva Convention,' said Weber.

'He's our man,' confided Kramer. When they reached the front of the line, the Germans were silent, but the American spoke up.

'Quarter for the dead?' His accent was from the deep south.

'Tell him we have something of interest,' Kramer said. Weber obliged. The American whispered something to Weber and then told them to move on. Weber looked behind him to see an ashen-faced prisoner retrieve a severed arm from the sack.

Later that evening, Kramer and Weber stood apart from their fellow prisoners. They ate their thin, flavourless soup and waited. Kramer was about to light a cigarette when the corporal approached them. Light was fading and the three soldiers lurked in the shadows of an adjacent farm building.

'What have you got?' the American said.

'That depends if you can help us,' said Kramer boldly. He looked at the corporal; he was nervous and filthy.

'What do you want?'

'To get to Heidelberg. We have family that need our help.' Kramer's English was simple, but accurate.

'And if I can help you?' Kramer then revealed his Knight's Cross.

'Given to me by the Führer himself.' Kramer closed the medal and its black, white and red ribbon in his palm and made it vanish like a magician. 'There are very few of these, my friend. Worth a lot of money, I think.' The American started to twitch on his feet, excited and anxious, and greedy.

'I will be back later,' he said, threw his cigar stub to the floor and walked into the gloom. Weber looked disbelievingly at Kramer, like he had just watched something from a movie.

Two hours passed when the corporal returned. The night was now thick and black, with a little drizzle spitting from the west.

'Okay, Fritz,' the corporal instructed, 'we go now. But first the medal.'

'Not yet,' replied Kramer calmly. They walked quickly, following the American to an idling truck.

'Get in,' said the American. Kramer and Weber climbed into the back of the truck and hid among its contents. It was full of loot. Boxes of uniform, helmets, wine, paintings, food, medicine and envelopes. Kramer guessed what was inside. He wasn't wrong.

'Now the medal,' demanded the corporal, his eyes

red with anger and good living. Kramer handed over his Knight's Cross. The American grinned and stared at his prize like a pirate. Without a further word, he tapped the side of the Jimmy with his rifle butt.

'You gave him your Knight's Cross?' Weber exclaimed with admiration and amazement. Kramer was unmoved.

'Would you want to keep anything that Hitler had touched?' he said. The truck moved slowly into the night. In a matter of months, Kramer would be walking the streets of London, clearing bombsites and the rubble of his past.

Fourteen

Hamburg - Summer, 1985

'A pre-prandial stroll in the park, Stephen, I think,' said Sir Charles with instruction more than question or invitation. 'Where would you recommend?' They left the Adenauerallee and took the short walk to Planten un Blomen. Sir Charles began to think of past times, vividly once more. He recalled Alexandria, just before Christmas, 1941. A distant relative had been killed aboard a British battleship after an attack by Italian frogmen. Sir Charles had repaid the debt by shooting one of their countrymen as a prisoner in cold blood. He had never regretted it. But larger in his mind appeared the foiled abduction in St John's Wood. And the dead man, O'Brien. Gifford ground his teeth with a visceral sound from the pit of his soul.

'Is everything alright, Charles? You look a little peaky.' Gifford's heavy brow was pale and sweating. 'A coffee, I think,' continued Carter. The two men bought drinks at a café and sat at a table.

'A sweetener?' Gifford offered a hip flask to Carter who declined. Sir Charles poured a large measure into his cup.

'Time to give up the chase, Charles. You're getting too old for this game.'

'I'd rather die on the battlefield than in a care home in Suffolk,' he replied. The lines were deep and pink in his face, the eyes sinking further back into his skull.

'Is there a battle, Charles? London would forgive you, eventually.'

'This is personal, Stephen. Fox is my enemy, my quarry. Our great country and our empire destroyed by the likes of him. And for what? West Germany is now the richest country in Europe. Japan is the third richest country in the world. Even the bloody French and Italians have a stronger GDP. We are a laughing stock. Yet, who stood alone for two years against the jackboot?'

'London needs level heads, Charles, not loose cannons from the Jurassic era.'

'To think we are doing deals with the French. It makes me sick.' Gifford was lost in his mad world; he wasn't listening to Carter.

'The world has changed. London has changed. Computers, intelligence, finance – these are the drivers now. The borders are blurring, merging. The age of Pax Britannica sank at Jutland, Charles. You of all people should know that.'

'Then I shall go down with the flagship.' Sir Charles hailed and gulped the last of his alcoholic coffee. 'Come, Stephen, let us go and stand on the bridge.' Carter left coins on the table and the two men walked on into the park.

*

'Three coffees,' said Rico with relief. Carlo caught one of the cups as it slipped from his nephew's grip.

'Do you have any regrets, Rico?' asked Carlo. Frank tried to contain laughter.

'Regrets?' Rico was stumped by the questions. 'Well, I regret buying that Ford Granada last year. All sorts of problems with that thing. Water in the fuse box. Electrics were a nightmare. The business I lost because of that car. I didn't dare drive it in the rain.' Carlo shook his head and smiled at Frank. They sat quietly for a while sipping good German coffee.

'There is one more place I want to see,' said Frank.

'Today?' asked Carlo.

'Yes.' Frank handed a piece of paper to Carlo.

'The only family I have left. She will be expecting us.'

'Of course,' said Carlo.

'But might I ask just one more thing before we go? I would like to see the sea one last time.'

'We can go today, my friend. Now my nephew is the proud owner of a Mercedes Benz, he will be delighted to take us for a day out at the beach.' Rico coughed on his coffee. Frank turned his face to the light breeze and the southerly sun. He squinted. A few hundred metres along the path, two men were walking slowly towards them.

*

'This is it.' Emily walked ahead of her sister and Ed, her hurried steps gathering pace. 'Isn't it beautiful?' Emily was spellbound and enchanted by the flower borders, the pond and the trees. It was a genuine and exaggerated enthusiasm. Anna and Ed could only stand and watch. The day was warming, and the clouds were thinning.

'Should we stay in one place? Or perhaps we keep walking around.' Ed was trying to be practical and helpful. He scratched the side of his head and looked around the park.

'Does it matter?' Anna whispered quietly. 'I think we let her enjoy her day, don't you?' Emily led them further into the gardens. Every now and then, she would stop and find something of interest, something of connection, something of her father.

Ed was the first to see it. Five men thick in confrontation about 200 metres away. Instinctively, he edged towards the fracas. He couldn't make out what the men were saying. Only the occasional salvo of syllables reached him through the air. Something drew him closer.

'Ed!' called Anna. 'Ed,' she called again, 'what is it?' Ed looked back at them silently and kept walking in the direction of the men. Anna and Emily then followed him. A park runner jogged past them in a garish tracksuit of purple, white and green, a dazzle ship in suffragette colours. As they approached, the argument became audible. The figures became clearer. Unmistakable and baleful, the thickset and shorter man turned to them with a wide-eyed, sickly grin. He casually swigged from a hipflask and wiped his lips with his sleeve.

'Well, well,' he began, 'quite the reunion. And on such a fine morning.'

'Oh my God – that's him – the man that left us to die at The Head.' Anna was white with fear and rage.

'Traitors, all of you. Traitors to Her Majesty,' said Sir Charles with unaffected menace.

'Bastard.' Emily spat the word at him like venom.

'It is time we sorted out this little charade once and for all.' Gifford concealed his small revolver in a gloved hand. He motioned to them all to stand and prepare to move.

'What are you going to do? Shoot us all in a public park?' Anna stared at him, unmoved.

'Not here, Charles,' interjected Carter. It was an error.

'So, you are not Colonel Hawkins?' said Frank. 'Who's playing games now?'

'This is no longer a game, Kramer. And you of all people should know about disguise. Now, shall we go, before one of you gets hurt?'

Within the hour, all eight were inside Carter's Reeperbahn apartment. Sir Charles helped himself to whisky. He leaned above the fireplace with his back to the wall, gun still loaded and ready.

'Rather like an Agatha Christie whodunnit, wouldn't you agree?' Sir Charles put his tumbler to one side. 'And who are the suspects in this sordid little case? The ex-

Nazi, still hellbent on bringing down our fine British institutions. The wife of a militant activist. A washed-up Wop with a grudge to bear, no doubt, and his accomplice nephew. But, who are these two?' Sir Charles had regained his ailing stamina, fuelled by the alcohol.

'My daughter.' Emily looked at Frank.

'The plot thickens,' laughed Sir Charles. 'And you are?' He flicked the gun barrel towards Ed.

'A family friend,' replied Ed quietly.

'Just thought you'd come along for the ride, did you?' Sir Charles lowered the gun. 'Now, let's start at the beginning. Herr Kramer, I think we will start with you. And let me warn you: tell me what really happened this time. I have lived too long on this godforsaken little planet to believe in coincidence.' A temporal artery bulged in his head.

'There is nothing to add. Whatever you believe we're involved in, we are not. I rescued a kidnapped girl from a park in London. That is all.'

'Liar,' Gifford roared. 'Why did you run away to the end of England if you had nothing to hide?'

'Because I was being followed, watched. But I assume you know all of this?' Frank's calm was impressive. He wiped a palm over his forehead. 'What is of more importance is why you would object to the rescue and protection of a child. Explain that, Colonel.' Frank emphasised the rank of address; the tone was mocking.

'Who are you working for, Kramer?' Gifford persisted. His hand movements were twitchy and deliberate. Frank laughed at him.

'Working for? Look at me! I am a dying old man. Do you really, truly believe I am working for somebody, as you put it?' For a moment, Gifford was unsure. But then his train of thought swerved.

'I am going to tell you all a story. When I have finished, I will give you one last chance to tell me the truth. Do you understand?' Before Gifford began his monologue, Carter slipped out of the room with head bowed and a fixed stare.

'When I was twelve years old my father died unexpectedly. Mother had sent for me from school. I didn't know why but thought it might be something exciting – early hols perhaps or maybe Daddy had come home for a bit. She told me in the garden. I remember this clearly because it was an early summer's day and there were tall foxgloves and lupins behind me. Isn't it odd what one remembers?

'Of course, I was far too young to understand everything. I barely knew my father anyway. He was mostly in London or up country, whatever that meant. But it was what happened next that really affected me. Do you know what that was? Do you know what that was?' Sir Charles repeated himself in some kind of dazed rhetorical gesture. Frank's lips moved to reply before Gifford continued. 'I was sent away to school, only this time overseas.'

'Where did they send you?' Frank interjected with fake pity.

'South Africa,' replied Sir Charles, his eyes falling on Frank's, holding out to them for a moment, like a sunken sailor's arm in the swell. 'How I missed my mother. She was such a kind and beautiful woman. I treasured those rare days when she would take me to Regent Street and the West End. We had a little flat near Portland Place and we would stay there. Occasionally, she would take me to the theatre and afterwards we would talk about the show. You wouldn't understand.' His face groaned like a dying engine, and he looked at his audience.

'No, I don't think I could,' Anna said coldly. Sir Charles reached for more whisky, swaying unsteadily as he did so.

'My mother remarried quickly. To a diplomat of sorts. They moved to Washington. I only saw her rarely – Christmases and summer holidays – well, some of them.' He looked again at the room. 'You are probably feeling sorry for me, but my upbringing made me what I am. And so, when war came, I was prepared to do my duty. I was ready. Unlike so many weak and feeble people in my homeland.'

'And your mother? What became of her?' Frank was playing with him, stirring the dark pools in his mind.

'Chamberlain, Halifax, Cadogan. Obloquy.' Sir Charles paused and then cast Frank a poisonous glare. 'My mother. How dare you mention her.' He stopped again, eyes awash with loss. 'She drowned in the middle of the Atlantic. With 600 others. Half of them women and children. She was trying to get home for Christmas. Left to die in a freezing November storm by Nazi scum like you, Kramer.'

'I almost feel sorry for you.' Anna was again the first to reply. 'But I don't. What are you doing now? Taking revenge for your mother's death?'

'Revenge? This isn't about revenge. This is about honour. Loyalty. Freedom and liberty. Qualities you people reject. You think you can appease the world with words, with diplomacy, with tolerance? By negotiation? Treaties?'

'Does anybody understand what he is saying?' Ed asked, his voice deep and calm. Sir Charles squeezed the mantlepiece as if he wanted to break it. His anger coiled like a viper's tail.

'You think the Soviets and the Chinese will stop their nuclear programmes? Kowtow to western demands for a peaceful world of free trade and ice-cream? You are naïve. These people exist on handfuls of rice and potatoes. They know hardship.'

'Better that than whisky and bullets,' said Emily.

'Your husband's actions threaten the free world, Mrs Groves.' Sir Charles had mustered some composure. He stroked his hand and then the barrel of his gun. 'So, you see, on behalf of Her Majesty and my country and its empire, I seek the truth from you.'

Sir Charles sat on the arm of a chair, spent by his words and the haunting memories of his long-dead mother. A single tear crept beneath his cheekbone.

'So, to the truth. Now is the chance to save yourselves. And your daughter, of course, Mrs Groves.' The room was silent. Anna looked to Emily and Frank. She offered a slight shake of the head.

'And if I tell you, will you let them go?' Frank spoke softly.

'Now we're getting somewhere,' Sir Charles replied.

'That doesn't answer my question.'

'That will depend on how you answer mine.'

'I would like a drink first.' Sir Charles handed Frank a glass of whisky. 'You are right to believe I was trying to foil the kidnapping.' Anna cast a startled look at Emily. Ed grabbed her hand, silently persuading her to stay quiet. 'But I was not working with Groves or any protest movement. You must understand this.' There was undiluted conviction in Frank's words.

'Then who were you working for?' asked Sir Charles with razor sharp precision.

'The British government.'

'Who?'

'Popplewell.' Sir Charles instantly turned a greyish-white colour of horror and sickness.

'You expect me to believe that?' Gifford could barely annunciate the words coherently. 'And what could you possibly be doing for him?'

'We needed to stop the kidnapping. Surely you understand why?' Frank was pretending – improvising.

'Enlighten me.'

'To allow it to go ahead would not have been in our interests.' It was a vague, seemingly hopeless statement, but somehow it worked. Sir Charles let out a gasp that was wretched and ugly. He threw his tumbler against the wall and brought the gun level with his eyeline.

'Johnny was bluffing. But I am not. Hands above your heads all of you – now!' Gifford moved the revolver in an arc from left to right. 'Who goes first? Ladies, perhaps it should be you. We mustn't forget our manners now, must we?'

'Put the gun down, Charles,' spoke a low and

commanding voice from the corner of the room. It belonged to Carter.

'Don't be ridiculous, Stephen.'

'I said put it down.' Carter's tone was now insistent, the volume louder.

'Or what?' boasted Gifford, almost slurring his words now. He glanced sideways to Carter.

'I shoot.' Carter was holding a double-action revolver. Gifford panicked – his hands were shaking. His gun fired with a deafening crack. Frank was thrown back into the chair he was sitting on. Carter responded. His bullet blew apart Gifford's hands to red pulp and bone. Sir Charles fell to the floor in whimpering agony and shock.

'Quickly!' screamed Emily. She rushed to Frank's side. A dark patch of blood had already soaked his shirt. His breathing was crackling, thin and tight. 'Can you hear me? Frank!' Frank's eyes were closing, shivering. 'Father!' Emily called to him in the dying light of the room.

'My love,' he murmured. 'I am sorry, I am so sorry.'

'No… no, you mustn't say this.' She held and kissed his forehead softly; he reached for her hand.

'I am sorry I wasn't there for you. When you were a child. For your mother.' His voice was breaking into dry whispers. Emily held his hand tighter. From her pocket, she retrieved her mother's letter.

'Listen, Father, listen.' Emily read Dorothy's letter. Where her German pronunciation faltered, Frank put right her mistakes; it was as if he knew the script already. At certain moments, words, phrases, he smiled and laughed, or wept. Whatever words Dorothy had written all those years ago, they were woven into a private code that only she and Frank would understand, as if protected from the cloaked censorship of war.

When she had finished, Frank lay against her side in his final breaths. Life was leaving him now; his soul already rising above the northern tides and shoals, and the sinking, westering sun.

'Sleep it is a gentle thing, beloved from pole to pole… the gentle sleep from Heaven, that slid into my soul.' Frank looked at his daughter for the last time, their eyes both blue as the summer sea. He smiled. A single tear, his final tear, reached Emily's hand, and his heart stopped.

Sir Charles lay moaning on the floor. He let out a pathetic cry for help which was greeted by Ed's heavy boot striking his rib cage.

'Do you know how one of these works?' Carter asked Ed. Ed shook his head in horror.

'I do,' said Carlo.

'You do?'

'I was an Italian infantryman in the war.'

'Then are you sure you know how it works?' Carlo and Carter exchanged a brief and knowing smile. They were old soldiers, and the battlefield humour wasn't lost on either of them. 'Shoot him if he moves.' He looked to Emily. 'An ambulance and police will be here shortly.' Anna was holding her tightly. Carter's attention turned to Sir Charles. 'A bit of a mess, Charles.'

'Why?' Gifford groaned.

'You lost your focus, Charles. Blaming others. The mistakes are yours.'

'What do you mean?'

'O'Brien. Switzerland. Mottram blabbed. And these people here. Coincidence, Charles, that's all it was. You gambled, lost and then chased. The bank wins.' If Sir Charles understood, he concealed it in agonies of silence. He was beginning to drift in and out of consciousness, shock and survival his masters now.

A rumble of footsteps pounded in the hallway of the apartment. Four medics arrived followed by armed policemen. It was clear Frank was dead. They attended to Gifford quickly and prepared to move him from the building.

'He won't be needing those,' said Carter gesturing to the handcuffs held by one of the officers. It was another macabre joke and only Carter's eyebrows chuckled. A whining Gifford was led away, beyond protest now. Polizei crowded the small apartment. Carter spoke to the commanding officer in German. The policemen retreated respectfully to the kitchen. Emily took her mother's letter. She folded it and placed it in Frank's inside coat pocket. Curiosity and impulse made her take out his wallet. She stared at the worn, brown leather, and then opened it. Carter was watching her.

'They will want to see it,' he said kindly. 'Take what you want and put it back.' Emily found some money, a photograph – presumably somewhere in Hamburg, a medical card and a prescription, but there was little else that marked Frank as anything other than an elderly man from London. And then she discovered an identity card. On it were Frank's name and photograph. She frowned and handed it to Carter.

'My God,' he said. Carter was for once speechless. All eyes looked to him for an explanation. 'Box,' continued Carter, mysteriously.

'Box?' said Emily.

'Military Intelligence.' He held the card for all to see. 'Frank was working for MI5.'

*

Charlotte Groves skipped and hopped in and out of the receding tide. The broad sands at Porthrowan were tawny brown, glossy and smooth. Emily stood at the water's edge, Anna, Di at her side.

'He was a brave and loving man, Em,' said Anna. Charlotte was talking to the waves.

'I just wish I had known him more,' Emily replied. A southwesterly breeze cut across the bay and dragged a wave across the tide. Anna called to Charlotte to come back on to the sand.

'Most of us never experience that kind of closeness in a lifetime. How many can say their father fought for their country?' Anna said.

'Both their countries,' added Di.

'I think he must have felt so guilty all his life. Fighting for Germany. That sense of displacement. His family killed by bombs.' Emily kicked some wet sand as she spoke.

'Then he more than made up for that with everything he did for British Intelligence,' Anna said, and the words reassured her sister.

'Give us a hand then, you lot,' called a voice from behind them. Ed was dragging a rickety buggy across the sand.

'Caerwen,' cried Anna gleefully. The dinghy had been recently painted in fresh colours of blue and white. It was the same small boat that Rosie and Ed had rowed all those years ago. 'I never knew you still had this thing.'

'It's had quite a life,' said Di mischievously.

'We don't have long, so let's get going,' instructed Ed. Di took Charlotte's hand and the two of them wandered towards the dunes looking for small adventures.

Ed clambered into the boat with middle-aged stiffness, waist high in waders amidst a gentle surf. They rowed towards Quies. The ocean was flat, but the current strong as it always was. On the horizon, a white container ship moved towards the Bristol Channel. They passed some floating crab buoys. The water was dark and deep beneath them. The rocks were a few hundred metres away, like a pancake, a shark, a fin and a small tooth poking through the white breakers at their bases.

'Here,' said Emily.

'Perfect,' agreed Anna. Ed relaxed his oars. Emily opened a metal urn and turned her back to the wind. She started to recite a well-known poem of the ocean.

'I must go down to the seas again,' she began in a voice choked with tears. 'And all I ask is a merry yarn from a laughing fellow-rover, and quiet sleep and a sweet dream when the long trick's over.' Frank's ashes flew over the waves and higher into the air before settling on the sea.

Emily looked one last time before turning to Ed. 'Let's go home,' she said.

They pulled little Caerwen along the beach and hooked its buggy to the trusty old Land Rover. Charlotte curled up with her mother on the bench seat. Emily and Di sat in the back gazing back at Porthrowan's breaking surf.

'I know now why you never take a holiday from this place,' Emily said.

'It's in your soul too – just like your grandmother,' Di replied.

'I think you're probably right.' The Land Rover's gears changed with a reassuring clunk. 'Thank you, Di.'

'You needn't thank me. Nor Ed. We're as much a part of this story as you are. If it wasn't for Frank, I wouldn't have known Ed, wouldn't have had the life I've had.'

'Sometimes I don't believe any of this is real.' They climbed into the slate grey lanes, the hedgebanks wild with bushes and thin trees.

*

'How are you feeling today, Sir Charles?' The accent speaking above his prison hospital bed hailed from the southern estuaries of England; it was a voice he had heard before, subterranean and menacing. 'Or should I perhaps just say Charles?'

'I have been better,' replied Sir Charles. He lay bedridden in a sterile, sanitised ward. There were no other patients.

'I have brought you a little something to ease the

trauma.' The man tucked a small bottle of single malt Scotch whisky into the bedsheets.

'How very kind, Doctor,' said Sir Charles with unfiltered sarcasm. The man pretended to write something on clipboard notepaper. He proceeded to carry out some routine tests of temperature and heartbeat.

'They saved your hands, at least. Bar the odd finger or two of course. But it's unlikely they'll spare your freedom,' said the fake doctor, returning pen to pocket.

'An inglorious day,' cavilled Gifford.

'You have let the side down, Charles. Badly and again.' A ward nurse shuffled past them with a trolley; her look suggested she was uneasy with the unfamiliar doctor's presence. 'Of course, time heals deep wounds. There might be another opportunity for you, but I wouldn't bank on it. You have made a lot of enemies this time.' The man produced a syringe and flicked it. 'No air in there.' And he smiled at his sinister punning.

'What are you doing?' Sir Charles turned pale and clammy like damp putty.

'Just a little tonic, Charles. Something to help you sleep. And forget of course. We wouldn't want you to remember every little detail now, would we? Goodbye, Charles, or should I say farewell?'

The man's footsteps faded into the long corridor. The clock ticked like a dripping tap on the ward wall. Sir Charles felt a shiver and then a slow, opiate calm. His eyelids flickered and he surrendered to the warm darkness that enveloped him. The pain in his hands was gone. There wasn't time to let his thoughts wander through the backstreets of his memory. There was nothing there to fight anymore. With a last gasp of effort, he tried to picture his mother, and a sunny day somewhere beneath English clouds, but he couldn't see her – her face lost forever. And then he lost consciousness, his heart beating in time to the rhythm of the hospital clock.

*

From the warm kitchen at Pentire the sea echoed like a faraway train. The late summer twilight closed with an autumnal breath. An animal called from a shed in the yard. Di was busy preparing supper.

'Will you go back to America soon?' Ed asked Emily.

'I don't know. I am thinking of taking a sabbatical. Maybe I will look to do some research in Europe.' Emily took a sip of tea. 'Somewhere closer to home,' she added. Anna smiled.

'Home?' she prodded playfully, and they both chuckled.

'Hamburg perhaps?' Ed offered. His suggestion was interrupted by a faint but persistent knocking at the porch door. Alfie barked half-heartedly from his basket, then slumped back into his cosy doze.

'Who on earth is that?' Di complained.

'It might be Joe,' said Ed. 'He wants to fix the baler. A bale got wedged. Didn't sound like him though.' He went to the door and moments later returned with a guest. Standing sheepishly with a limp bunch of carnations and an awkward half-smile was Alex Groves.

'Hello, Alex.' Anna greeted him confidently.

'Hello,' Alex replied uncomfortably.

'Are you coming in?'

'Yes.' He paused and handed her the cartoonish flowers. 'I wondered if we could talk?' Anna put him out of his misery and led him to the dining room. They stood beneath the harsh glare of the ceiling light, standing metres apart. Alex moved to embrace her, but Anna stopped him with an outstretched palm.

'I'm sorry,' Alex began, 'I know I have let you down. Let Charlotte down. I haven't been here for you both. I know that. I have been stupid. I haven't listened and I want to change all of that.' He cut a miserable figure. 'Come back to London – please.' Anna turned and walked to the window; she looked out over the farm.

'It's not as easy as that, Alex. You don't know what I have been through recently.' She turned to face him with eyes as hard as granite. 'You have no idea.' The strength of her statements silenced him. 'I don't want Charlotte to grow up in London. It's a frightening place. It's no place for children. I don't want to live in London.'

'Then we could move. Go to somewhere quieter. Hertfordshire.'

'To live near your mother. No thanks. I have made up my mind. In fact, I've made up our minds.'

'What do you mean?' The tone of his voice was high-pitched and brittle.

'Charlotte and I are going to stay in Cornwall.'

'Here? What will you do? Where will you live?'

'In the cottage – where else do you think we would

live? And as for what I will do, well, in a sense, that's none of your business.'

'In what sense?' he said both pleadingly and demandingly.

'In the sense that I never knew what you did.'

'I couldn't tell you. My work is confidential. It relies on secrecy.' Before he could finish, Emily cut through him.

'There you are. In the present tense as always. Never the past or the future. It doesn't matter, Alex – you won't change.'

'But I can, and I will.'

'No, you won't. Charlotte will probably see more of you anyway. This will mean you will have to come to see her – if you want to.' The words stung him like a dwarf nettle.

'And how will you live? How will you survive?'

'Survive? I have been surviving for a long time. You can keep the flat. I don't want it. I will be in London next week to collect our things. I have a couple of Italian friends who will help me, so please make sure you're not there.'

'There's a payphone in Trenance,' Anna called as Alex stumbled along the farm track and into the dark.

'And where's that?' he replied, colliding painfully with a rusted hay turner.

'A short stroll for an explorer like you.' She closed the door firmly and returned to the kitchen. The others were seated at the table, expectant, muting their talk.

'What did he want?' Emily was the first to speak.

'A reconciliation, I suppose,' Anna replied.

'And you said?' continued her sister.

'That Charlotte and I have moved to Cornwall.'

'Are you serious? You are moving to Penrose?'

'It makes perfect sense. There is a lovely little school in St Merryn.'

'And what will you do for money?'

'You can help me on the farm,' said Ed. 'God knows we could do with an extra pair of hands.' Di rolled her eyeballs but said nothing more.

'I can help.' Emily unfolded a piece of paper she had taken from her bag. It was a letter from a solicitor. She passed it to Anna.

'Oh my God,' she said, her face circular in shock. 'He's left you everything.'

'Yes,' replied Emily. She nodded to Ed who read the letter.

'It seems Frank was a wealthy man. A flat in London. And there seems to be a property in Hamburg.' Ed adjusted his reading glasses and examined the letter in more detail. 'Not to mention his other assets.' Di touched his arm, quietly showing him to be quiet.

'So, you see, we can both have our little piece of freedom.'

'Perhaps this calls for a small celebration,' Ed suggested with clumsy eagerness. The sisters shared a momentary glance.

'I think we should just shelter from the storm for a bit, don't you, Em?'

*

Sunrise the following morning cast a deep pink glow across the cliffs. A tired Rico arrived at the farm and was carefully loading cases into the boot of the Mercedes. Di stood in her dressing gown at the porch door. Charlotte was cuddled into her blanket, sleeping in the car. Anna and Emily stood beside the house breathing in the fresh early breeze.

'It's time to go,' Emily said wistfully.

'But we'll be back in the blink of an eye,' replied Anna, 'and you will be too.'

'I hope so. I do hope so.'

'Hamburg is a lot nearer than California. You can come here for long weekends.' A lone gull perched on a barn gantry and called to the sea.

'Ready, ladies?' Rico called cheerily.

'As we'll ever be,' said Anna. They got into the car. Ed and Di exchanged goodbyes at the windows and Rico slowly pulled away along the farm track. The taillights faded into a mist.

'Looks like a misty morning,' said Di to her husband as she closed the garden gate. Ed looked skywards and then back out to sea.

'I think it's a fog coming in, love.' He followed his wife back into the soft orange glow of the house. He was right. Beyond the farm and the cliffs, a thick and dense haag was creeping across the surf towards the breaking shore. It would soon arrive, and it would stay awhile.

Epilogue

Oxford – December, 2019

The barman called last orders. The fire's last flames were dying in its embers.

'Is that really a true story?' Angus was spellbound.

'What happened to your grandmother?' asked Ollie.

'She's still alive and living in Cornwall. It's a different place now. Little London she calls it. Loads of rich bankers and celebrity chefs. The villages are holiday homes mostly. The Merrimans are still there.'

'I think I know it. It's near Padstow, right?' Angus drank the last of his warm ale.

'Everyone knows Padstow,' said Dotty.

'I think my parents stayed there with some friends who know David Cameron,' Angus continued.

'Fascinating,' Dotty replied with unguarded sarcasm.

'Anyway, it's late and I have to get the early train tomorrow.'

'Home for Christmas?' said Ollie.

'To Penrose, of course.'

'I'm going to be in Rock for New Year.' Angus looked at Dotty with a playful glint in his eyes.

'Have fun,' she said. They got up and left the pub. Angus lit a cigarette, inhaled on the orange-tipped tube and blew out a tunnel of smoke into the night air. They walked a short distance southward towards the colleges near the Christchurch Meadows. The old, narrow streets were empty.

'Was that a seagull?' said Ollie.

'It's a long way from home,' answered Angus, flicking his half-smoked stub into the side of the lane.

'Aren't we all?' said Dotty.

*

Inside the pub, the barman collected glasses and wiped down tables.

'Time to go, sir,' he said to the old man by the window.

'I think it is,' replied a well-spoken voice.

'Will you be okay getting home, sir?'

'I will, young man, but thank you for asking.' The old man climbed unsteadily to his ancient feet and reached for a walking stick that leaned against the wall.

'Did you hear the story that girl was telling?' the barman enquired.

'I did. Very enjoyable, I thought.'

'Unbelievable,' concluded the barman.

'Funny – I think I've heard it somewhere before.' The old man began to shuffle out of the pub.

'Goodnight, sir.'

'Indeed, it was.' The pub door closed behind him. Sir Charles Gifford walked towards the mist of the Cherwell. He was looking for the river but searching for the sea. The beam of his wartime flashlight marked a lonely path through Grove Passage. And then caught in his light, a pair of bright eyes, the thin upright body and tag of a fox. The creature did not move or flee in fright but waited for the old man. Sir Charles plodded cautiously, a cold sweat around his neck. He reached a junction in the path. To his left, Deadman's Walk skirted the edge of Merton Field. A sickening dizziness struck Gifford. He froze, unable to plot his course. The river mist was thickening in the freezing night. Undisturbed, unafraid, the red animal sniffed the ground beneath his shoes, and then, in calculated strides began to circle its quarry. It came closer and closer, calm and silent, like the fog from the black river.

Acknowledgements

I would like to thank my family, particularly my parents, who have supported me through the writing of Quies. The journey started for me in 1975 – my first visit to the bay named Porthrowan in the novel. Any seasoned visitor to this part of the world will know exactly where this is, and like me will have quickly fallen in love with its wild seascapes and cliffs on this rugged stretch of the north Cornish coast, so beautifully captured by Toby Ray's cover artwork. Many of the families and characters of yesteryear have sadly passed away or moved on, but some are still there, and some are reborn in the story. Some events in the book are factual and some imagined. You will have to work out which of those are true, and which are not. I hope to have given a voice to the underrepresented and those who deserve dignity, our love and compassion. It's no coincidence that these voices are usually Cornish.

Finally, I would like to thank my friends who have supported me through what has been, and what will continue to be, an extremely tough time in my life. So, thank you Anth Barton, Claire Barton, Cam Brock, Steve Dudley, Louise Elliott, Steve Evans, Paul Laird, Tom Morgan, Tasos Papastamou, Neil Pinney, Jo Ronxin, Anne Thomsett, Anna Williams, my brothers, parents and family. And to those I haven't named, thank you too.

It goes without saying that all the errors are my own.

This book is printed on paper from sustainable sources managed under the Forest Stewardship Council (FSC) scheme.

It has been printed in the UK to reduce transportation miles and their impact upon the environment.

For every new title that Troubador publishes, we plant a tree to offset CO_2, partnering with the More Trees scheme.

For more about how Troubador offsets its environmental impact, see www.troubador.co.uk/sustainability-and-community